PRAISE FOR THE

Candy

"A sweet tale of the c[...] with a dash of murder [...] get *Candy Apple Dead*, [...] and highly entertaining [...] fast-paced story of sweet and sour." —*The Best Reviews*

"A promising new mystery series. Abby is a wonderful new character . . . Anyone with even a minor sweet tooth will enjoy the various descriptions and recipes included here." —*The Romance Readers Connection*

"Small-town intrigue, a juicy conflict or two, and some fun characters are the highlights of this story, which launches what will probably be an exceedingly popular new series. Carter has a very accessible style—and is equally talented at inducing sugar cravings in the reader. Dieters beware!" —*Romantic Times*

"Delightful start to a new mystery series featuring a feisty heroine . . . An engaging, entertaining tale . . . Abby is a sensible, believable heroine. She's strong, yet vulnerable, and definitely feisty! The story moves along at a quick pace . . . And the Divine Almond Toffee . . . yummy!" —*Fresh Fiction*

"A delicious whodunit full of interesting, well-developed characters. I can't wait for the next installment!" —*Affaire de Coeur* (four and a half stars)

"An exciting one-sitting amateur-sleuth tale . . . Readers will appreciate [Abby's] spunk and desire to insure justice occurs." —*Midwest Book Review*

A Candy Shop Mystery

Sucker Punch

Sammi Carter

BERKLEY PRIME CRIME, NEW YORK

THE BERKLEY PUBLISHING GROUP
Published by the Penguin Group
Penguin Group (USA) Inc.
375 Hudson Street, New York, New York 10014, USA
Penguin Group (Canada), 90 Eglinton Avenue East, Suite 700, Toronto, Ontario M4P 2Y3, Canada
(a division of Pearson Penguin Canada Inc.)
Penguin Books Ltd., 80 Strand, London WC2R 0RL, England
Penguin Group Ireland, 25 St. Stephen's Green, Dublin 2, Ireland (a division of Penguin Books Ltd.)
Penguin Group (Australia), 250 Camberwell Road, Camberwell, Victoria 3124, Australia
(a division of Pearson Australia Group Pty. Ltd.)
Penguin Books India Pvt. Ltd., 11 Community Centre, Panchsheel Park, New Delhi—110 017, India
Penguin Group (NZ), 67 Apollo Drive, Rosedale, North Shore 0632, New Zealand
(a division of Pearson New Zealand Ltd.)
Penguin Books (South Africa) (Pty.) Ltd., 24 Sturdee Avenue, Rosebank, Johannesburg 2196,
South Africa

Penguin Books Ltd., Registered Offices: 80 Strand, London WC2R 0RL, England

This is a work of fiction. Names, characters, places, and incidents either are the product of the author's imagination or are used fictitiously, and any resemblance to actual persons, living or dead, business establishments, events, or locales is entirely coincidental. The publisher does not have any control over and does not assume any responsibility for author or third-party websites or their content.

PUBLISHER'S NOTE: The recipes contained in this book are to be followed exactly as written. The publisher is not responsible for your specific health or allergy needs that may require medical supervision. The publisher is not responsible for any adverse reactions to the recipes contained in this book.

SUCKER PUNCH

A Berkley Prime Crime Book / published by arrangement with the author

PRINTING HISTORY
Berkley Prime Crime mass-market edition / June 2009

Copyright © 2009 by Penguin Group (USA) Inc.
Cover illustration by Jeff Crosby.
Interior text design by Kristin del Rosario.

ISBN: 978-0-425-22706-0

BERKLEY® PRIME CRIME
Berkley Prime Crime Books are published by The Berkley Publishing Group,
a division of Penguin Group (USA) Inc.,
375 Hudson Street, New York, New York 10014.
BERKLEY® PRIME CRIME and the PRIME CRIME logo are trademarks of Penguin Group (USA) Inc.

PRINTED IN THE UNITED STATES OF AMERICA

10 9 8 7 6 5 4 3 2 1

For Abigail

Chapter 1

"What are you talking about?" my cousin Karen demanded, her expression a mix of horror and hurt feelings. "You *can't* hate Valentine's Day!" Even her auburn curls seemed to droop, as if my slip of the tongue had affected them, too. A lifetime spent in the candy business has turned her into a full-fledged romantic. But why not? She and Sergio had been married forever. She had reason to believe.

Weak winter sunlight spilled into the candy shop through the front windows and winked off the glass containers on the shelves. The day looked warm and sunny, but that was a delusion. The temperature in Paradise had been hovering below zero for more than two weeks, ever since a February cold front swept down from the Arctic and swallowed the northern half of Colorado.

I'd grown up hanging around Divinity, just as Karen had, but I'd only been owner of the shop for two years. I hadn't been bitten by the romance bug, but I still knew better than to open my mouth around Karen about some things. My attitude toward Cupid was one of them.

If I hadn't unexpectedly found myself standing beneath a cascade of carelessly stacked gift boxes—every one covered with red and pink heart stickers—I would have kept my opinion to myself. At least, that's what I told myself. I picked up one of the boxes and grimaced. "Are they *all* like this?"

They were gaudy, and they weren't the only thing bothering me. I'd run a few errands yesterday afternoon, and I hadn't come back until after the shop was closed. Apparently Karen and my new clerk, Liberty, had been busy while

I was gone. The entire shop was now filled with hearts, so much red and pink my head had started to pound when I came inside a few minutes earlier.

Karen snatched the box away from me and skewered me with a look. "Yes, they're all like this. They're festive. And you didn't answer my question. How can you say you hate Valentine's Day? You're a candymaker for Pete's sake. It's like our national holiday."

Karen had worked part-time for our Aunt Grace from the time we were teenagers until Grace died. She's been my assistant manager since I came back to Paradise, Colorado, to run the shop. When it comes to Divinity, she and I agree about almost everything. But not this time.

I tried to pick my way through the mound of boxes without crushing any. They're usually pretty classy looking—white with gold trim. Classic. Elegant. The heart stickers moved them from the "refined" column right over into "cheesy."

"I didn't say that I hate Valentine's Day. I said that I try to avoid thinking about it. This"—I waved a hand to encompass the hearts hanging from the ceiling and walls—"makes that kind of hard to do. When did we decide to . . . decorate . . . and why wasn't I consulted? These stickers were a huge waste of money, not to mention the cost of the boxes you've ruined." The shop wasn't struggling to make ends meet anymore, but that's only because we watch every penny and never spend when we don't have to. Until today.

Karen's scowl etched lines into her face. She's a few years younger than I am, but she's also married with a teenage daughter, and she sometimes forgets she's not my mother. "We haven't *ruined* anything," she said.

"That's a matter of opinion."

Karen dismissed my concerns with a flick of her slender wrist. "It was Liberty's idea," she said, "and I happen to think it's a good one. Liberty says—and she has a point—that we're cheating ourselves by not getting more into the spirit of the day."

"Great," I snarled. "Now you're taking business advice

from someone who thinks the alternative rock station is the perfect background music for a candy shop." Karen's quick glance into the showroom set my teeth on edge. "Give me some credit. I'd never talk about Liberty when she was around to hear me."

"You still don't like her, do you?" Karen said, but it was more accusation than question.

"I like her. I just don't like some of her ideas. She's only worked here for a few months. I'm sure she'll eventually get a feel for how we do things."

A challenge flashed through Karen's brown eyes. "Well, *I* like it." She'd thrown down the gauntlet with that. She'd been asking for more authority in the store, and I'd been obliging little by little. After all, she's the one who stayed in Paradise while I was gone for twenty years. She's the one who *should* have inherited the store. It had been a touchy subject between us since the day I came back, and I owed her more than just a job. But I wasn't sure I could go along with this. The store looked garish, and that was the nicest word I could think of to describe it.

I finally reached the edge of the boxes and looked around for a place to escape the hearts. "It can't stay like this, Karen. It's—"

"It's festive," she insisted again, cutting me off. The frigid temperature outside seemed warm when compared to the wall of ice forming inside Divinity. Much as I hated the decorations, I relied on Karen too much to risk offending her.

"Can we at least scale back a little?"

"I like it," Karen said stubbornly. "And the only reason you don't is because you're still bitter over your divorce. I understand that Roger hurt you, and I know you've had issues with the idea of falling in love again, but your attitude toward love is cynical and unnatural, especially for someone who does what *you* do for a living."

Her observations stung, and cousin or not, she'd stepped across the line. "My attitude has nothing to do with Roger," I snapped. Maybe that wasn't entirely true, but I wasn't going to get into a discussion about my ex-husband, his new wife, or the havoc that coming home from work to find them rolling around on my bedroom floor had inflicted on my psyche.

I could tell by the scowl on Karen's narrow face that she didn't believe me. She's one of those people who seem to know everything about everything. Want to know how to treat psoriasis, the definition of "a jiffy," or how to keep rubber bands like new? Call my cousin.

Karen knows where to find the best price on everything, from aspirin to zucchini, and can tell you without pausing to think who fits where in any family tree. She also has a serious sugar addiction, but you'd never know it because she's rail thin—something *I* think is "unnatural" in a candymaker.

So when her eyes widened and her face took on an "aha" expression, I knew I was in trouble.

I had someone new in my life. And if Detective Pine Jawarski and I weren't exactly ready to commit to a life together, at least we were inching in that direction. Karen's expression warned me that her thoughts had moved in the same direction as mine. "Does Jawarski know you feel this way?"

We were in dangerous territory now, and I knew I had to nip this conversation in the bud. "Jawarski and I don't talk about it. Why don't you stand there and I'll hand you the boxes. The least we can do is get the mess off the floor."

Karen was too busy gaping at me to move. "You haven't talked about what you're going to do for Valentine's Day this year?"

"He hasn't brought it up, and neither have I." I picked up a few boxes and held them out to her. When she made no move to take them, I caved. "It's no big deal. He'll probably be working. And I'll be breaking my neck that whole week to keep up around here. I'll probably just want to crash."

Karen took the boxes reluctantly and said something I was pretty sure I didn't want to hear.

I'd finally reached the point in my relationship with Jawarski where I could actually call it a relationship. I'd adjusted to the fact that most everyone in Paradise considered us a couple. I'd even adjusted to the fact that we spent most weekends together as a matter of course. They were huge concessions for me, and I thought they might make up for the fact that Jawarski's growing importance in my life made me feel weak and vulnerable—and the fact that I don't like feeling weak and vulnerable.

Karen stacked the boxes on the shelf and turned back for more. "All I'm saying is you'd better start thinking about what you're going to do that night. Valentine's Day is only two weeks away, and Paradise isn't the quiet little town it used to be. If you don't have a reservation for dinner, you'll be scraping something together out of the cupboard."

I thought about my kitchen in the apartment upstairs and made a mental note to pick up a frozen dinner, just in case. Make that two. "Thanks for the warning," I said. "What time is Liberty coming in today?"

Karen shot a look over her shoulder. "In about fifteen minutes. So is that it? 'Thanks for the warning,' now mind your own business?"

"Something like that."

She stopped working and turned to face me, hands on hips. "You're going to lose him, you know. With that attitude."

"Just because I don't want to agonize over Jawarski all night and day doesn't mean I don't care about him. Maybe what we have isn't what you'd want, but it works for us, so leave it alone, okay?"

"Does it work? Are you sure?"

She was really fighting dirty today. Karen isn't usually like that. She's not mean or vicious, so why did she keep aiming at my weakest spots? "Are you trying to make me insecure?"

"Of course not." She sounded hurt that I'd even suggest such a thing. "I'm just trying to help."

Some help. I'd never had self-esteem issues until the day I'd discovered the truth about my marriage. Twenty years of blind trust had been blown away in an instant, and the blast had been the emotional equivalent of a nuclear explosion. Try as I might, I couldn't just flip a switch and get over it.

Not even for Jawarski.

I knew there were times when he felt impatient with me, but I didn't think I was in danger of losing him. But what did I know? I hadn't known I was in danger of losing Roger, either. "It works for us," I said again. "And I don't want to talk about it anymore."

"Fine."

"Fine."

"Just don't blame me—"

"I mean it, Karen. Drop it, okay?"

She clamped her mouth shut and turned back to the supply cupboard. A strained silence stretched between us as we each pretended to concentrate on the task at hand. Only the steady slap of boxes hitting the shelves broke the unnatural quiet.

When the bell over the front door jangled to signal a customer, both of us turned toward it gratefully. My eagerness turned to dread when I saw Jawarski come into the shop. Karen beamed as if she'd personally arranged for his arrival.

While he scraped snow from his boots, I tossed off a desperate prayer that he hadn't come to talk about Valentine's Day or anything else remotely related to our relationship. That was one hassle I didn't need.

Chapter 2

❧

Blissfully unaware of the tension between Karen and me, Jawarski came toward the counter, a smile on his solid face, a key dangling from one finger. He's in his mid-forties, tall, dark, and, yeah, handsome. He's also in fantastic shape thanks to his job as a detective with the Paradise Police Department.

"Hey there, good-looking," he said. "Got a minute?"

I've almost grown accustomed to the little *zing* of pleasure I get when I see him. Any woman would get a little *zing* watching him walk toward her. But there was no *zing* today, only a growing sense of panic.

With Karen's predictions ringing in my ears, I made sure I sounded happy to see him when I answered. "For you? Sure." I nodded toward the key. "What's that?"

"What do you think it is?"

His eyes were sort of sleepy and sexy, and I got a bad feeling in the pit of my stomach. "Looks like a key to me."

He leaned on the counter and ran those sexy blue eyes up and down my body. "As a matter of fact, it's a key to my place. What do you say? You interested?"

"A key? To your house?" I could feel Karen watching us, but I refused to make eye contact with her. I already knew what I'd see if I did. "You're kidding, right? You're giving me a key? Just like that?"

Jawarski's smile dimmed. "You don't want it?"

"Did it ever occur to you that I might want to talk about this first? In *private*?"

"Whoa! Hold on. Relax, slick. It's not what you think."

He tossed the key onto the counter where it clattered, metal on glass. "I have to leave town for a couple of weeks. I just came by to ask if you'd mind taking in my mail while I'm gone."

Embarrassment came hard on the heels of anger, and I shot Karen a look that might have killed a weaker woman. "Your mail?"

"Yeah. Do you mind? I can put in a delivery hold at the post office if you don't want to."

I waved away his last suggestion and managed a thin smile. "Don't be silly. Of course I can take in your mail. Is that all?"

He shrugged. "No plants. No pets." As if I didn't know that already. "Mail's it."

I tucked the key into my pocket and tried for a genuine smile this time. "That should be easy enough. When are you leaving?"

"Tomorrow morning." He eyed me cautiously, as if he expected me to wig out or something. "I know it's short notice, but it's really a last-minute thing."

This is the beauty of an uncommitted relationship, I told myself. There's no pressure. One partner can flit off at a moment's notice and the other one is just fine with it. No drama. No hysterics. No jealousy. I shot an I-told-you-so look at Karen and practically beamed at Jawarski. "I think it sounds wonderful. Where are you going?"

"Montana. Ridge's birthday is next week, and Bree called last night to suggest I come up there. She thought I might like to spend some time with the kids."

All those ugly insecurities bashed me, and my smile grew brittle. One whack with a kitchen mallet and it would have shattered into a hundred pieces. Don't get me wrong. I didn't begrudge him a visit with his kids. But the one time I'd met Cheyenne and Ridge had been a total disaster. He wasn't ready for me to be part of their lives, so every time he slipped into dad mode, I was left out. Some day I might become a part of their special triumvirate, but I wasn't yet.

But that wasn't what made my nerve endings tingle. Somewhere along the way I'd developed a case of ex-wife-itis—probably because Jawarski mentioned his ex so rarely, I was never certain where things stood between them.

It was hard to ignore the smug look Karen flung at me, but I did my best. "The trip was your ex-wife's idea?"

Jawarski nodded as if dropping everything to accept an invitation from the ex was the most natural thing in the world. "I haven't seen the kids in a few months, and I have a couple of weeks of vacation saved up."

Jealous girlfriend questions rose in my throat, but I bit them all back. My reaction had nothing to do with Jawarski and everything to do with Roger. Karen's earlier comments had just made me more susceptible to doubt, that's all.

"What a great idea," I said, trying very hard to mean it. "I'll bet the kids are excited."

Jawarski smiled, relief evident in every line on his face. "They seem to be."

See? We were fine. And Jawarski leaving for two weeks should prove, even to Karen, that there are some couples who are just fine without hearts and flowers . . . and even candy.

Apparently satisfied that I wasn't angry with him, Jawarski leaned across the counter and kissed me briefly. "Listen, I've gotta run. There's some kind of trouble over at the theater and I need to check on it. But I'll call you while I'm gone. And I should be back by Valentine's Day, so think about what you want to do that night." He walked backward for a couple of steps and spread his arms wide. "I'm all yours, babe. Just name it."

Babe?

It was a good thing he left when he did, because if I'd named it right then, we'd probably both have been sorry.

The door had barely closed behind Jawarski when the bell tinkled to signal another customer. We get a fair amount of walk-in traffic since we're situated in a prime location, one I could never afford if I were trying to set up a business today. Paradise is growing rapidly, and in the tourist season

we get a lot of spillover from Aspen and Vail. So it's not unusual for someone I don't recognize to walk into Divinity.

It *is* unusual for that someone to be barking into a cell
phone so intently he doesn't pay any attention to where he's
walking. The customer, a twig of a man with reddish hair
and hard blue eyes, plowed into a display table loaded with
old-fashioned candy sticks and sent half of them crashing to
the floor. He glared at them as if they'd bashed into him and
shifted his cell phone to his other ear.

"No, no, no. I said today. It *has* to be here today. Which
part of that word do you have trouble understanding?"

Karen was still busy with the boxes and Liberty wasn't in
yet, so guess who got to wait on him. *Lucky me.*

I pasted on a bland smile—the best I could do considering what he'd just done to half my stock of candy sticks—
and waited for him to acknowledge me. He plowed across
the mess he'd made, crunching candy underfoot. I swear, I
could smell money burning.

"If you can't do it, say so now," he snarled into his phone.
"I'll find someone who can." An ugly smile curved his thin
lips as he listened to the response. "That's what I thought.
The Summit Lodge, no later than five. Got that?" He snapped
his phone shut and fixed his hard little eyes on me. "How soon
can you deliver a two-pound box of candy across town?"

"I'm sorry," I said, making my best effort to look sincere,
"but delivery isn't one of our services." Unless you placed a
really big special order or I liked you. Which left this guy
out in the cold. "We do offer gift wrapping though, and you
can handpick the chocolates you want to include in your se-
lection."

He wagged his narrow head from side to side and let out
his breath in an irritated huff. "You've got to be kidding,
right? What kind of Podunk town is this? Do you know who
I am?"

I was pretty sure he wouldn't like my answer to either
question, so I ignored them both and gave up trying to smile.
"If you need something delivered, maybe you should—"

Before I could finish, Karen bolted through the door and

nudged me out of the way. "Of course we'll deliver your order, but depending on where you want it delivered, we may have to charge a small delivery fee."

He shot me a haughty look and pulled out his wallet. "Money's not the issue. Time is. You ought to teach your girl here a thing or two about customer satisfaction."

"Her *girl*?" Furious, I nudged Karen out of the way. "Now you listen here—"

Karen locked eyes with me. "Why don't I help the gentleman so you can get back to the kitchen?"

An indignant refusal rose to my lips, but I swallowed it and turned away. I'd have loved to order him out of the store and tell him what he could do with his money, but maybe Karen was right. I wasn't in the best mood. Maybe I should let her handle the situation.

Leaving Karen with Mr. Personality, I pulled sugar, corn syrup, and flavor oils from the cupboards and dug out my large copper kettle. A few months ago I'd run through Divinity's sales records for the past five years and I'd created a game plan for what to make when so we could get through the holiday season with relative ease. Today's schedule called for ten dozen red rose lollipops in assorted flavors and two batches of cherry divinity. If I didn't get started soon, I'd still be pouring syrup into molds at midnight.

A few minutes later Liberty blew into the kitchen, *oohing* and *aahing* over the decorations as she shed her coat and tucked her purse into a drawer. "This is so exciting!" she said, clapping her hands in delight. "It looks even better in the daylight than it did last night. What do you think, Abby? Isn't it great?"

Usually, I'm a stickler for the truth, but I knew what Karen would do if I told Liberty to pull everything down, so I kept my eyes on the pan and said only, "You two certainly were busy."

"I know. It took us forever to do it all, but if you're happy, then it was worth it."

What was I supposed to say to that? The argument over the decorations was between Karen and me. It wouldn't be fair to put Liberty in the middle. Luckily, another customer came into the shop and Liberty hurried away to help her before the silence dragged out too long.

I spent the next few minutes taking out my frustrations on the thick mixture of sugar and syrup with a wooden spoon. When the bell jangled again, I glanced up just in time to see Mr. Personality leave.

Don't let the door hit ya—

Karen finished up at the cash register and turned to look over the half wall that separated the shop from the kitchen. "Do you know who that was?"

"No, and I don't care either. He was rude and obnoxious."

Karen tilted her head to one side, a silent acknowledgment that I had a point. At least she gave me that.

"So who was he?"

"His name is Geoffrey Manwaring, and he's Laurence Nichols's manager."

Okay, she had my attention. Laurence Nichols is to Colorado what Donny Osmond is to Utah. Without the brood of siblings. Or the teeth. Or the Mormon background. Laurence started out in Paradise as a kid, and the folks around here practically idolize him. I have to admit, I was a little starstruck, myself. But only a little.

"That doesn't excuse the way he acted. Why would Laurence Nichols keep such an annoying person on his payroll?"

"Probably because he can get things done. He doesn't take *no* for an answer."

I snorted a laugh. "I could have made him."

"I'm sure you could have, but that wouldn't have been the best move for Divinity."

"Neither is pandering to awful people."

"He wanted a box of chocolates delivered," Karen said, growing impatient with me. "Was that so awful?"

"He called me *your girl*," I reminded her. "And yes, it was awful. If we deliver for him, we're going to have to deliver for everyone who flashes a little cash or thinks they're special. It's setting a bad precedent, one we can't afford."

"We already deliver under special circumstances," Karen said, coming into the kitchen and lowering her voice so it wouldn't carry. "You just didn't want to deliver for him because he was rude."

"Bingo!"

"Well, relax. I'll have Liberty make the delivery so you won't even have to think about it again. Meanwhile, we made a nice sale and we can now say that Laurence Nichols is a customer."

I glanced at her sharply. "They were for Laurence?"

"Yes they were. A nice gift from Laurence to a woman who lives right here in Paradise. If he's happy with our service, maybe he'll order more. Can you imagine what it would do for the store if he bought Valentine's Day candy from us?"

I had to admit, he'd make a nice addition to our client list. "As long as I don't have to deal with Mr. Manhandle," I bargained.

Grinning from ear to ear, Karen sketched an *X* across her chest. "I promise, you never have to see Geoffrey Manwaring again if you don't want to."

She had good reason to grin. So far, the score was Karen 2, Abby 0, and all I could do was hope the worst was over.

Chapter 3

We had a rush of customers after Manwaring left, and we all stayed busy for the next several hours. I didn't have a chance to think about anything but rose-shaped lollipops and cherry divinity until Vonetta Cummings strolled into the shop with Paisley Pringle on her heels late in the afternoon.

Liberty had left a few minutes earlier to deliver Manwaring's order, and the shop was crowded with teenage girls making plans for the Sweetheart Ball that weekend, but they seemed to be shopping in a pack and Karen had taken charge.

Vonetta stood out from the crowd for several reasons. First, she's tall, slim, and regal and the rest of our customers were mostly short and giggly. She's also closer to sixty than sixteen.

She wore a long chocolate-colored coat and boots. Paired with matching leopard print hat, scarf, and gloves she looked as if she'd just stepped out of a fashion magazine. She's the only woman I know who can wear that much animal print and not look overblown.

Vonetta has been manager of the Paradise Playhouse for as long as I can remember, and I've always admired her. Even when I was a girl and African Americans were rare in Paradise, she dressed to celebrate her heritage. Her choices might not seem remarkable now, but in those days her wardrobe created quite a stir. Back then, Paradise wasn't known for its forward thinking.

Paisley, on the other hand, dresses like most of us—jeans,

old sweater stuffed under last year's ski jacket, feet laced into an inexpensive pair of black igloo boots. She owns the local beauty shop and changes her hairstyle at least once a month. February's choice: a sleek mop of burgundy curls that spilled into her eyes every time she moved.

I was happy to see Vonetta. Paisley, not so much.

I finished ringing up the customer I'd been helping, then let myself out from behind the counter and found them looking at the one-pound milk chocolate assortment. I nodded at Paisley and told Vonetta, "We have some of those marshmallow caramels you like in the alcove if you're interested."

Vonetta looked up with a warm smile. "I'll definitely pick up a box. How are you, Abby?"

"Fine. We've been swamped all day, but that's good. How about you?"

Vonetta pulled off her gloves and slipped them into her coat pocket. "Busy. We're starting a new production this week."

We? As in Vonetta and Paisley? When had that happened? It's not that I dislike Paisley. Or that I think she's incompetent. She's been running the Curl Up and Dye successfully for years. But there's something about her that just rubs me the wrong way.

I tried not to let my reaction show. "Does this mean you're involved in the theater now?" I asked her.

Paisley nodded and dark red curls bounced across her forehead. "I'm Vonetta's assistant. Just part-time, of course. In the evenings. Because of the salon. But it's so exciting. I just love it."

"We're giving it a try," Vonetta clarified, but the almost maternal glance she sent Paisley erased any hint of rebuke. "If things work out with this production, we'll talk about something permanent."

"Oh. Sure. Sounds great." Okay, yeah, I was a little envious. I'd been in one production at the Playhouse, and that was almost twenty-five years ago. But I'd been friends with Vonetta's daughter, Serena, and I'd spent hours hanging out with her at the Playhouse watching the companies put their performances together. Apparently, I still felt a proprietary interest in what happened there.

I shoved the envy aside and said, "I heard there was some trouble over your way this morning. Anything serious?"

Vonetta's smile faded slightly. "Thankfully, no. Just a bit of youthful exuberance. A member of the stage crew tied one on last night and forgot to sleep it off before he came to work. He didn't like being told to go home." She shook her head indulgently. "Life in the theater is never dull. But your handsome young policeman showed up and set everything to rights."

I still felt a brief jolt whenever someone referred to Jawarski as "mine," but I was learning not to flinch when they did. "I'm glad to hear it. What can I get for you?"

"I'll take the caramels," Vonetta said, "but we didn't come in to shop. I'm here to talk with you about the play."

I'd been placing ads in the playbills almost as long as I'd been owner of Divinity, so I assured her, "I'll take a quarter page. Do you need the check today?"

Vonetta shook her head. "Drop it off any time in the next couple of weeks." She glanced at the small seating area in the center of the shop. A handful of girls had taken over two of the wrought-iron tables, but the third was unoccupied. "Do you mind if we sit for a minute? Do you have time?"

"Sounds serious," I said with a grin. "Sure. I can take a quick break." While Vonetta and Paisley dealt with coats, gloves, and scarves, I rounded up a spare chair and carried it to the table. "So? What's going on?"

"I need your help," Vonetta said. "I'm here to ask a favor, and I hope you'll say yes."

"I will if I can," I promised. "What do you need?"

"We're doing a musical comedy. A fun new piece from a playwright in Utah." She looked me square in the eye and added, "This play is important to me. It's important to the reputation of the Playhouse, and I want to make sure I have people I can rely on in the cast and crew."

She looked so serious, I laughed uneasily. "What does that have to do with me?"

"I want you in the cast. And don't tell me you aren't interested because I know better. As for talent, you've acted before, so I know you can do it."

I bleated another uneasy laugh. "Nothing like cutting my arguments off at the knees." Sure, I'd nursed dreams of becoming a great actress once upon a time, but that was a dream for another lifetime. Besides, although I'm not one to carry a grudge, I hadn't forgotten that Vonetta had cast me as one of the nameless, faceless wives of the King of Siam while propelling Chrissie Montague into the spotlight with the dancer position I'd wanted. "I'm sorry, Vonetta, but *The King and I* was both my debut and my swan song."

The girls at the other tables roared with laughter over something. Paisley leaned closer and almost shouted, "Don't say no. It's going to be a blast."

"I'm sure it will be, but I really have to pass. It's not that I don't want to help, just ask me something else. Something I can actually do. Why are *you* casting, anyway?" I asked Vonetta. "Don't tell me you're directing?"

"I haven't directed in years," she said. "I don't have the energy to produce and take on other jobs anymore, but I'm making an exception this time. Alexander Pastorelli has agreed to direct, but he doesn't do his own casting."

I knew the name, of course. I think just about everyone in the tri-peaks area did. Like Laurence Nichols, he's a local celebrity, and recently his star had risen high enough to catch the attention of a producer with connections to Broadway. If I remembered my trivia right, Laurence and Alexander had even started out at the same time. I wondered whether there was a connection between Vonetta's play and Laurence Nichols's visit to Paradise, or if it was just a coincidence.

"I've been hearing rumors for weeks that he's heading to New York. Does this mean he's not?"

"He's not leaving for a few weeks, and he's agreed to put on a farewell performance at the Playhouse before he goes."

Which explained why the production was so important to her. "You must have offered him a terrific deal."

Vonetta's lips curled into a soft smile. "We don't have the money to offer terrific deals. I've had to trade shamelessly on his sentimental nature. He has a soft spot in his heart for the Playhouse. It's where he got his start."

"He said yes, so he must not have minded too much. So you're his casting director?"

She nodded. "I need reliable people in the cast," she said again. "The play is likely to have a larger audience than usual. We've already scheduled a longer run than normal."

"Not to mention the media," Paisley said.

Vonetta waved off the suggestion. "There may be some media attention, but let's not get ahead of ourselves. I can't even think about that until I know I have the cast in place."

"But I'm not really an actor, Vonetta. You know that."

"You did a fine job in *The King and I*."

"That was a long time ago," I reminded her. "All I had to do was sit in the corner and look like a devoted member of Brian Hubbard's harem."

Vonetta laughed softly. "You did more than that. As I recall, you had quite a nice singing voice."

"I have a lousy singing voice," I said firmly.

"I seem to recall you being quite disappointed when you were cast as a member of the chorus. Weren't you interested in one of the more prominent roles?"

"I wanted to be a dancer, but I was sixteen and in shape. And I had no idea that I had absolutely no talent."

"Don't be ridiculous." Vonetta waved a hand and beamed up at me. "It doesn't really matter anyway. I *don't* need a singer, I need someone with rhythm. You don't have to be a professional dancer."

"I'm sorry, but I can't. And you really should believe me when I say I wouldn't be any good. I haven't danced in years. I'm so out of shape, I'd embarrass the entire cast if I tried now." Not to mention myself. "My thighs haven't come within speaking distance of dance tights in years, and they aren't about to renew their acquaintance now."

Vonetta laughed. "Then I guess it won't make any difference to you that Laurence Nichols is musical director?"

So there *was* a connection. But she wasn't fighting fair. Anyone with an interest in music or theater would trip their mother for a chance to work with him. Not that I *had* an interest.

"So that's why Laurence Nichols's manager was in here this morning. They're here for your play."

Vonetta's expression changed subtly. "You've met Geoffrey."

I nodded. "Yeah. Lucky me."

"Don't let him turn you off," Paisley urged. "Laurence has agreed to work on the production as a favor to Alexander. And Alexander hired Colleen Brannigan—you remember, Colleen Miller?—as stage manager. Come on, you know you want to see her again."

For all four years of high school, Colleen and I had been inseparable. In fact, she'd been another member of Brian Hubbard's harem, and the time we'd spent hanging out together offstage had almost made up for the disappointing roles we'd been assigned. Knowing that she'd be at the theater every day for the next few weeks exerted a powerful tug.

But I couldn't ignore the facts. "It's almost Valentine's Day," I said. "I have no time, no talent, and no training."

"We're casting now," Vonetta said. "We won't even start rehearsals for a few more days. You'd have plenty of time after the holiday to become familiar with the part."

"But I—"

Paisley glowered at me. "I don't know how you can turn Vonetta down. She's never been anything but supportive of you. Didn't she start selling some of your candy from the concession stand a few months ago?"

"You don't have to tell me how supportive Vonetta has been," I said, trying not to let my irritation show, "and I appreciate everything she's done."

"You have a funny way of showing it."

It had been a long day, and I didn't have the energy or the patience for this. Before I could zap Paisley back, Vonetta rose majestically from her chair. "Ladies, please. Don't create bad feelings over something so minor. If you really don't want to be in the play, I won't press you."

She looked disappointed, and I suffered a sharp pang of guilt. "I *can't* be in the play," I said again. "There's a difference."

"You can't blame me for trying, right? I'm sure I'll find people to fill all the roles eventually."

"Of course you will. Everyone loves the Playhouse, and they love working with you."

"We'll hope, won't we?" She gathered her coat and scarf, and smiled fondly at Paisley, who was shooting daggers at me from beneath knit brows. "It looks as if you'll get your wish after all, Paisley. If you want the role of Isabel, it's yours. I just hope you aren't taking on more than you can handle."

Paisley gave me one last look and turned to Vonetta with a smile. "I'll be fine. Mom's at the salon every day, and she knows how much this means to me."

"If you change your mind," Vonetta said as she pulled on her coat again, "you know where to find me."

I stood there for a minute after they left, trying to get a handle on what I was feeling. I hated turning Vonetta down. I could have kicked myself for passing up the chance to meet and work with Laurence Nichols. And that slow curl of envy for Paisley hadn't gone away.

But what choice did I have? I couldn't turn my back on Divinity either. Not to mention the fact that Karen would have killed me if I'd said yes.

Chapter 4

The next two days passed in a blur of sugar, cream, caramel, and chocolate. A large order of white Russian truffles for a luncheon at the golf course kept me working late into the night so I couldn't even slip away to check Jawarski's mail. On Saturday evening, I turned the key in the lock promptly at seven and went up to my apartment on the third floor above the shop to gather Max, my Doberman pinscher, and head over to Jawarski's house.

Since we used the second floor to store orders waiting for delivery and candy that wouldn't fit into the displays, Max had been confined to the apartment while I worked. Judging from the bits of wicker in the middle of my living room floor, the claw marks on the kitchen door, and the mound of dirty clothes Max had dragged into the hall to sleep on, the long hours I'd been working had taken their toll on both of us.

The temperature still hovered right around zero, so cold it hurt to breathe, and the Jetta coughed a couple of times before it finally cranked over. Max didn't seem to mind, but he was so glad to be around people he wouldn't have minded anything.

While I chugged across town, I phoned my nieces, Dana and Danielle. They're seniors in high school and involved in everything. They're also tough negotiators, but the promise of an empty apartment for a few hours after school gave me the upper hand for once. After some discussion, we struck a bargain. They'd spend time with Max every afternoon until after the holiday, I'd provide soda and chips, and Max would stop chewing my stuff.

I hung up as I pulled into Jawarski's driveway in front of his unnaturally dark house. *I* would have left a light on, but I'd spent twenty years in the city, so I also locked the Jetta when I parked it. Just another way Jawarski and I were different.

Max and I climbed out into the cold and trudged to the mailbox on the curb. I pulled out a handful of junk mail and a couple of bills and carted it up the walk to the front door. "Well, this is it, Max," I said as I turned the key in the lock. "Feels a little weird to be here without him, doesn't it?"

Max didn't seem to think so. He nudged open the door with his nose and trotted into the kitchen with his stubby tail wagging expectantly. Unfamiliar shadows danced across the walls as I fumbled for the light switch.

When I could finally see, I tossed the mail onto the kitchen table and stood for a minute just breathing in the atmosphere. It smelled like Jawarski in here—a mixture of coffee and spice and something else that was pure Jawarski. At least *that* was familiar. I'd been married to Roger for twenty years, and I'd known him almost as well as I knew myself—or I'd thought I did. Jawarski and I had only been flirting with this relationship for two years, and he was still an unknown quantity. If Jawarski and I decided to make a commitment, would he ever become as familiar as Roger had? Did I want him to?

Maybe that's why I was having so much trouble letting Jawarski past my internal security gates. I missed the idea of belonging with someone and having a routine that felt as comfortable as my own skin. But the thought of living with a relative stranger, of waking up to unfamiliar tousled hair and morning breath made a spiny knot of panic twist in my stomach.

A shiver rattled me out of my thoughts, and I realized for the first time that the house was icy cold. Either Jawarski had turned down the heat while he was gone, or the wind had blown out the pilot light.

Hoping I wouldn't have to crawl around in the basement to get the furnace going, I nudged up the thermostat a few degrees. A few seconds later I heard the gratifying sound of the furnace kicking on, followed by the smell of burning dust.

I thanked my lucky stars and turned the thermostat down again, then turned on the kitchen faucet to a low trickle to keep the pipes from freezing. After checking the windows and doors to make sure they were all shut and locked, I led Max outside and locked the door behind me.

On my way back to the Jetta, I realized that I was going to have to sort through my commitment issues or Karen's predictions would come true. Eventually, Jawarski would get tired of my uncertainty. Anyone would.

But that was a job for another night. I had two whole weeks to think about our relationship. I didn't have to do it tonight.

As I drove back through town, I cranked up the stereo and warbled along with Carrie Underwood. Snow, unmelted since the last big storm, lay piled against the sides of the road. Slush and dirty spray from passing cars had turned it all an ugly shade of gray.

My voice cracked on a high note, and I lapsed into silence. Why on earth Vonetta would want *this* voice in her play was beyond me. But I'd heard Paisley singing along to the piped in music at the Curl, and I knew she wasn't any better.

Two blocks from home, I decided to be smart and pick up dinner rather than relying on the questionable supplies in my kitchen. I ran through my options quickly and settled my taste buds on a bratwurst sandwich and macaroni salad from the deli. The perfect comfort food for a cold winter night.

I pulled into the first empty parking spot I came across, clipped on Max's leash, and climbed out into the freezing cold. Two cars away, Dylan Wagstaff and Richie Bellieu stepped onto the curb in front of me.

The two men have been life partners for years. They also own the Silver River Inn, a bed-and-breakfast on the north end of town. When you meet Richie, you're left with no doubt about his sexual preferences. Dylan's a bit less obvious.

Neither of them noticed me at first. Dylan was arguing mildly with Richie, whose attention was riveted on something inside the satchel slung over his shoulder.

"Hey there," I said as they drew even with me. "What are you two doing?"

Richie's head shot up in surprise. When he saw Max and me, he flapped a hand at me and flung himself on Max's neck. Richie and my dog are members of an elite mutual admiration society, and they never let a chance to indulge slip past them.

As he watched them, a smile replaced the frown on Dylan's face. "Hey there yourself," he said to me. "Haven't seen you around in a while. You must be busy."

"Valentine's Day," I said. We'd been friends through two seasons already, so he knew how things were. "Have you guys eaten? I was just going to pick something up, but if you're free—"

Richie gave Max one last air-kiss and stood. "Sorry, Abs. We ate before we left home." He started walking slowly, and the rest of us followed. "If you don't want to eat alone, why don't you grab some takeout and bring it to the Playhouse? I'm sure nobody would mind."

Ice crunched beneath our feet as we walked, and the cold made talking difficult. Or maybe it was the unexpected jolt of envy that snuck up the center of my chest. "You guys are going to the theater? Does that mean you're in the play?"

Richie nodded so fast, he looked like a bobblehead doll. "*I* am. Dylan volunteered for the stage crew so we could do something together." He grinned at his partner and added, "Something away from the inn."

I tried to imagine Jawarski and me searching for extra-curricular activities to share, but the picture wouldn't form. We were both too independent, I guess. Or we had nothing in common. I wasn't sure which.

"Sounds great. I had no idea you were interested in theater."

"Oh, sure," Richie said. "I've always wanted to be on stage. Besides, *Laurence Nichols* is the musical director." He shot a guilty smile at Dylan. "I'm sorry. I know I'm taken, but there's just something about him, you know?"

I think we all knew.

"Snaring him for the play is quite a coup for Vonetta," Dylan said. "I wonder how she managed to get both Laurence Nichols *and* Alexander Pastorelli for the same production?"

"Either the theater is doing better than anyone realized," Richie speculated, "or she's blackmailing them."

"Vonetta? Blackmail?" I laughed. "Not likely. She's one of the most ethical people I know."

"Then she must be rich. All I know is, I'm dying to meet Laurence." Richie touched Dylan's arm briefly, reassuring him that he had nothing to worry about.

Dylan didn't appear concerned, and I felt another pang of envy over that. More than anything, I wanted to feel that kind of absolute trust in someone again. "What's going on tonight?" I asked. "I thought rehearsals hadn't started yet."

"They haven't," Dylan said, swerving to avoid a patch of ice on the sidewalk. "Vonetta called a mandatory meeting for the whole company."

"Oh. In that case, I shouldn't bring my dinner in."

Richie slipped behind us as we passed a couple walking in the other direction, then scurried up to walk three abreast again. "I'm sure it will be fine. Who's going to care?"

"I don't know," I said with a shrug. "Alexander Pastorelli maybe? Or Laurence Nichols? Or both? I'm sure neither of them wants spectators hanging around before opening night."

We reached the glass doors of the theater and stopped walking. I could see people milling about in the lobby. Some, I recognized—Gavin Trotter, Rachel Summers, Paisley Pringle—and some I didn't, but this time the longing to be part of the group didn't surprise me.

I'd been struggling ever since I came back to Paradise to find my place back among my friends and neighbors. Here was the perfect opportunity to get more involved, and I was turning my back on it.

Dylan followed my gaze, then slid a glance at me. "I'm surprised Vonetta hasn't tagged you for a part."

I wondered if he could sense my ambivalence. "She tried," I admitted, "but the shop's just too busy with the holiday right around the corner. I had to turn her down."

"You're going to be sorry you did that," Richie predicted. "The script is hilarious. It's one of those plays within a play about a group of silent movie actors making a talking version of *The Pirates of Penzance*. They're all beautiful, but none of them can sing a note and their speaking voices are hideous so the director hires a bunch of ugly people to hide out in the sound booth and provide the voices."

"It's very clever, really," Dylan said. "Like *Singin' in the Rain*. I read the script when Richie brought it home. You should come with us and see what you think."

It sounded fun, but my practical side held out. "Another time, maybe."

"Oh, come on," Richie urged. "What can it hurt? Who knows? Maybe you'll get a chance meet Laurence Nichols."

That got me moving. The promise of warmth after standing outside in subzero temperatures *and* a chance to see Laurence Nichols in person? Didn't I deserve that much?

I trailed them inside and looked around for an out-of-the-way place to leave Max. I knew Vonetta wouldn't mind him being in the Playhouse, but the rehearsal hall at the far end of the building was already crowded and I didn't want to make things worse by squeezing a large dog into the mix. Besides, some people get nervous around Dobermans, and there might be strangers here tonight who didn't know that Max is a total teddy bear.

I tried the door to the box office, found it unlocked, and settled Max in the corner with a promise to come back soon. I closed the door to keep him from wandering and followed the sound of voices to the center of activity.

I could almost picture two Abbys sitting on my shoulders, one urging me to turn around and walk away before I got caught up in the excitement, the other telling me that I could be in the play without ignoring my responsibilities at work. *Besides*, Bad Abby asked, *what kind of friend was I to turn my back on Vonetta after she'd come to me for help?*

Experience has taught me that I shouldn't listen to that Abby. She's the one who gets me into trouble. The one at the heart of all my regrets. She doesn't care about my obligations, the success of the store, or my mental well-being. She doesn't worry about making ends meet. She only cares about doing what seems fun or feels good at the moment. I know all that about her . . . but I followed her anyway.

It wouldn't be long before I realized my mistake.

Chapter 5

A wave of heat rolled over me as I stepped down into the rehearsal hall. Someone had cranked up the thermostat, and the warmth that had been so welcome in the lobby became oppressive in the crowd.

The rehearsal hall is a long room that runs the width of the building, front to back. It's about a third as large as the stage, and it's in this room that most of the preproduction work on any play being staged at the Playhouse takes place.

Overflow props too large to fit in the storage closets teetered in precarious-looking stacks in the corners. Mirrors lining two walls allow dancers to see their moves as they practice, and posters from previous productions cover another wall. A bank of windows looks out on the alley that runs between the Playhouse and the insurance office next door.

Dylan and Richie melted into the crowd, but Rachel bounded up to me before I could get both feet through the door. I wasn't exactly surprised to see her in the cast. She's been telling me for the past two years that her life's ambition is to be a plus-sized model, and she rarely steps outside unless she's ready for a photo shoot. Meanwhile, she runs the candle shop a few doors down from Divinity, and she's in and out of my shop almost as much as she is her own.

"I didn't know you were in the play!" she said, grabbing my arm and tugging me further into the room. Her short brown hair was carefully styled, her makeup perfect. Next to her I always feel like somebody's frumpy older sister. "You should have told me. We could have come together."

"I'm not in the play," I told her. "No time. Dylan and Richie dragged me in with them tonight, but I'm only staying a minute."

"Oh. Well that's too bad. It would have been fun." She craned to see over the crowd. "Can you believe this? What a zoo!"

That was an understatement. People had gathered in knots around the room. Some were catching up with each others' lives, some were reciting lines, some singing—although no two seemed to be singing the same song. A couple of women made practice runs at dance steps, and I had to dodge the enthusiastic twirls of a young woman with pale blond hair.

The creative energy swirling around the room was almost palpable. Vonetta had obviously stirred up plenty of interest in the play, so it wasn't as if she needed me. I could safely ignore the guilt trips my conscience kept trying to send me on.

Rachel spotted someone she needed to talk to and scooted off, leaving me to fend for myself. I felt out of place and uncomfortably conspicuous, so I hovered on the edge of the crowd where I wouldn't have to keep explaining what I was doing there.

I caught a glimpse of Vonetta, who looked imperial in an emerald-colored caftan embellished with a bold design in gold, talking to Geoffrey Manwaring and a short man with a stocky build on the other side of the room. Paisley hovered at her side, almost embarrassingly eager to please. A few steps behind, almost hidden from view, a plump woman wearing a bored expression watched the chaos.

Since I wasn't expecting to see her, it took almost a full second to recognize the bored woman as Vonetta's daughter, Serena. Years ago, when we were both enamored of the theater, we'd spent hours in this room, but Serena's love of the stage had clearly evaporated somewhere along the way. She didn't look enamored of anything tonight.

I was surprised to see her in the rehearsal hall—not only because of her antipathy for the world of the stage, but because she'd been gone from Paradise almost as long as I had. I wondered why Vonetta hadn't told me that she was back.

"Abby? Is that you?"

Making a mental note to connect with Serena later, I turned to see who was calling me and found Colleen Miller—Colleen *Brannigan*—surging through the crowd toward me. Colleen looked exactly the same. Her short hair was the same buttery blond it had been in school, and if she'd gained an ounce, she hid it well.

She hugged me as if we'd seen each other just yesterday. "I can't believe you're here. They told me you weren't going to be in the play. Did you change your mind?"

I shook my head, but it was getting harder and harder to say no. "I just stopped by to see if Vonetta found enough people for the cast. Apparently, I didn't need to worry."

Colleen trailed her gaze around the crowded room. "We've had a pretty good turnout," she agreed, "but the show isn't completely cast yet."

"Really? I'd have thought that people would be fighting each other for the chance to work with Laurence and Alexander."

"They are," Colleen said with a rueful smile. "Vonetta's turned away so many people it makes my head spin. We could have had three casts already if she'd stop being so picky."

"She has to be discriminating, doesn't she? She's casting for a couple of bigwigs."

Colleen shrugged and tilted her head toward the men Vonetta was talking to. "Alexander knows what he's getting into. This is semiprofessional theater, not Broadway. None of these actors are getting paid, and you're not going to get star quality performances for nothing."

"Is that Alexander?" I asked, feeling a faint flutter of disappointment. Aren't superstars supposed to be tall, well-built, and handsome?

Colleen nodded. "And he's on one tonight. I don't know what's going on over there, but he hasn't been happy since he walked through the door."

Sure enough, Alexander's face had turned a mottled

shade of red, and from where I stood it looked as if he could have throttled Geoffrey Manwaring cheerfully. *Get in line, buddy. Me first.* I wondered what Mr. Personality had done now.

Before I could find out, a sullen-looking man of about fifty came up behind us. His hair was more salt than pepper, and his stocky build was just starting to run to fat. He said something in Colleen's ear and her smile faded. For a heart-beat she looked almost as unhappy as he did, but she smiled again and the shadows fled.

She took Smiley's arm and pulled him forward. "This is Abby Shaw, an old friend from *way* too many years ago. Abby, my husband Doyle."

Her husband? That surprised me. I would never have matched the two of them in a million years. I said I was pleased to meet him. Doyle mumbled something under his breath and pumped my hand once. Whether he'd said he was pleased to meet me or told me to go to hell was anyone's guess.

"Well, I wish you were going to join us," she said, return-ing to our conversation. "Are you sure I can't convince you to change your mind?"

I laughed and shook my head. "I'll admit it's tempting, but I run the candy shop now, and Valentine's Day . . ."

"Yeah, I know. Vonetta told me. We should at least get together for lunch now and then. Doyle and I are just over in Leadville."

As the crow flies, Leadville is less than twenty miles from Paradise, but it takes at least forty-five minutes to drive there. I said "Yeah, we really should," but I wondered if we ever would. "So you've stayed active in the theater," I said. "Vonetta tells me you're going to be stage manager."

"Yes, and it's a terrific opportunity. I can't believe she hired me for this production."

"Don't be so modest. Vonetta's loyal to her friends, but she wouldn't risk this production just for friendship. You must be good at what you do."

"I've worked with Laurence a few times," Colleen said,

ducking her head as if the admission embarrassed her. "And I've met Alexander. I just happened to be free when they needed someone." The gleam of triumph in her eyes gave her away. She hadn't landed this job by luck. She'd worked hard to get here.

Doyle spoke again, still too low for me to hear what he said, but the softness evaporated from Colleen's expression and she rounded on her husband. "Stop it, Doyle," she snarled. "I mean it. This is not the time or the place."

Doyle snorted a harsh laugh, and I wondered if he'd been drinking. "You expect me to just sit back and pretend like I don't know what's going on?"

I didn't have any trouble hearing him now, and neither did anyone around us. A few people fell silent, and several turned to see what was going on.

Colleen's face flamed and anger sparked in her eyes. "*Nothing's* going on. I've told you that a hundred times."

Doyle barked another ugly laugh. "Yes. Yes, you have. So why don't I believe you?"

What a jerk.

Colleen's eyes turned to stone. "I don't know, and I don't care," she ground out, her voice almost too low for me to hear. "You have absolutely no reason to suspect me, and I *refuse* to let you destroy another job for me. If you can't keep your suspicions to yourself, then please leave."

I inched away, convinced that Colleen wouldn't want me to hear their argument any more than I wanted to listen. Suddenly, the idea of staying long enough to meet Laurence Nichols didn't sound nearly so appealing.

Doyle seemed oblivious to the audience he was drawing. "You'd like that, wouldn't you? Kick me out. Make me look like some kind of lunatic, and you stay here with *Nichols*." He spat out the name and his face contorted, as if it had left a bad taste in his mouth.

My feet stopped moving. *Colleen and Laurence Nichols?* Was he serious?

The sparks in Colleen's eyes flashed again. "I mean it,

Doyle. Either shut up, or leave. Go back to the Avalanche and polish off the gin. I'll know where to find you when the meeting's over."

The noise level in the rehearsal hall rose by another decibel or two and some kind of activity broke out near the wall of posters. Grateful for the distraction, I turned to see what was going on. Colleen moved to stand beside me, wearing a look of grim determination, and a few seconds later I saw Doyle slinking out the door. Apparently, she'd won the argument—for now anyway.

"I'm sorry about that," she said. "Doyle's . . . well, he's—"

"Don't worry about it," I said, trying to spare both of us the discomfort. "Is everything all right now?"

She nodded and some of the tension seemed to leave her. Frankly, I thought she was either unbelievably naive or a master at self-deception. Pouring alcohol on top of Doyle's suspicions wasn't likely to make things between them any better. But her marriage wasn't any of my business, and I was in no position to offer advice.

Just then, Vonetta clapped her hands and called out, "All right, everyone. Let's get to work."

Both Colleen and I turned toward her eagerly.

"I promised we'd be out of here by nine, and I intend to keep my word. Casting is nearly complete; I expect to fill the open roles by early next week. Those of you who have already been cast or assigned positions on the stage crew will stay in this room so Alexander and Laurence can run through a few things with you. Those of you who are here to audition will come with me into the auditorium. That should give the rest of you room to move around."

A few people shifted closer to the door, ready to move on. Vonetta gave a few basic instructions about rehearsal schedules and explained where the call-board would be, reminding everyone to check it frequently. "I'm not going to hold your hands," she said. "Don't expect individual phone calls. It's your responsibility to check the call-board and to know when you're needed."

Paisley held out a file folder, and Vonetta took it almost without looking. She spoke over her shoulder to Serena, who shrugged but stood and scowled down at her fingernails.

Serena had always seemed like a shadow of her mother, and apparently nothing had changed. Vonetta was the strong, vibrant one who commanded attention. Next to her, Serena seemed almost invisible. She'd been out on her own for two decades, yet here she was, melting into her mother's shadow as if she'd never left.

"As most of you know," Vonetta continued, "we have an impressive array of talent lined up for this play already, and our production team is top-notch. Colleen Brannigan will be our stage manager."

As if Vonetta had thrown a switch, Colleen beamed and waved one hand over her head. Her smile might look genuine from a distance, but I was close enough to see how fake it was. A polite spattering of applause greeted her introduction, and even the most stubborn whispers finally died away.

Vonetta waited for the applause to fade before making her next introduction. "Alexander Pastorelli is someone I'm sure you all recognize. He's the reason you're here, and I'm delighted that he's agreed to direct this play for us."

Her introduction spawned another round of applause and even brought on a few cheers. His expression almost grim, Alexander turned toward the crowd and nodded, accepting the applause as his due.

"We're so lucky to have this next man in the company," Vonetta said when the noise quieted. "You all know and love him—the multitalented Laurence Nichols will be musical director." For such a small crowd, the cheers that rose up were almost deafening. Vonetta held up both hands in an appeal for them to quiet down. "Please, people. Quiet, please." When she could go on, she said, "Before I introduce him, I want to share an exciting piece of news. This morning, Laurence graciously offered to add four original pieces to the score. Some of you will have the honor of performing those pieces in public for the first time."

Another roar went up from the crowd. I caught a glimpse

of Richie, bouncing with excitement. Even Dylan looked interested. But what caught and held my attention was the look on Serena's round face. She wasn't looking at her mother, but at the man of the hour, Laurence Nichols himself. And the look on her face was one of pure, unadulterated hatred.

Chapter 6

On the television screen, Laurence Nichols looks like he's over six feet tall, well-built, with short dark hair and intense brown eyes. In person, he's probably five nine and his dark hair is flecked with gray. Still, a good-looking guy, even if he is a little too thin for my taste.

He rose to his feet and bowed to the crowd. Even from a distance, charisma radiated from him. Most of the women and half the men in the room were immediately under his spell. Colleen was one of the few who seemed unaffected, but I wondered if her reaction was genuine, or if she'd just learned how to protect herself from her husband's jealousy. Laurence might not be a Greek god, but it was easy to see why a squat little toad like Doyle Brannigan might feel threatened.

The crowd on the other side of the room shifted as people craned to see our resident superstar, and I caught a glimpse of Richie almost wetting his pants with excitement before he was swallowed up again. Vonetta beamed, obviously pleased by the reaction of the group. Alexander scowled, as if the rousing cheers annoyed him.

After the applause went on for a while, Vonetta held up both hands and called out, "Quiet everyone. Please. Settle down."

While she waited for the applause to die away and the noise level to subside, Richie worked his way to the front of the room. At the same time, Dylan appeared at my side wearing a slight scowl on his handsome face.

"Well, there he is," Dylan said with shake of his head.

"Almost close enough to touch. The poor fool's going to have his heart broken."

"You can't really think he's interested in Laurence," I said.

Dylan smiled ruefully. "Not in that way. But since he heard the very first rumor that Laurence Nichols might be coming to Paradise, he's been reinventing himself. He's managed to convince himself that being on stage is his life's calling, and that Laurence is going to discover him while he's here."

"It could happen," I said.

"Sure. If he could act." Dylan looked away from Richie and smiled at me. "But if you ever tell him I said that, I'll tell him what a horrible liar you are."

"Your secret's safe with me," I assured him. "I'd never get in the way of Richie's fantasies."

Dylan grinned. "Now *that's* a friend." He looked as if he intended to say more, but a loud bang cut him off and pulled my head around with a snap.

Laurence had moved from Vonetta's side to the piano in the far corner, and his expression had gone from pleased to furious. "Where in the hell is it?" he demanded. Before anyone could answer, he whipped around and jabbed a finger at Serena. "You took it, didn't you?"

I exchanged a glance with Dylan and inched a little closer—not that it was easy to do. Everyone in the room was trying to get close enough to see and hear everything they were saying.

Vonetta has always been like a mama bear when it comes to Serena, and tonight was no exception. She stepped in front of her daughter. "Don't be ridiculous," she said, but the reassuring tone of her voice didn't match the hard glint of anger in her eyes. "Of course Serena didn't take your music."

"She was in here alone earlier," Laurence accused. "I came in and found her snooping around my things."

"I wasn't snooping," Serena snapped. "And I wasn't alone. There was a stagehand in here with me almost the whole

time." She craned to look over the crowd and pointed toward
a young man of about twenty-five. His thin blond hair was
combed carefully forward in a David Beckham cut, but he
seemed uncomfortable with all the sudden attention. "What's
your name?" she demanded.

"Jason. Dahl."

"There you go," Serena said, as if his name proved something. "Jason can tell you I didn't steal your stupid music. I
don't know why you're making such a big deal about it anyway. Unless you're a complete idiot, you must have copies."

Laurence shoved past Vonetta and grabbed Serena by the
shoulders. Serena jerked away and gave him a look that
would have frozen someone less angry. "Take your hands
off me."

A few people gasped at her audacity, but the rest of us
could only stare at the drama unfolding in front of us. Why
would Laurence accuse Serena, of all people, of taking his
music? What possible reason could she have for doing that?
For that matter, what possible reason could *anyone* have?

Vonetta asked something similar, and Laurence rounded
on her as if she'd suggested that he'd stolen the music himself. Geoffrey Manwaring threw himself into the fray, and
whatever Laurence said in reply got lost behind his bluster.

He clapped a hand on Laurence's shoulder and murmured
reassuringly. It was clear Manwaring was telling his client
that everything was fine, Laurence was not to worry, that
he—Geoffrey—would take care of everything.

With Laurence under control again, Vonetta put an arm
around Serena's shoulders and led her toward the door that
opened into the shop area.

When they disappeared, Dylan let out a low whistle. "Well
that was interesting."

"To say the least," I agreed.

"What do you think that was all about?"

I shrugged and pulled my gaze away from the door.
"Which part? The music is missing part, or the Laurence
accusing Serena part?"

"Oh. My. God." Richie bounced to a stop in front of us,

his eyes wide with excitement. "Can you believe what just happened?"

"I'd have to understand it to believe it," Dylan said.

"We must have missed something," I told Richie. "Why did Laurence accuse Serena of taking his music?"

"I don't know. Nobody does." Richie glanced over his shoulder to make sure nothing was happening without him. "Vonetta's fit to be tied. I thought she was going to kill Laurence for accusing Serena, but then when Serena said that to Laurence . . ."

"It didn't sound like Serena," I mused. "Did it?"

Dylan shook his head. "Sorry. I don't know her. I can't say."

"Vonetta's *royally pissed* at her," Richie said, bouncing on the balls of his feet. "That's all I know. And I can't say I blame her. I mean, she almost single-handedly destroyed the whole production."

I grabbed the hem of his sweater in an attempt to stop the bouncing. "I think that's a bit harsh, don't you? Things are bad enough. Let's not make them worse by spreading all sorts of gossip."

Richie scowled and the skin between his eyes formed an accordion wrinkle. "Well, ex-*cuse* me. I thought you'd *want* to know what was going on."

He knew me too well. "I do," I said, lowering my voice a notch. "I just don't want to make things worse for Vonetta. There's going to be enough speculation as it is." For the first time in a while, I remembered Colleen and looked around to see where she'd gone. I found her standing a few feet away, watching Laurence closely and wearing a deep scowl. From where I stood, her expression looked a lot like jealousy. I had no idea whether she and Laurence were lovers, but I was pretty sure they were more than professional colleagues.

Vonetta reappeared in the doorway and waved Colleen over. She spoke briefly to her, punctuating the conversation with a gesture here, a nod toward Laurence or Alexander there, then disappeared again.

Colleen took charge at once. "All right people, calm down.

We'll sort out what happened to the sheet music, but in the meantime maybe we can convince Laurence to play something else for us. What do you say, Laurence? Will you play for us?"

For one fleeting second, Laurence's displeasure showed clearly on his face. In the next moment, his professionalism took over and a broad smile replaced his irritation. He bowed deeply in Colleen's direction and sat on the piano bench. Music we all recognized drifted into the room and the conversations around me hushed. One by one, people began to sing along. Those who didn't sing stopped chattering to listen. Two young women battled for position beside the piano while he played, apparently hoping that he'd take notice of them. Nearby, a heavyset woman of about forty alternated between glaring at the two young hopefuls and gazing adoringly at the object of everyone's desire.

Laurence seemed delighted by the attention, and the crumbs he tossed each of the women were just enough to keep them hanging on. For sheer entertainment value, it was the best thing I'd seen in a long time.

Vonetta returned to the rehearsal hall a few minutes later, smiling as if nothing unusual had happened. She gave cast and crew a brief rundown of the schedule for the next two weeks, glancing my way once or twice to see if I was grasping how little the schedule would impact my work schedule.

I did my best not to make eye contact. Not because I didn't want to be involved, because I did. The excitement of the theater, along with its pure craziness, was working on me almost like an aphrodisiac.

I don't know how long I'd been standing there when I caught a movement out of the corner of my eye and saw Serena leaving her mother's office and turning down the long corridor that led to the dressing rooms at the far end of the building.

Caught up in the drama of the night, I slipped out of the meeting and followed her. Curiosity has always been a weakness of mine, and I was dying to know why she'd reacted to

Laurence the way she had when everyone else in the building would have traded their firstborn for one smile.

Instead of going into a dressing room, she turned the corner at the end of the hall and let herself into the adjoining ladies' room. She was already inside one of the three stalls by the time I let myself in, so I killed some time checking my reflection, noting that it was about time for a haircut, and wondering when I'd developed those crow's-feet around my eyes.

I was still frowning over my newly discovered wrinkles when I heard a flush and the stall door opened. Serena smiled when she saw me, but there was something self-conscious about the way she looked away as she came toward the short bank of sinks.

I tried to pretend that I hadn't purposely cornered her in the bathroom. "Hey, Serena. I didn't realize you were back in town. How long have you been here?"

She met my gaze in the mirror. I thought she looked relieved that I hadn't asked about the confrontation with Laurence. Under the relief lurked a sadness so deep it made me ache. I wondered what had happened to cause it, but I wasn't crass enough to ask. I have my limits.

"I've been back a couple of months," she said, turning on the faucet and pumping soap into her palm. "I just haven't gotten out much."

"I know how that is," I said. "It took me forever to get settled when I moved back. Where are you living?"

Her soft brown eyes met mine again, but only for an instant. "I'm staying with Mom right now, but just until I find a place of my own. She keeps trying to talk me into making it permanent, but . . . well, you know."

I laughed. "Yeah, I know firsthand. I'm sure it's hard enough to move back after just a couple of years, but after twenty?" I gave a mock shudder and checked for a dry spot on the counter so I could lean against it. "What made you decide to come back?"

"Oh, you know. This and that." She shook the water from

her hands and moved around me to reach for a towel. "I got tired of the city, for one thing."

"You were somewhere on the East Coast, right?"

She nodded. "I was in Virginia for a few years, and then I moved to Atlanta." Crumpling the paper towel in her hand, she tossed it into the trash. "You might as well ask what you really want to know. You're wondering why I snapped at Laurence Nichols."

I thought about denying it, but no doubt she'd see right through me. "The question *did* cross my mind."

A tight smile curved her lips. "Yours and everybody else's, I'm sure. The answer is simple. He's a complete asshole."

A laugh slipped out before I could stop it. "Well, that's clear enough, I guess. I take it you two know each other?"

Her gaze danced up to meet mine, then skittered away. "Not exactly."

I waited for her to go on.

She didn't, but that might have been because the door burst open and we both jumped back to avoid being hit. Vonetta loomed in the opening and split a disapproving glance over the two of us. "What's going on?"

I felt fifteen again. Young and uncertain and afraid of getting into trouble. "I was just saying hello to Serena," I said. "I didn't realize she was back in town."

"She's been back for several weeks now." Vonetta stretched out one arm toward her daughter—a mother hen movement that clearly said *come here right now*—and the years seemed to melt away for Serena, too. Ducking her head, she scurried out of the ladies' room like a kid who'd just been sent to time-out.

"Hold on," I said, and started after her.

Vonetta's arm swept down in front of me, blocking my exit. "I'd rather you didn't, Abby. Serena hasn't been feeling well lately. I think it would be best if you leave her alone just now."

Was she kidding? Did she really think I'd buy that lame excuse? Something was going on here, and I was dying to know the whole story. "I'm not going to bother her," I said with an innocent smile. "We were just catching up."

"I'm sure you were, but I really must insist. Now, if you'll excuse us . . ."

She turned around and followed Serena into the hall. By the time I got there, they were halfway to the front of the building, one of Vonetta's arms wrapped protectively around Serena's shoulders.

Chapter 7

Still reeling from my encounter with Vonetta, I turned in the other direction and made my way through the shop area toward the rehearsal hall. I'd never seen that side of Vonetta before, and I wasn't sure I liked it. Obviously, she wanted to keep me from talking to Serena about Laurence, but why? What did they have to hide, and how long did she think she could keep Serena from talking about it?

She'd piqued my curiosity, but I decided to leave it alone—at least for tonight. Serena would be on guard, and Vonetta would be watching. Besides, it was late and I was tired, and I still hadn't eaten dinner. Interesting as things were here at the Playhouse, it was time for me to rescue Max and get back to the real world.

When I opened the door to the box office a few minutes later, Max greeted me with a flurry of grateful doggy kisses. That's both the best and the worst thing about dogs. Whether you go outside to check the mail or leave for an entire day, they're always excited to see you when you get back. But they can also dish out guilt. I think it's the expectation and trust in those big, sad, puppy dog eyes that does it. The *How could you leave me?* look they give as you're closing the door. It gets me every time.

Before Max came to live with me, he'd been the constant companion of a friend who owned a clothing store. When Brandon was murdered, Max became my dog. Alas, unlike his previous owner, I couldn't take the dog to work with me at the candy store—health regulations don't allow it—and Max wasn't happy with the change. His adjustment to long days spent on his own had taken a toll on my wardrobe and my apartment.

Tonight, as he slathered me with kisses and wagged his nubby tail in excitement, I felt like a jerk for leaving him alone so long. I sat beside him on the floor and indulged in a scratch-fest to make up for my neglect. Max forgave me immediately. He's far more understanding than most people. But I didn't get up right away. I had a lot to make up for.

I think Max would have indulged me for hours if we hadn't been interrupted by the sound of strident voices coming our way. Max got to his feet and tilted his head to listen. Even before I could make out what they were saying, I could tell that another situation had exploded.

What *was* going on around here?

While Max and I inched out of sight, Laurence Nichols strode into the lobby. Vonetta followed close on his heels. Her voice was low, but her anger was unmistakable. "I mean it, Laurence. Get the hell out of my theater."

Ooo-kay. That was a switch.

Intrigued by Vonetta's sudden change of heart, I nudged Max further into the darkened box office. This abrupt about-face must have something to do with Serena. Naturally, that made my curiosity shift into high gear.

Laurence glanced over his shoulder, a thin smile on his handsome face. "That's a helluva thing to say, Vonetta. Especially since you practically begged me to take this job."

"That was then. This is now."

Laurence's smile grew a bit wider. Unlike Vonetta, who looked angry enough to hurt someone, Laurence seemed to be enjoying himself. "You're hysterical, Vonetta. You're not thinking clearly."

"I'm thinking clearly for the first time in *years*. There's nothing further to discuss, Laurence. You're a despicable man. You don't care who you hurt, and I don't work that way. You're through here. I'll find another musical director."

He shifted his whole body to face her. That charming smile still stretched across his face, but the expression in his eyes had turned to ice. "Don't be a fool. How easy do you think it will be to find someone Alexander Pastorelli will be willing to work with? Especially on such short notice."

"I'll take my chances." I'd never seen Vonetta so angry. Until tonight, I hadn't even known she could *get* angry.

Laurence barked a disbelieving laugh. "You'd rather let the production fail than have me around? That's a bit melodramatic, isn't it?"

"Think what you want," Vonetta snarled. "If I'd known the truth about you, I never would have hired you."

What truth? I edged forward a fraction of an inch so I could see them more clearly.

I was pretty sure her comments had hit their mark, but Laurence hid his anger well. Smirking, he leaned against the wall and folded his arms across his chest. "Oh come on, Vonetta. Lighten up. You're making a mountain out of a molehill."

"How dare you." The words ground out of her throat, and she drew back her arm as if she intended to strike him.

Laurence caught her hand and barked another laugh, but his expression changed in the blink of an eye, and I saw something cold and calculating beneath his handsome exterior. "I'd be careful if I were you. Once you get up on a high horse like that, the only way off is down. Maybe it's slipped your mind, but we have a legally binding contract. If you want out, take me to court. Otherwise, I have a job to do. I suggest you stay out of my way while I do it."

Vonetta jerked her hand out of his grasp and massaged her wrist. "You're the one who'd better be careful," she snarled. "Stay away from my daughter. Stay away from the cast. Stay away from the crew. And don't do *anything* to jeopardize this production or I swear I'll make you regret it."

She pivoted away and a second later I heard the door to her office shutting behind her. Laurence watched her go, an odd expression on his face. After a moment, he stuffed his hands in his pockets and strode into the auditorium, whistling as if he didn't have a care in the world.

I stayed in the shadows of the box office, my mind whirling as I replayed the argument I'd just witnessed and thought back over everything else that had happened tonight.

What would Vonetta do next? There was no way she could take Laurence to court and win. If nothing else, he'd just keep spending money on delays until her bank accounts all ran dry. Even if she won, the publicity involved would destroy her reputation. A man like Laurence Nichols would win hands down in the court of public opinion. But neither could I see Vonetta just backing down and letting Laurence stay.

One thing for sure, Vonetta had been right the other day. Life in the theater was never dull.

"I have four more orders for one-pound mixes, three for chocolate caramels, and five more for chocolate-covered strawberries," Liberty announced as she strode into the kitchen at Divinity the next morning. We'd only been open an hour, but we'd had a steady flow of customers into the store since we unlocked the doors, and the phone had been ringing off the hook.

At this rate, I wouldn't have time to miss Jawarski or envy those who were in the play, and that was fine with me. In the space of twenty-four hours, I'd managed to misplace my last bottle of cinnamon flavor oil and I'd already wasted half an hour looking for it. I didn't need any distractions.

I stepped off the stool I'd been standing on and brushed past a hanging heart to take the order forms from Liberty. "All of these came in during the last hour?"

Liberty nodded, and the black and blond hair she'd piled loosely on top of her head threatened to escape its clip. "Can you believe it? The phone hasn't stopped ringing since I walked through the door."

I was happy to see the brisk sales, but a little worried about my ability to keep up with them. Swallowing my rising panic, I forced a smile. "I've noticed. You haven't been promising exact dates for delivery, have you?"

Liberty gave her head another shake. "By the fourteenth, just like you said."

Gratified, I pulled in a calming breath and reminded myself that Elizabeth, my sister-in-law, would be here next weekend to help. So would Dana and Danielle. All I had to do was keep my head above water until then.

After scanning the orders briefly for special requests, I handed them back to Liberty. She crossed to the area we'd designated as control central and began sorting the slips into piles. "I heard you were at the theater last night. Are you thinking of auditioning after all?"

Word always travels fast in Paradise, but sometimes the speed of our grapevine still surprises me. "Where did you hear that?"

Liberty shrugged and plunked another sheet into place. "A friend of mine was there to audition. She said she saw you." Grinning over her shoulder as if she'd caught me trying to hide something, Liberty said, "I guess Vonetta got to you, huh?"

Her smile made me edgy, but only because I'd been trying so hard not to think about last night's excitement. "I'm not auditioning," I said, sounding like a broken record. I wasn't even sure which of us I was trying hardest to convince. "I ran into Richie Bellieu and Dylan Wagstaff on their way to a meeting and decided to tag along to see how things were going."

Liberty shrugged and turned back to work. "Hey, if you want to be in the play, I say go for it."

"With all of these orders waiting to be filled?" I shook my head and climbed back onto the stool to search for the flavor oil. "It's not going to happen."

"If you say so. I heard that somebody stole some music from Laurence Nichols. Is that true?"

I shrugged. "I don't know if it was stolen, but it was missing."

"My friend said he was really pissed. *And* she said that Vonetta's daughter called him an idiot."

"He was upset," I said as I moved from one shelf to the next. "But Serena didn't actually call him an idiot. She was just trying to figure out whether or not he had copies of the missing music. It was no big deal, and it was all over in a second." Not entirely true, but I saw no reason to mention the argument between Vonetta and Laurence.

Liberty's eager expression turned into disappointment. "Really? That's it?"

"That's it," I said. "Sorry."

She might have pushed harder, but the bell over the front door jangled to signal another customer. Karen was busy with a couple of middle-aged women, so Liberty set the orders aside and scurried into the showroom.

I pulled the first row of bottles out of the cupboard and dug through some that had been buried in the back. It seemed unlikely that I'd put the cinnamon back there, but stranger things had happened.

"Abby? Do you have a minute?"

Startled, I dropped a bottle and almost lost my balance on the step stool. I glanced over my shoulder and found Paisley standing at the counter, looking at me over the half wall that separates the kitchen from the showroom. Her burgundy hair gleamed an odd shade of purple in the sunlight, and her curls corkscrewed away from her head in every direction.

I couldn't imagine why she needed me, but I nodded and abandoned the search again. "Sure, what's up?"

"I know you're busy," she said with an apologetic smile, "and I hate to interrupt. It's just . . . well, I'm worried about Vonetta, and I wonder if you know what's going on with her."

"With Vonetta?" I shook my head. "I don't know anything. Sorry." Maybe I should have let that be the end of it. After all, Paisley does love to talk, and I didn't want to encourage her to spread rumors. But it would have been rude to turn her away, and besides, Vonetta's a friend. If there was something wrong, I should care enough to find out what it was.

I motioned Paisley toward the seating area where we could talk without being overheard, and carried two cups of coffee to the table with me. "What are you worried about?" I asked as I put one in front of her.

Paisley wrapped her hands around the warm cup with a grateful sigh. "*You* were at the theater last night," she said after a moment. "You saw what happened."

I opened two sugar packets and dumped the contents into my cup. "I was there, but I'm not sure I know what you're talking about."

"The missing music?" Paisley said, incredulous at my slow-witted response. "The way Serena talked to Laurence? Don't tell me you didn't hear *that*."

I added a touch of cream to my coffee. Okay, a dollop. I deserved at least that much. "I heard all that," I agreed, "but I didn't think it was a big deal. The missing music didn't seem to bother Laurence."

"Oh, it bothered him all right." Paisley waved away the offer of cream and sugar and sipped her coffee black. "His manager came in this morning demanding that Vonetta ban Serena from the theater until the production is over."

I almost choked on my coffee. Considering the argument I'd witnessed between Laurence and Vonetta last night, the demand came across like a declaration of war. "What did Vonetta say?"

"She said that Serena's part of the company, and she'll be at the theater whenever Vonetta needs her there." Agitated, Paisley moved a paper heart out of her way and went on. "And *then* she told him that Laurence is free to stay away if that's what he wants, but he'll be in breach of contract if he does."

Obviously, Paisley knew way more about what was going on than I did, but I didn't say so. Instead I asked, "What did Manwaring say to that?"

Paisley glanced around the shop, then leaned in close and whispered, "I don't think you want me to repeat it here."

"Probably not. But emotions are running high. I'm not sure there's anything we really need to worry about."

Paisley scowled at me—hard. "Well, I *am* worried, and I thought maybe you knew something I don't."

"I'm afraid not," I said with a thin smile.

"But you talked to Serena, right?"

How did Paisley know that? "I talked to her for a minute," I admitted, "but she didn't really say anything."

"How did she seem to you?"

"I don't know. Why?"

"Doesn't she seem different? I think she's quieter than she used to be. I thought for sure *you'd* notice."

"She was always quiet," I said, although that wasn't exactly true. Around her mother, she'd always been quiet and reserved. Away from Vonetta, Serena had been much more gregarious. "Neither of us have seen her in twenty years. People *can* change."

Paisley frowned thoughtfully for a second, then gave her head another firm shake. "It's not like that. She's . . . well, she's almost secretive. She never talks about all the years she lived away."

"That's not a crime," I pointed out. "Maybe she's just trying to move on with her life."

"Maybe." The look on Paisley's face made it clear that she didn't think so.

"Is that what you're worried about?"

Her eyes flew to mine and she shook her head. "No, not really. I can't put my finger on what it is, but something weird is going on around the theater. You could feel it last night, couldn't you?"

"There was some tension," I admitted. "But I don't think there's anything to worry about. I'm sure Vonetta has everything well under control."

The picture of dejection, Paisley propped her chin in one hand and picked at the lacy edges of a heart with the other. "I wish I could agree with you, but I can see the front of the Playhouse from the window of the salon."

"Are you saying you saw something?"

"I saw Laurence Nichols and Richie going at it about an hour ago. Arguing, I mean."

"Laurence and Richie?" Okay, *that* was odd. "They were fighting?"

"Not throwing punches, but they were definitely arguing. And it looked like things were getting pretty heated."

It would be hard to find someone less confrontational than Richie, which made me place the blame squarely on Laurence's broad shoulders. "What did he do? Freak out because Richie asked for an autograph?"

Paisley shook her head. "I have no idea, but it seemed like something bigger than that. I mean, Richie was . . . well, for a minute I thought he might deck Laurence."

"You're talking about *our* Richie? From the Silver River Inn?"

"Yep."

"Did you hear what they were arguing about?"

"No, I was too far away. And inside." Paisley pushed the heart away and brushed bits of lacy edging into her hand. "But I do know that Richie has been making a pest of himself, hanging around the theater and whatnot. He's been underfoot almost constantly since he found out Laurence was coming to town. Vonetta doesn't need that on top of everything else she's dealing with."

I doubted it was that bad. Richie had a business to run, after all, and I couldn't imagine Dylan just taking on everything that needed to be done without a complaint. "I'm sure the novelty of having a celebrity around will wear off in a few days and Richie will calm down again," I said.

Paisley glanced around for someplace to throw away the garbage, gave up, and put the lacy bits on her napkin. "That's the trouble, Abby. I'm afraid that might be too long to wait."

Chapter 8

Paisley was starting to freak me out a little with her predictions of doom and gloom. "What do you mean, that might be too long to wait? What do you think will happen?"

"I don't know! I only know that something's wrong, and I'm worried."

"You know how emotional those creative types can be."

"Okay, then, how do you explain this? Last night, after they thought everyone was gone, I heard Serena and Vonetta arguing."

"They're family. Families argue."

"Not like this they don't," Paisley insisted. "It was late. Everyone else was gone. I should have been gone, too, but I forgot my scarf and had to go back in to get it. They had no idea I was there."

I didn't want to ask, but I couldn't help myself. "What did you hear?"

"I heard Vonetta telling Serena that she didn't know if she could ever forgive her. Does *that* sound normal to you?"

She had me there. "Are you sure she was talking to Serena?"

"I'm positive," Paisley said with a stiff bob of her head. "I'm telling you, Abby, something's wrong."

Let me be perfectly clear about this: I'd hate for someone to dig into my personal life and listen in to my arguments with family members. I certainly didn't want to disrespect Vonetta by sticking my nose in where it didn't belong. But like I said, curiosity has always been my weakness. "What else did you hear?"

"Serena begged Vonetta not to make trouble, but Vonetta said it was far too late for that. See what I mean? That doesn't sound like Vonetta at all."

"No, it doesn't." I rolled my head on my neck, trying to work out the kinks that had suddenly appeared.

"Will you do me a favor?" Paisley asked.

"If I can."

"Just keep your eyes and ears open. If you hear or see anything I should know about, tell me?"

I ignored a rush of guilt and nodded. "Okay, sure."

"Thank you. I knew I could count on you." Paisley reached across the table and squeezed my hand, looking as grateful as if I'd just agreed to let her cut and style my hair.

Which wasn't going to happen—but then, I was pretty sure I wasn't going to hear anything that Paisley *needed* to know, either. At least not until pigs flew over Paradise—and maybe not even then.

I managed to push Vonetta and the play to the back of my mind for the rest of that day. I had work to do, customers to serve, candy to make. Orders kept stacking up, and I didn't have the luxury of giving in to distractions.

That's what I kept telling myself, anyway. I took out my frustrations by lining a dozen cookie sheets with foil, then crushing six boxes of graham crackers the old-fashioned way. A food processor might be quicker, but nothing beats a rolling pin for getting the crumbs to the right consistency.

When the crackers were ready, I set them aside and opened a package of bamboo skewers. I pulled several containers of homemade marshmallow from the storage room, and melted dark chocolate on low heat until it was silky smooth and ready for dipping.

Maybe it's because we live in the mountains, but S'Mores Pops are a local favorite. Every classroom with a Valentine's Day party scheduled had a corresponding order for thirty pops. If I did nothing else between now and the fourteenth, I'd barely keep up with the demand for those.

I was crazy for even thinking about getting involved with Vonetta's production, but the idea still danced around at the back of my mind all morning. Trying to shake it off, I slid three pieces of marshmallow onto each skewer, drizzled chocolate until each trio was completely coated, and then sprinkled cracker crumbs over the chocolate. But no matter how hard I tried to concentrate on the recipe in front of me, the drama at the Playhouse was never far from my thoughts.

Of course, it didn't help that everyone in town knew that Laurence Nichols was around, or that every customer who walked through the door had some bit of gossip to share. We heard that Laurence had been seen dining at Gigi, that he'd flirted with the clerk at the post office, and we even picked up claims that he'd purchased artwork or antiques from half the businesses in town.

Far from packing up and slinking out of town, it seemed he was going out of his way to make his mark on Paradise. Between picking up on gossip and wondering how Vonetta was feeling now about all of it, I had a hard time concentrating on the work I should have been doing.

I was still trying to convince myself to ignore the talk when I took Max for his walk that evening. The cold front was still firmly settled in our valley, so I bundled up in layers, wrapped the scarf my mother had sent for Christmas around my nose and mouth, and headed into the glacial night air.

Five minutes later, I opened the door of the Playhouse and stomped the frozen snow from my boots before leading Max into the lobby. According to the call-board I'd just happened to notice the other night, the production team would be meeting tonight to discuss scenery. I wasn't even sure why I'd stopped in, but I hadn't been able to stay away.

Last time I was here, the building had been bustling with activity. Tonight, it felt deserted and a little creepy. I laughed at the way my imagination could fly off in all directions with very little provocation, but I also decided not to leave

Max in the box office. I didn't intend to stay long, and only a handful of people would be here. Max would be fine sticking with me.

We started off in the rehearsal hall, but the room, like the lobby, felt completely deserted. "Vonetta?" I called softly. "Are you here?" My voice bounced off the walls, and the echo only added to my uneasiness.

If they weren't in the rehearsal hall, they must have been meeting in the auditorium—which I supposed made sense if they were discussing scenery. Still a little creeped out by the silence, I kept up a steady stream of chatter as Max and I followed the dark hallway that twisted past the green room, turned at the prop room, and circled around the wardrobe and shop area.

The shops, if you could call them that, were areas of one large room separated by temporary walls. Each space was designated for work on the lighting, props, or scenery for the current show. Of course, there were always a few old things hanging around, but Vonetta kept most of the stuff she wasn't using in a storage space on the edge of town.

Two small rooms in the midst of the chaos were routinely turned into makeshift offices, one for the director and one for the stage manager. I suspected that Laurence outranked Colleen in this case, and that he'd claimed the second office for himself. I glanced briefly into both, but only to make sure I wasn't missing someone.

Framed pictures lined the desk in Alexander's office, each one a shot of him with another person, and all posed in front of a poster from some play he'd worked on. A half-empty wine bottle and two dirty glasses sat on the desk of the other room.

I walked a few feet further, and found myself at one of the entrances to the auditorium. If I went through this door, I'd end up in the walkway between the stage and the front row of seats, or I could walk another fifty feet and use the crew's backstage entrance. While I tried to decide which door to use, I listened for the sound of voices, but all I heard was more of that unnatural quiet and the sound of Max's panting.

"Vonetta? Paisley? *Anybody*?" I started to move on, but a soft sound stopped me in my tracks. "Vonetta?"

I heard it again, and this time I was almost certain it had come from inside the auditorium. Climbing the gently sloping ramp, I pushed aside the velvet curtain that hid the work areas from the audience. The theater was dark, so I had to wait a second for my eyes to adjust. A couple of emergency lights and three Exit signs were all that relieved the darkness, but they were enough to let me see someone kneeling on the stage. Heavy breathing punctuated the silence, and I crossed mental fingers that I wasn't interrupting Laurence and some young lady in the middle of a tryst.

"Hello?" I said as I took a couple of steps closer. "Who's there?"

The sharp intake of breath cut through the relative silence and the panting silenced.

"Nice try," I said with a laugh. "I can see you, you know. You're on the stage."

"Oh my God." The whispered words seemed to come out of nowhere, but I recognized the voice immediately.

"Vonetta? Is that you?" I glanced around as if a light switch might have materialized at my side. "What are you doing in here in the dark? Are you all right?"

"Don't—" Her voice caught, and she broke off. When she spoke again, she sounded shaky. Frightened, even. "Abby, I think we need to call the police."

"The police? Why? What's wrong?"

"It's Laurence," she said quietly, and sat up, shifting slightly so I could see a figure stretched out on the stage beside her. "I think he's dead."

Chapter 9

With my heart in my throat, I secured Max's leash to the arm of a chair in the front row and moved closer to Vonetta and the shadow on the stage. Laurence lay on his side, his body lifeless, face frozen forever in a grimace of pain. A spotlight wrapped in thick metal casing lay a few inches away, and a dark pool of blood spread out across the stage from beneath Laurence's head.

I took an involuntary step backward. "What happened?"

Vonetta sat back on her heels and shook her head. "I don't know. He was like this when I found him."

Still acutely aware of the sweet smell of blood, I forced myself to move closer. I thought I knew the answer, but I asked anyway. "Are you sure he's dead?"

"I think so. I've been trying to revive him, but I can't get a response." She reached out as if to touch him again, but drew her hand back sharply before she actually made contact. "We need to call an ambulance."

If he was dead, an ambulance wouldn't help, but I didn't know who else to call. On the off chance he was still breathing, I clenched my teeth and reached past her to feel for a pulse. Laurence's skin was still slightly warm, but it felt waxy beneath my fingers. He *might* still be alive, but if so he was barely hanging on.

"Is he alive?" Vonetta whispered.

I shook my head. "I don't think so."

Lights suddenly blazed on in the auditorium, blinding me momentarily. I blinked, trying to regain my sight as Paisley called out, "Has anyone seen Vonetta? I need to know what to do about the callbacks."

Shading my eyes with one hand, I tried to focus in the glare. Paisley's voice sounded far away, and as my vision cleared, the scene in front of me took on a surrealistic feel. It occurred to me that Paisley had been right—something bad *had* happened. What a senseless tragedy.

Paisley saw the two of us—or should I say the three of us—and stopped abruptly. One hand flew to her chest and her eyes grew round with shock. "My God! What happened? Is that—?"

I tried to shake off the mental heaviness, but it clung persistently. "I think he's dead," I said, surprised at how calm my voice sounded. "If not, he's seriously wounded. You need to call 9-1-1."

"Right," Paisley said, bobbing her headful of cherry curls a few times before she realized I meant for her to make the call. When the dots finally connected, she raced from the room and left me alone with Vonetta again.

Splotches of Laurence's blood stained Vonetta's blouse and hands, but she didn't seem to notice. Obviously in a daze, she sat on the floor and stared at his still form. "Dead. What a nightmare. We're going to be blamed." Her head snapped up and her gaze met mine. "*I'm* going to be blamed for this, aren't I? Once the press gets hold of this the theater will be ruined."

The media would be on the prowl, all right. They'd be looking for someone to fault. And Vonetta was the person most likely to take the brunt of the blame. "I wish there was a way to keep this quiet," I muttered. "At least until we figure out what happened."

Vonetta turned a deep scowl in my direction. "Isn't it obvious? That spotlight came loose and hit him."

"You're probably right," I glanced at the fly system overhead, and wondered where the light had been. I couldn't see any obvious holes in the lighting system, but I was no expert. The C-clamp was still attached to one end, and the safety cable stretched away through the pool of blood. I couldn't be sure, but it didn't look to me as if the cable had snapped. The loose end, which should have been shredded or frayed, looked as if someone had sliced through it with a knife. And if they had, Laurence Nichols's death was no accident.

No, I told myself firmly. There was a reasonable explanation for the way the cable looked. But I suddenly found myself wishing that Jawarski hadn't picked this week to leave town.

I realized that Vonetta was watching me closely, but I didn't want to start a wholesale panic so I tried to hide my suspicions. "I'm just confused, I guess. What were you doing in here with the lights out?"

She looked at me, her eyes blank. "I don't know what you mean."

"You were in here with the lights out when I came in," I said. "You were kneeling beside Laurence . . . Leaning over him."

Her expression turned to stone. "What are you implying?"

"Nothing," I said quickly. "But I thought you were all in a meeting. That's what the call-board said. So why were you in here with Laurence alone?"

"I told you. I found him like that."

"Yes, but—" The sound of running feet reached us, and I swore under my breath. Don't get me wrong—I didn't for one minute think Vonetta had bashed Laurence over the head with that light fixture, but thanks to the arguments Laurence had been involved in over the past few days, I was having a little trouble buying the accident theory.

The footsteps came closer, and I just had time to warn Vonetta, "Don't let anyone onstage," before Alexander Pastorelli burst through the velvet curtains that separated the auditorium from the lobby. Jason, the David Beckham lookalike, came in hard on his heels, with Colleen Brannigan right behind him.

Alexander jumped onto the stage before I could stop him,

demanding, "What the hell happened here?" The words were barely out of his mouth when he saw Laurence and bolted toward the body. "Larry? Are you all right?"

"Don't come any closer," Vonetta warned. "I think he's dead."

Alexander stopped abruptly, his face a mask of disbelief and horror. Colleen let out a whimper, covered her mouth with both hands, and dropped heavily onto the steps stage left. Even from a distance, I could see that her whole body trembled. I thought about her husband's suspicions and wondered again if he had reason to doubt her.

But that didn't matter right now. What mattered was keeping people out of the auditorium, preserving the scene, preventing widespread panic. Or maybe I just wanted to keep myself busy so I wouldn't have to think about the body on the stage.

Noticeably shaken, Alexander ran a hand through his hair. "He can't be dead. I just saw him ten minutes ago."

I knew how he felt. After I'd walked in on my ex-husband and his girlfriend having sex on *my* bedroom floor, I'd struggled for months with how quickly life could change. It seemed inconceivable that the man who'd once inhabited the lifeless body in front of us could have been striding around the theater barking orders just a few short minutes ago.

"Call the police," Colleen said softly. When nobody moved, she struggled to her feet and shouted, "Call an ambulance. Do *something*. Don't let him just *lie* there like that."

"Paisley's calling 9-1-1 right now," I said, hoping I sounded reassuring. "We're doing everything we can. Why don't you all go back to the rehearsal hall—?"

Colleen folded her arms and jerked her chin in stubborn refusal.

Jason stared at the grisly scene. "Are you sure he's dead?"

"Not 100 percent," I admitted, though it was harder to believe there was even a flicker of life left in Laurence's body now that I could see it in the light. The kid moved closer, but I blocked his path. "I don't want to be rude, but unless you're a doctor, I don't think you should touch him. I checked for a pulse, but I couldn't feel one. I don't think there's anything we can do for him."

Jason nodded without taking his eyes from Laurence's inert form. "Okay. But shouldn't we—" He pulled his gaze away and looked at me. "Shouldn't we cover him up or something?"

Vonetta slowly got to her feet. "That's a good idea. Why don't you see if you can find a blanket or something in the back?"

Obviously happy to be useful, Jason dashed from the auditorium.

Alexander watched him go, a deep scowl on his broad face. "How did this happen?"

"It looks like a spotlight came loose and fell," I said.

"I can *see* that. What I'm asking is how a spotlight could *come* loose. What are we looking at here? Negligence?"

Vonetta bristled, but I didn't want a scene, so I answered before she could. "It was an accident. That's all."

"An accident?" Colleen's head bobbed up. "Are you sure?"

"Well, of course we're sure," Vonetta said, her lips drawn into a thin, disapproving line. "What else could it be?"

Colleen moved unsteadily toward a seat in the front of the house. "You're right, of course. An accident." She looked up at us, a helpless expression in her eyes. "It's just that he—he—"

Jason burst though the curtain carrying a thin blanket. He thrust it at Vonetta, then sat beside Colleen and put a hand on her back. "I just realized how tough this must be on you especially. Are you all right?"

Colleen jerked away from him as if his hand had burned her. "Laurence was a *friend*, nothing more. And yes, I'm fine. Just shocked, like everyone else."

Color flooded Jason's cheeks. "Oh. Sure. Sorry, I—well, you hear talk, you know?" He looked at the rest of us, as if we might back him up. When no one did, he finished with a lame, "I didn't mean anything."

"There's always way too much gossip around a theater

troupe," Alexander said, his tone frosty. "You might as well learn right now that you can't believe everything you hear." Jumping from the stage apron, he nudged Jason out of the way and took over as Colleen's moral support. "Where the hell is Geoffrey?"

"He left about an hour ago," Jason said. "I think he was going to the hotel to check on a package he's been expecting."

"Somebody ought to call him," Alexander said. "And one of us should stay with the—with Laurence until the ambulance arrives, but I don't see any need for us all to hover. Why don't we go back to the rehearsal hall, Colleen? I'm sure you'll be more comfortable there."

With an uneasy glance at the body, Jason tried once again to be helpful. "I'll stay if you want me to."

"Thanks," I said, "but since Vonetta and I have already been near the body, we're the ones who should probably stay. I'm pretty sure the police will want to look at everything to figure out exactly what happened. It's probably a good idea not to muddy up the scene more than we already have."

As if I'd snapped the lock that had been holding her in place, Vonetta started toward the lobby. "You stay. I'll make sure everyone else in the building stays put."

"Wait!" I called out before she could reach the curtains. "Don't you think you should stay here with me?"

Vonetta stopped and turned back. She held back the curtain with one hand, clearly intending to keep walking, and the scowl on her face made it obvious that she didn't appreciate my suggestion. "I don't see why. I'm sure you can handle things here just fine."

"Yeah, but you're the one who found him and . . . Well *look* at you. If there's anyone else around, one look at all that blood will create a panic."

She stared at her chest and hands for a long time. "I suppose I'm a bit of a mess, aren't I? I should clean up."

"I'd wait," I said. "We have no idea what the police will want to see. Why don't you stay here with me? Just until the police come." She still didn't look convinced, so I added some more incentive. "There are probably half a dozen ways into this room alone, not to mention all the different ways someone could get onstage. It's going to be hard for one person to watch them all, and I'm sure you don't want people disturbing things before the police have a chance to see that this was all just a horrible accident."

A horrible, poorly timed, senseless accident. At least, that's what I hoped it was.

Chapter 10

The paramedics arrived about ten minutes later, and the police came with them. Since Jawarski was out of town, the lead in the investigation of Laurence's accident fell to my old nemesis, Nate Svboda. Nate's a good ol' boy and a friend of my brother, who is also a good ol' boy, though not quite as bad as most of his friends. I'm convinced that Nate resides permanently in the early 1970s, back when the concept of treating women like equals was a relatively new idea, one that men could—and frequently did—ignore.

Since Laurence had been a celebrity, I knew the mayor would be in a panic and pushing everyone to figure out what had happened. Nobody in Paradise wanted the negative publicity the city would get from this, and the more unanswered questions left hanging out there, the unhappier they'd all get.

I was still trying to convince myself that Laurence's death was an accident and arguing with myself over whether or not to point out the cable to Nate. He's a notoriously lazy cop, and he never needs encouragement to tie up a case as quickly as possible, which means that "thorough" usually drops by the wayside.

Nate's creeping up on fifty—a dangerous age for men, in my opinion. I can't prove it, but I'm also convinced that he's been miserable for a long time—a dangerous outlook in general. Give a miserable person a little power, and there's usually trouble.

Nate burst into the auditorium like an invading general, barking orders at the uniformed officers who came with him and swaggering around as if he owned the world. He took a cursory look at the stage, studied the spotlight for a few minutes, and strode out again, leaving a couple of men to keep curious onlookers out. He sent two other men to guard the outside doors, and directed two others to herd all unofficial personnel into the rehearsal hall.

He did all this without saying a word to those of us who'd been waiting for him to arrive, and without asking a single question. Finding Laurence had made us all uneasy, and being herded like cattle into the rehearsal hall didn't help. Except for Vonetta and I, who sat together on a sagging prop couch, everyone seemed to want to put some distance between themselves and the rest of us.

Colleen had claimed a folding metal chair near the wall of posters. She sat ramrod straight, eyes closed. If it hadn't been for the occasional shudder that racked her body, I'd have wondered if she were still awake.

Alexander sat in a wingback chair that had seen better days. His gaze traveled steadily from one of us to the next, and I wondered if he had his own suspicions about how Laurence died.

Jason sat at the piano, slumped over the keyboard and plucking at a key now and then. The effect was so discordant and irritating, I wanted to tell him to stop. But he was probably the one person in the room whose image of Laurence hadn't been destroyed before he died. The one person who was genuinely grieving over the loss of an idol.

Even though we'd left the body on the stage, that sickly sweet smell still filled my nostrils and made me want to retch. I couldn't get the image of Laurence's body—or of Vonetta leaning over it—out of my mind. I couldn't stop wondering if the safety cable had been cut, or keep myself from thinking about the argument Vonetta and Laurence had a few nights earlier.

It wasn't that I suspected Vonetta of killing Laurence. The very idea would have made me laugh if the situation hadn't been so serious. Vonetta wasn't the type to commit murder. Oh, I know, I know. Anyone can be driven to kill with the right provocation. But we were talking about *Vonetta*! It just wasn't possible.

Was it?

Paisley came to stand behind us, muttering constantly. "I *knew* something bad was going to happen. Didn't I say that, Abby? I just *knew* it." She nudged me in the back and waited expectantly, so I agreed that she had, indeed, predicted trouble. Which didn't shut her up, but only made her start all over at the beginning. "I *told* you there was going to be trouble, didn't I?"

I rubbed my forehead and wished I could step outside for a few minutes. Maybe that would take away the smell. "You told me," I said again.

"I just knew it. *Now* look what's happened."

Vonetta twisted the hem of her blouse nervously in both hands. "People are going to blame me, aren't they? They're going to say this is my fault."

"It's nobody's fault," I said firmly. "There's been an accident, and yes it's a tragedy, but it was just an accident."

Vonetta shot me a look of pure derision. "You heard Alexander. Laurence hadn't been dead ten minutes and he was already talking about negligence on my part. And Geoffrey Manwaring will probably be even worse." Her shoulders sagged. "The press will crucify me, won't they?"

"I knew it," Paisley muttered. "I just *knew* it."

I ignored her and stayed focused on Vonetta. "You haven't done anything wrong," I said with a reassuring smile. "You can hardly be blamed if there was an equipment malfunction."

Vonetta's lips curved slightly. "I wish that were true, but the press just loves to play the blame game—or haven't you noticed?"

"I'm just trying to stay optimistic," I said.

Vonetta covered my hand with one of hers and gave it a squeeze. "I appreciate that, but I'd rather have you be realistic."

Unfortunately, reality looked pretty bleak to me. A dull ache formed in the back of my head, and my nerves were stretched so thin they threatened to snap when Paisley launched into another chorus of the I-told-you-so blues. To make things worse, Nate positioned himself near the main door of the rehearsal hall, slid a fresh toothpick between his teeth, and asked, "All right. Who found the body?"

Nate and I get along much better when we don't interact, so I waited for Vonetta to say something. When several seconds passed and she still hadn't spoken, I caved in and raised my hand. "We did."

Nate's mouth pursed around the toothpick, and I suspected he was no happier to see me than I was to be seen. "You have something to do with this, Abby?"

"Not really. I just happened to walk in a few seconds after Vonetta found Mr. Nichols lying on the stage floor."

"Yeah? What are you doing here?"

I hesitated, but only for an instant. "I'm in the play. I came to pick up the script."

Vonetta shot a look at me, but she didn't contradict me. Nate shifted the toothpick from one side of his mouth to the other and ran a glance over Vonetta's bloodstained clothes. He nodded toward the door and said, "I need both of you to come with me."

This wasn't the first dead body I'd seen, but I hadn't been around enough of them to take away the horror. My knees buckled as I stood, and my head swam.

Nate led us into the hallway and closed the door on the rehearsal hall. "We're trying to figure out what happened to Mr. Nichols before the press starts hounding us for details. You got some place where we can talk in private?"

"Of course." Vonetta smiled as if Nate had just invited her for tea. "Feel free to use my office. It's the second door on the left."

Nate jerked his head toward the door, and a young man in his midtwenties wearing a black suit, white shirt, and tie hurried off to conduct reconnaissance. He came back a minute later, pronounced the office clear, and we were ushered inside.

Vonetta's office isn't large, and what space there might be

is taken up with copies of screenplays, broken props, and bits of costumes. I expected Nate to claim her desk for himself, and he might have tried if Vonetta hadn't made a beeline for it first.

She linked her hands together on the blotter pad and waited while Nate and I settled into the two old wooden chairs facing her. The young man who'd given us the all clear stood sentinel at the door in case one of us decided to make a break for freedom.

Nate pulled a notepad and pen from his shirt pocket and got down to business without missing a beat. "So the two of you found the body, eh?"

I shook my head. "Not exactly. Vonetta got there a minute or two before I did."

Nate switched the toothpick from one side of his mouth to the other. "In the other room you said it was a few seconds. Which was it?"

I shrugged. "I guess minutes."

"I see." He turned away as if I'd outlived my usefulness and focused on Vonetta. "*You* found the body, then."

"I did."

"You want to tell me about it?"

Vonetta seemed surprised by the question. "I went into the auditorium and found him lying there."

Nate smiled—almost. "Maybe you could give me a bit more than that.. He was dead when you found him?"

"I assumed he was."

Nate quirked an eyebrow and ran another glance over her bloody clothes. "You're covered in blood. How do you explain that?"

"When I found Laurence, he was bleeding profusely. I tried to revive him, but he was already gone."

Nate exchanged a glance with the young man by the door, and I wondered if her answer meant something to them. "You tried to revive him," Nate said as he turned back to Vonetta. "How did you do that?"

"I don't remember exactly," Vonetta said. "As you can imagine, I was quite upset."

"Is this really necessary?" I asked. "Couldn't she go to the station tomorrow and answer your questions?"

Nate jotted something in his notebook and looked up with an almost friendly smile. "I'm afraid not. There'll be reporters sniffing around by tomorrow, and I'd like to have my ducks in a row by the time they show up."

He was acting almost reasonable, which wasn't like him at all. Usually, he struts around like a banty rooster, waving his authority in everyone's face. I had no idea how to deal with Nate Svboda if he didn't do that, so I sat back in my chair and bit my tongue.

"I'm sure that finding Mr. Nichols was upsetting," he said to Vonetta. "But why don't you think about it for a bit? When you're ready, start from the beginning and tell me everything that happened from the minute you walked into the theater until we arrived."

"Why are you so concerned about what happened when I found him?" Vonetta asked. "It was an accident."

"It sure appears to be," he agreed. "But we're just trying to make sure of our facts."

Vonetta considered that for a long time. At least, it felt like a long time to me. Judging from the way Nate began to fidget in his chair, he was growing impatient, too. Just when I thought he might snap out of his unnatural rationality, she spoke.

"I was just leaving a meeting with Alexander and Colleen. We'd been talking about scenery for the production. Making plans. That sort of thing. I was in a hurry, so I cut through the auditorium and I found Laurence lying there. But it's quite obvious what happened, isn't it? That spotlight must have come loose and hit him."

Nate shared another meaningful glance with his man by the door. "It would appear that way," he said again. "Anybody else in the theater when you were having your meeting?"

"Not that I know of." She glanced at me and added, "Obviously, Abby was here, and anyone might have wandered in and out, I suppose. I tried to keep an eye on the lobby, but I might have looked away."

"You leave the door unlocked, then?"

"Most of the time," Vonetta said. "We have cast and crew coming and going at all hours."

I got the distinct impression that Nate was getting at something he didn't want to voice aloud, and I had a gut feeling I knew what it was. "You don't think Laurence's death was an accident?"

"I didn't say that." His lips quirked upward again, but his smile seemed a trifle cooler than it had a minute ago. He turned again to Vonetta. "So you saw him lying there. Did you see anyone else?"

"No. No one."

"No one leaving by one of the other doors as you came in?"

The question made me sit up straight. "What are you getting at, Nate? You think someone else was here?"

"I know someone else was here," he said without looking at me. "I have an eyewitness who saw somebody leaving the theater just a few minutes before you folks raised the alarm about Nichols. According to my witness, he looked mad enough to kill. And according to my guys in there, that spotlight didn't fall on its own. The safety cable was cut."

Vonetta gasped in shock. "Cut? But that can't be!"

"Oh, it can be," Nate said, "and it is. We'll run it through the lab just to be sure, but it looks to me like we might have a murder on our hands. At the very least, we're looking at involuntary manslaughter."

I wish I could say that Nate's pronouncement made *me* gasp in shock, but it only made my stomach hurt. "Who is your eyewitness?" I asked. "Is it someone credible?"

"She's credible, all right. It's Molly Flanders from over to the post office."

He was right. Molly ranked right up there on my list of people I'd believe. "And who does she say left the theater? Was it someone she recognized?"

Nate tucked his notebook into his pocket and sat back so he could look me in the eye. "It was. You sure you want me to tell you? I don't think you're going to like it much."

Colleen. It had to be. Besides Vonetta, no one else I cared about had been here at the time. I steeled myself for his answer and nodded. "You might as well tell me. I'm going to find out eventually anyway."

"It was that funny fella you hang around with. Richie Bellieu."

Chapter 11

Bam! Bam! Bam! Bam! Bam! "Abby? Are you in there?"

Startled by the unexpected noise, I jumped about three feet and slammed the door to my microwave so hard it swung open again. What in the—?

The police had kept us all at the Playhouse for a couple of hours, asking the same questions over and over again before they'd finally let us leave. While we sat around waiting, my headache had grown steadily worse. Since I didn't know whether the pain was caused by hunger, exhaustion, or tension, I was trying to treat all three. I had a frozen chicken dinner ready to nuke, a margarita-flavored wine cooler I'd found in the back of my fridge ready to drink, and a hot shower and bed waiting for me down the hall. I wasn't sure which I wanted more, but I knew I didn't want company.

Telling myself that whoever it was would leave if I ignored them, I shut the microwave and punched numbers on the keypad. I unscrewed the top on my cooler and chugged enough to kill the pain in my head.

Bam! Bam! Bam! "Abby? It's me, Dylan. I need to talk to you. It's an emergency."

Okay, so I didn't want company, but for Dylan and Richie I'd make an exception. Abandoning my makeshift dinner, I hurried toward the front door of my apartment and flung it open just as Dylan raised his fist to bang again.

His hand dropped, and he stood in front of me looking like something the cat had dragged home after an all-night prowl. His dark hair spiked all over his head, his shirt looked as if he'd slept in it for two days, and the shadow of a beard darkened his cheeks and chin.

"They're going to arrest Richie," he said, fixing a pair of wounded eyes on me. "I don't know what to do."

Ignoring the rumble of my stomach, I pulled him inside and settled him on my ugly plaid couch. I curled up on the other end and put a bowl of Caramel Marshmallow Pillows in the space between us. They were good enough to solve almost any problem, and the sugar rush might help me stay awake. "Tell me what happened."

"The police came to the inn," Dylan said, hunching forward in a posture of abject misery. "They said that somebody saw Richie leaving the theater right before they discovered Laurence Nichols dead."

"I heard about that," I told him. At the stricken look on his face, I hurried to add, "Don't worry. It's not all over town yet. I was at the Playhouse when Laurence was found. Did they actually arrest Richie, or did they just question him?"

Dylan wagged his head back and forth a few times. "They questioned him, but you should have seen them, Abby. They think he murdered that man. Which is utterly ridiculous. You know as well as I do that Richie couldn't hurt a fly."

"What did Richie tell them?" I asked. "And where is he now?"

"He's at home. Locked in the bedroom." He plunged the fingers of both hands into his hair and stared at the floor. "He won't let me in, and he won't come out. He says his life is ruined."

"Richie says that all the time," I reminded him, trying to ease some of the tension. "He said that when he couldn't find fresh cilantro for the salsa last month, remember?"

Dylan slid a glance at me. "Yeah, well this time he might be right." His sour outlook was completely out of character.

"Why do you say that? You don't really think he killed Laurence do you?"

Dylan shook his head. "No. Richie couldn't have. It's just not in him. But I think the police are satisfied with him as a suspect. You know what some of them are like. They'd love to put Richie away just for being Richie."

Unfortunately, I believed he was right about Nate Svboda and some of the others. What a time for Jawarski to leave town. Unlike the members of the good ol' boys' network, Jawarski didn't prejudge people for their lifestyle choices or the color of their skin. "Was Richie at the theater when Laurence was killed?"

Dylan nodded. "He was supposed to be picking up milk and eggs for tomorrow's breakfast at the inn. Instead, he went to the Playhouse. I *warned* him to stay away from there, especially after—" He broke off suddenly and rubbed his face with his hands.

"After the argument he had with Laurence?"

Dylan gave a reluctant nod. "You know about that?"

"Paisley saw them."

"Which means everybody knows about it by now."

"They're going to find out anyway," I pointed out. "Laurence's death is bound to bring reporters out in droves. Do you know what they argued about?"

Dylan looked sick at the idea of reporters coming to town. "It was no big deal," he said. "He went there to invite Laurence to the inn for lunch. I told him not to, but he never listens to me."

"I take it Laurence didn't leap at the invitation?"

"I'm afraid not. He laughed and told Richie he didn't swing that way."

Ouch. "How did Richie take that?"

"Not well. It pissed him off. He went there as a fan. He wasn't trying to seduce Laurence or anything."

"Did he tell Laurence that?"

"I think so. You'd have to ask him about it. He was too distressed when he came home to say much, but I knew he was upset."

That didn't bode well, but I kept my opinion to myself. Something about Laurence's death was bothering me. There was something that didn't add up, but I couldn't figure out what it was and I was too tired to think straight.

With a heavy groan, Dylan covered his face again. "What are we going to do, Abby? We've put every penny we have into the inn; we don't have the money for a lawyer. And you know as well as I do that Nate Svoboda would be thrilled to get rid of us."

"Some people in this town are seriously behind the times," I said, "but that doesn't mean they'll let Richie be railroaded for a crime he didn't commit. Try not to panic yet. The police have talked to him. They *had* to, since Molly Flanders says she saw him leaving the theater. But they haven't arrested him, and there's no reason to think that they will. I'm sure they'll also be talking to everyone." I unwrapped a Caramel Marshmallow Pillow and bit into it, barely resisting the urge to swoon at the sweet, buttery taste. "Did Richie say whether he even saw Laurence tonight at the theater?"

Dylan shook his head. "He says he didn't. Laurence was in a meeting. Richie says he hung around for a while, hoping the meeting would end, but left when he finally realized how long he'd been gone from the inn."

"What about Laurence's manager, Geoffrey Manwaring? Did Richie mention seeing him at all?"

"Richie didn't mention him at all, why?"

I shrugged. "No reason, really, except that Manwaring wasn't at the theater when Laurence died. Jason Dahl said that he'd gone to the hotel to check on a package he was expecting, but I don't know if that's true or not."

Dylan actually looked encouraged. "You think he might have killed Laurence?"

"It's possible. The point is, there are plenty of people the police need to question, and I'm sure they'll realize that Richie's telling the truth."

"You really think so?"

"Of course." I nudged the bowl toward Dylan, mostly because I felt kind of guilty for pigging out on caramel marshmallow heaven while he was in such hell. "It's all going to work out. You'll see."

Looking almost optimistic, Dylan plucked a Pillow from the bowl and unwrapped it slowly. "So is it true? Was Laurence really murdered?"

I nodded and popped the other half of my candy into my mouth. "It looks suspicious. We won't know for sure until the lab finishes analyzing everything, but I'm almost certain the safety cable on that spotlight didn't break on its own, and Nate said the same thing. I'm pretty sure someone cut it."

"They'll say that Richie did it," Dylan predicted dourly. "He was alone in the theater for quite a while."

"Maybe." Aunt Grace's Caramel Marshmallow Pillows worked their magic and the elusive piece of logic finally clicked into place. "But even if somebody cut the cable, how could they know when it would break and what it would do? If you ask me, it's a pretty sloppy way to commit murder. It's too uncertain."

Hope flickered in Dylan's eyes. "You're right. Cutting the cable might make the light fall, but you wouldn't be able to make it fall precisely where you wanted it to."

"Exactly! Which means that Laurence's death might have been caused by the person who cut through the cable, but I don't think it was premeditated murder. And obviously, Richie had no reason to be crawling around in the fly system cutting safety cables anyway."

Dylan let out a breath loaded with relief. "You're right. What possible reason would he have had for doing that?"

"None, as far as I know."

"That's right. None. And the police will have to establish a motive, won't they? And Richie doesn't have a motive— for anything."

"That's right. Everything will be fine, you'll see." A little quiver of warning raced up my spine, but I ignored it. The idea of anyone—even Nate—seriously considering Richie a suspect was too ridiculous for words. The most aggressive thing I'd ever seen Richie do was overdecorate for a dinner party. He simply wasn't a threat. To anyone.

"Why don't you go home for now?" I said, doing my best to stifle a yawn. "I'm sure the whole situation will look better in the morning."

Which only goes to show how wrong a person can be.

Chapter 12

After Dylan left, I climbed into a hot shower and let the water wash away the scent of death. I stood there until the water ran cold, then slipped into a pair of sweats and a T-shirt and climbed under the covers of my warm bed. I curled up with Max on my feet and waited for sleep to carry me away. But every time I closed my eyes, I saw Laurence's lifeless body, and each time the image floated through my mind, I jerked awake.

More than anything, I wanted to call Jawarski and talk about the case with him. Nate had seemed unusually reasonable, but I still had a hard time trusting him. Besides, I knew what Jawarski would say if I did call him. He might be dating me, but he was loyal to his brothers on the force. Nate would have to pull a major screwup for Jawarski to stop defending him.

And I had to think about Jawarski's kids. The time he spent with them was so rare and precious, I didn't want to intrude.

When my alarm went off the next morning, I was still exhausted. Dragging myself out of bed, I dumped food into Max's dish and hauled myself into the shower again, hoping that the water would wake me up.

I was just stumbling out of the shower when my phone started to ring. Nobody I know calls to talk at six thirty in the morning, so a lump of dread formed in my stomach as I hurried to answer. It doubled in size when I saw "Silver River Inn" on my caller ID screen.

"The police were just here," Dylan shrilled when I answered. "They took Richie down to the station."

My stomach tried to turn over, but the rock-solid ball of apprehension wouldn't let it. "Did they arrest him, or did they just take him in for questioning?"

"I don't know. How would I know that?" The questions came rapid-fire, a sign of panic. "They came while I was in the kitchen and took him away right in front of our guests. I couldn't even go with him."

Poor Richie. Poor *Dylan*. At least Richie had some idea what was going on. "Did they read him his rights?"

"I don't know. I don't think so."

"Then they probably didn't arrest him," I said. "Chances are they're just asking him more questions."

"Why couldn't they talk to him here? They did last night."

I was asking myself the same thing, but I did my best to sound calm and reassuring. Hysteria wouldn't make anything better. "I don't know, Dylan. Just try to be calm and take care of your guests. That's the best thing you can do for Richie right now. I'm sure you'll hear something soon."

"I hope so." I heard someone talking in the background and Dylan covered the phone to muffle their conversation. When he came back to me, his voice was low and hushed. "I don't know what I'll do if they arrest him, Abby. It's not as if we can afford an attorney."

"It probably won't come to that," I said, ignoring the twinge of warning as I had last night. "And if by some odd chance it does, Richie can see if he qualifies for court-appointed counsel." I didn't add that the chances of that were probably slim. Not that many people can meet the narrow guidelines involved, which is a good thing if you're a member of the public whose pocket is being plundered to pay for someone's defense. Not such a good thing if you're in desperate need of an attorney and living on an overextended budget.

"Try not to worry," I said, even though we both knew that

Dylan would worry himself sick. "Let me know when you hear from him."

The news left me chilled, so after we hung up I piled on a few warm layers and clipped Max to his leash. Maybe a brisk morning walk in subzero temperatures would warm me up.

The weather seemed a little more moderate this morning than it had last night, which lightened my mood a bit. With any luck some of the dirty mounds of snow that had been piled up around town for the past two weeks would melt.

Max and I set off, deliberately walking away from the Playhouse and thoughts of death. I tried to keep my mind on other things. The recipe for the Marshmallow Caramel Pillows I'd be making later that morning. My relationship with Jawarski, and whether or not I'd be able to move past my commitment phobias. How to convince Karen that the hearts hanging all over Divinity were as hideous as I thought they were. Important things. Things I stood a chance of doing something about.

Unfortunately, I was also wondering about who else might have been in the theater when Laurence Nichols died, and whether Richie would be able to convince Nate that he was innocent. I wondered about Colleen Brannigan's husband, and what he'd been doing when the lethal spotlight fell from the fly system. I wondered if Nate knew about Doyle Brannigan's jealousy, and whether he planned to ask everyone involved in the production where they'd been when Laurence died. And I told myself over and over that I could trust Nate Svoboda to conduct the investigation. He was a good cop. Jawarski believed in him, didn't he? So I should, too. I just wished I could make myself believe it.

Max and I walked along Prospector Street, past Rachel's shop, Candlewyck, and Iris Quinn's Once Upon a Crime. I was so busy trying to find answers to the questions dancing in my head, I barely paid attention to traffic when I crossed the street.

Much as I hated to admit it, I hadn't told Nate everything I knew when he questioned me last night. In fact, I'd told him very little, really. Out of loyalty to Colleen, I hadn't mentioned her husband's suspicions about her relationship with Laurence. I'd also failed to mention the argument I'd overheard between Vonetta and Laurence the night of the meeting. I'd planned to tell him about both if the lab verified that the safety cable had actually been cut, but Dylan's late-night visit had convinced me to bump up my timetable. I hated casting suspicion on anyone, but I hated knowing that the police were focusing on Richie even more.

I don't know how long I'd been walking when the cold air finally bit through the layers of clothing I'd piled on and pulled me back to reality. We'd wandered several blocks from home, and as I got my bearings, I realized Max and I were standing across the street from the Wagon Wheel family restaurant, which had been one of my dad's favorite places to grab a bite when Wyatt and I were kids.

Back then, life wasn't like it is now—mothers rarely worked outside the home, and eating out had been a special occasion. A trip to the Wagon Wheel meant Sunday clothes and best behavior for my brother and me. We'd both hated wearing our Sunday best, but we'd looked forward to those rare treats with such anticipation, we'd have done anything our parents asked. For months before Mom's birthday and Mother's Day, we'd think about what was coming, and once in a blue moon Dad would get a hankering he just couldn't ignore, and we'd come to town for a spontaneous dinner.

I hadn't eaten at the Wagon Wheel since I moved back to Paradise. The years in Sacramento had dulled my appetite for greasy food. But I'd missed dinner the night before and suddenly nothing sounded better than the Wheel's all-American breakfast, eggs over easy cooked in bacon grease, and white toast slathered with butter.

As long as I shared my leftovers with him later, Max wouldn't mind waiting, so after a slow-moving truck passed by, we jogged across the street to the restaurant. I made Max comfortable in the vestibule and let myself inside. The aromas of bacon, sausage, and coffee filled my senses as I walked through the door, and my stomach growled with anticipation.

A harried-looking waitress poured coffee for a couple of guys seated at the counter, then glanced at me with a weary smile. "Sit anywhere, hon. I'll bring you a menu in just a sec."

I pondered my breakfast choices as I looked around the long, narrow dining area for a place to sit. Ham and eggs or chicken-fried steak and gravy? I couldn't make up my mind. But when I saw two people I recognized sitting together at the far end of the room, all thoughts of food flew right out of my head.

Nate Svboda sat with his back to me, but I'd have known him anywhere. Across the table, Doyle Brannigan mopped up egg yolk with a piece of toast and laughed at something Nate said. I know it seems unreasonable, but seeing Doyle sitting there, looking as if he didn't have a care in the world, made me angry. If anyone in Paradise had a motive for wanting Laurence Nichols out of the way, it was Doyle Brannigan. So why did he get to enjoy breakfast with his friendly neighborhood police detective while poor Richie agonized over his fate?

My heart slammed against my rib cage, and I backed up a couple of steps, hoping they wouldn't notice me. I could almost hear Jawarski telling me not to jump to conclusions, but this conclusion didn't require much of a leap.

It was pretty obvious that Nate and Doyle were friends, and I knew how the good ol' boys network functioned. My dad had been a card-carrying member for years. Doyle could have walked down the street holding the murder weapon in plain sight, and Nate would have just come up with a way to excuse him.

My mind raced as I backed out of the door and unclipped Max's leash. "Sorry, boy," I said as I turned for home. "No bacon for you this morning."

I'd be beating my head against a brick wall if I tried to convince Nate to check out what Doyle was doing last night. But *somebody* had to make sure he hadn't been crawling around the upper levels of the theater with a knife, cutting cables. I stepped off the curb and crossed the street, tossing a silent apology to Jawarski into the Universe. I knew how much he'd worried about me in the past, and I wouldn't have gotten involved this time if he'd been here to investigate.

That's the honest truth.

But Richie is a friend, and the odds were seriously stacked against him. Sure, Jawarski would be back eventually, but Nate and the boys could do a helluva lot of damage in the meantime. I wouldn't get *involved*, I promised myself. I'd just ask a few questions. See if I could figure out what Doyle Brannigan had been doing last night. Make sure that if Nate left Doyle walking around free as a bird while he kept Richie boxed up in an interrogation room, there was a good reason for the difference in the way they were being treated. That's all.

And Nate had better hope he hadn't overlooked something. Because if he had, there would be hell to pay.

Chapter 13

"I can't believe it. Laurence Nichols? Dead? Inside *our* theater?" Karen stopped polishing the glass container in her hand and shook her head in amazement. "Do you know what this is going to mean?"

"Yeah," I said. "It means that Richie Bellieu is considered a 'person of interest,' and it means that we're going to have to deal with a bunch of reporters and rotten publicity that nobody needs." In the time it had taken me to walk from the Wagon Wheel to Divinity, I'd gone from grimly determined to furious.

While I put a pot of Chocolate Mudslide on the coffeemaker, I'd given Karen and Liberty a brief rundown of the mess at the Playhouse, leaving out almost nothing except the part where, less than twenty-four hours before Laurence died, Vonetta had threatened him with harm if he didn't get the hell out of her theater. I just couldn't picture Vonetta climbing around in the fly system and sawing at safety cables with a knife. If she'd wanted to kill him, she'd have been more straightforward. Besides, the first order of business was satisfying my curiosity about Doyle Brannigan.

Liberty must have found some hidden square inch of the shop she hadn't decorated because she was carefully attaching ribbon streamers to yet another stack of hearts. "People are going to come from all over the place to see where he died. Don't you think that's kind of creepy?"

I rubbed my neck, trying to get rid of the knots of tension that had started forming as I walked through town. I hated thinking about the reporters who'd try to interview Richie and Dylan, and about the negative publicity all of this would mean for the inn. And not just the inn, either. The Playhouse certainly wouldn't benefit from the attention, and neither would Vonetta. But short of locking away the entire cast and crew until the reporters disappeared, I couldn't see any way to avoid them.

Karen set aside the glass container and sat, putting her feet on an empty chair. She flexed one foot, then the other several times. "Do you really think Nate will try to railroad Richie into court?"

"He might not railroad him," I said, trying to be fair, "but I don't think he'll go out of his way to look for other suspects."

"But surely Richie's not their only suspect?"

"I hope not," I said. "But you know Nate as well as I do. Maybe better. He's not a big fan of the alternative lifestyle."

Karen scowled at her feet as she began rotating both at the ankles. "I know he's not, but he wouldn't send someone to jail just for being gay."

"I don't think he'd send Richie to jail for being gay," I clarified. "But you know how some of these guys are around here. If he thinks Richie is sick and twisted—and you know he does—it's not much of a stretch for him to believe Richie's a murderer, too."

Liberty held up a heart so she could admire her handiwork. "Poor Richie. He must be scared half to death. Have you heard anything yet? Is he still at the police station?"

"As far as I know." I pulled three mugs from the cupboard and carried them to the table. "What do you know about Doyle Brannigan?" I asked Karen.

"Doyle? Colleen's husband?" Karen stopped rotating her feet and glanced up at me. "Not a lot, but he seems like a good guy."

Liberty set aside one heart and started working on another. "Why are you asking about him? Do you think he did it?"

I shrugged. "I don't know, but I intend to find out where he was last night." I sat at the table and sighed with frustration. "The trouble is, a falling light seems like such a careless way to commit murder. I can't even get to *who* could have done it yet, because I'm having a hard time wrapping my mind around *how* it was done. There's just no way to guarantee that that would do the job."

Karen put her feet on the floor and straightened one leg in front of her. "You don't know for sure that the light killed him, do you? It was there, and you say the cable was obviously cut, but do you know for sure that it's what struck the fatal blow?"

I stared at her, dumbfounded that I hadn't even considered that. "No, I guess I don't know."

"Wow," Liberty breathed. "So somebody, like, cut the cable and dropped the light to make it *look* like the light was what killed Laurence?"

"It's possible, isn't it?" Karen asked.

"Yeah, it's definitely possible." I grabbed the coffeepot and carried it to the table. "The police will be able to say for sure when they get the coroner's report back, but I have no idea how long that will take. I wish Jawarski was here. He'd be able to find out where things stood for me."

"So the murder weapon could have been anything?" Liberty seemed to be enjoying herself. "He could have been shot or stabbed or anything for all we know."

"Yeah. Maybe." We were straying from the subject I wanted to discuss, so I tried dragging us back. "You said you don't know Doyle well," I said, fixing my attention on Karen. "But it seemed to me that he has a pretty bad temper. Do you know if he's ever been in trouble before?"

Karen put both feet on the floor again and sat ramrod straight. "Not that I know of, but I'm hardly an expert on who's done what in the past twenty years. I'll bet you could check the archives at the *Post* and find out."

"If *you* can't remember anything," I said, "there probably isn't anything to remember."

"I wouldn't be too sure about that." Karen stopped rotating, flexing, and stretching, and picked up another freshly washed container to check for water spots. She knows everything about everyone, but she never seems to recognize her own ability.

"Maybe it wasn't him," Liberty said as she glued ribbon to yet another heart. "Maybe his wife is the killer. Didn't you say she was at the theater when Laurence died?"

I nodded reluctantly. Much as I hated knowing that the police suspected Richie, I didn't want to cast my old school friend in the role of cold-blooded killer either. "What about Geoffrey Manwaring? Did he say or do anything to make you think he was unhappy with Laurence when he was in here the other day?"

Karen shook her head slowly. "He didn't say much of anything except that I should fire you."

"Well, I'm not going to cross him off my list yet. You know what a miserable human being he is."

"Unfortunately, being a jerk doesn't automatically make somebody a murderer," Karen said reasonably.

She had a point. "There's always a chance that the killer was someone completely unrelated to the production," I said. "When I left the theater last night, Nate was still trying to figure out whether Laurence had any family."

Liberty finished with the hearts and sat back with her mug in her hands. "I don't think he did," she said. "I don't remember ever reading about any. Isn't that sad?"

"Family is everything," Karen agreed.

"Well, I'm sure the police know by now," I said. And if they hadn't figured out how to use Google, the reporters (who were bound to show up soon) would fill them in.

We sat in silence for a minute, each of us pursuing our own line of thought until Liberty asked, "So what are you going to do?"

Cradling my cup in both hands, I inhaled the scent before treating myself to a taste. "Wait to hear from Dylan and hope the police don't decide to arrest Richie without a lot more evidence."

"You should go see how Dylan's holding up," Karen said. "He's going to need a friend."

"Good idea. I'll go after work."

She shook her head firmly. "I wouldn't wait that long. Liberty and I can handle things for an hour or two this morning. You should go now."

The suggestion surprised me, but I didn't argue with her. That's the thing about Karen. She's one of the most compassionate people I know. Even if my leaving inconvenienced her, she was more concerned about Dylan than herself. Which is great, except that all that compassion made it even harder for me to stick to my guns on the gaudy paper heart decoration issue inside Divinity.

Ten minutes later, I had Max in the Jetta and we were chugging sluggishly toward the Silver River Inn.

The good news was that Richie was back by the time I got there. The bad news? I'd never seen him so depressed. He barely acknowledged me when he saw me, and instead of showering Max with air-kisses, he gave the poor dog a half-hearted scratch behind the ears before flopping onto a cushioned window seat that overlooked the street.

I sat beside him while Dylan turned a wingback chair away from the fireplace and perched on the edge of his seat, ready to leap up if Richie needed or wanted anything. After checking to make sure we were alone, I asked, "How are you two holding up?"

Dylan lifted one shoulder. "As well as can be expected, I guess."

Richie sat hunch-shouldered and staring at his hands. "It was humiliating, Abby. One of the worst things I've ever been through, and that's saying something."

"They didn't arrest you, though," I said. "That's good, isn't it?"

"They haven't arrested me *yet*." He lifted his eyes to meet mine, and I was shocked by the despair I could see in them. "Give them a few more hours and they'll probably be able to trump up enough evidence to execute me."

"I'm as worried as anyone about Nate's investigation," I said, "but I don't think he'd manufacture evidence just to get a conviction. I'm more concerned that he'll ignore evidence because he's made up his mind that you're guilty."

Richie's lips curved slightly. "With all due respect, Abs, I have a little more experience with homophobes than you do."

"Yeah, but Nate's not just prejudiced against gay people. He's also firmly convinced that women need to be kept in their place. He's an equal-opportunity bigot."

Richie let out a sharp laugh, and Dylan shot me a look of gratitude. "All evidence to the contrary," Dylan said, "we're trying not to panic or assume the worst. It's not easy, though. We lost three couples this morning after the police showed up and hauled Richie off. They heard the word *murder* and they couldn't check out fast enough."

I hated hearing that, but it didn't surprise me. It was just one more reason why clearing Richie of all suspicion was so important. "What did the police want to know?" I asked Richie.

He shrugged listlessly. "The same old stuff. What was I doing at the theater last night? Somebody told them that Laurence and I had an argument, so they asked about that. They wanted to know how I felt about him. Was I interested in him romantically? *As if!* They're convinced that I was trying to seduce him, and he spurned me. They've cast me in the role of 'woman scorned' and they're determined to prove that I climbed up into the rigging and bashed his skull in."

"With a well-placed and very lucky swing of a spotlight," I muttered. "That's all they asked about?"

"They asked about my relationship with Dylan," Richie said with a scowl. "They wanted to know how the two of us were getting along and whether our relationship was in trouble. And then they asked if I'd seen anyone else hanging around the theater, and whether I knew of anyone who wanted Laurence dead."

"And did you? See anyone, I mean."

He shook his head. "Besides Alexander and Vonetta and Colleen and Jason? No."

"I knew about all of them," I said. "They were there when

we found the body. But where were they right before Laurence's body was found? I thought they were there for a meeting, but I walked all through the Playhouse and couldn't find anybody."

"Probably out on the loading dock," Richie said. "Alexander had some special piece of equipment he wanted to bring in, and Jason was trying to show him what our limitations were and why it wouldn't fit."

"What about Colleen's husband? Was he there?"

Richie looked surprised by the question. "Not then. He was with her when she first got there, but he left."

Which put him in the vicinity. My heart did a little quickstep. "What about Geoffrey Manwaring?"

Richie thought about that for a second, then shook his head. "I didn't see him at all. I don't think he was there."

"Was Laurence on the loading dock with the rest of them?"

"At first. He got pissed off at Alexander for being such a prima donna, and went back inside."

"And where were you when he did that?"

"In the men's dressing room," Richie said, looking embarrassed. "I was waiting, hoping to get a chance to talk to Laurence."

I didn't want to grill him. The police had already badgered him enough. But if I was going to help at all, I needed to know exactly what he'd seen and done. "This was after the misunderstanding you and Laurence had over your lunch invitation?"

Richie shot a withering look at Dylan. "You told her about that?"

"She'd already heard about the argument," Dylan explained. "And I was groveling at her feet, begging her to help us. I wasn't in any position to hide things. Besides, Abby's on our side. She knows you weren't trying to seduce anybody."

Richie dragged his gaze back to mine. "Can you believe that? I mean, I hate to speak ill of the dead, but that guy was a real piece of work. I'll admit I was a bit starstruck at first, but I wasn't after . . . *that*."

"Of course you weren't," I said. "But why did you want to talk to him? If he'd already been so nasty to you, why didn't you just steer clear?"

"It was stupid, I know, but he'd asked me to do him a favor a couple of days earlier, and I decided not to be a jerk. I went back there to deliver a message."

I sat up a little straighter. "What kind of favor?"

"He wanted to talk to someone privately, and he asked me to arrange it."

"I warned him not to get involved," Dylan said. "I knew it was just asking for trouble."

"Who did he want to talk to?" I asked. "And why didn't he just make the arrangements himself?"

"He tried. She wouldn't talk to him, so he asked me to get her alone somewhere and then tell him so he could meet us there."

The only woman I could think of in Paradise who would have avoided a conversation with Laurence Nichols was the one whose husband was convinced she'd been having an affair with him. I have issues about infidelity, so I was glad to know that Colleen had refused to meet Laurence alone.

Even though I was pretty sure what the answer would be, I asked again anyway. "Who was this mystery woman?"

Richie looked uncertain for about half a second, then laughed uncomfortably. "I promised Laurence I wouldn't tell anyone, but I don't suppose it matters now. He wanted to meet with Serena Cummings."

I hadn't seen *that* coming. "Serena? What did he want to see her about?"

"I don't know. He didn't tell me, and I didn't ask. I wish I had. Serena told the police I was lying, and I can't prove that I'm not."

"So you did set something up with her?"

Richie nodded. "She was going to meet me for lunch the next day. Which would make it today, wouldn't it?" He snorted a laugh and closed his eyes. "I told her that I was having trouble with Paisley and I needed some advice about getting around her so I could talk to her mother. She bought the whole story at the time. I guess she knows it was a lie now."

We all fell silent at the sound of footsteps coming down the stairs, and an instant later a young couple stacked their bags near the front door and came into the great room. The woman held back and smiled nervously while the man strode toward the polished counter that serves as the inn's front desk.

Dylan stood and did his best to put on a happy face. "You're not leaving us, are you?"

"I'm afraid so. Something's come up. Family . . . thing."

Yeah, and I was Queen Elizabeth. The guilt on Richie's face and the weariness in Dylan's posture tugged at my heart. They couldn't afford to watch business walk out the door any more than I could. If the mantle of suspicion wasn't removed from Richie soon, these two could lose everything. I didn't know how much good I could do, but I couldn't just sit around and wait for a miracle.

Chapter 14

❀

As I saw it, I could start asking questions in one of two places: the Paradise Playhouse or the Victorian-style house on Lucky Strike Road that Vonetta had called home for the past thirty years. I timed my visit for an hour when I was pretty sure Vonetta would be at work, and even drove past the theater to make sure her Buick Regal was parked in its usual spot.

Setting my sights on Serena, I drove to Lucky Strike Road and began the search for a parking space. Paradise used to be a mining town, and these old streets are narrow. Ever since the town began growing a few years ago, parking has been at a premium. It's hard enough to find a space when the weather's good. In the winter, when the streets are lined with several feet of plowed snow and street parking is prohibited, people are forced to become creative.

After searching for several minutes, I managed to cram the Jetta into a few inches of space about two blocks away between someone's garage and a No Parking sign. While Max and I walked back to the house, I ran through what I'd say when Serena found me on her doorstep.

The temperature had warmed to slightly below freezing, and the sun hung high overhead in a cloudless blue sky. Sunlight reflected off the snow, making the day look far warmer than it actually was. In spite of the chill, I turned my face to the sky and soaked up the sunlight as I walked. Fresh air and sunshine can always lift my mood.

It took me a minute to figure out the latch on Vonetta's old-fashioned gate, but I finally climbed the steps to the porch and knocked on her door while Max nosed through snow piled up against the porch. Vonetta's house is an original Painted Lady design, built in the late 1800s. It's long and narrow, built into the hillside like most of the buildings in that neighborhood. Between productions, Vonetta had restored it to its original glory, and I'd been hearing rumors for years that it was about to be placed on the historical register.

Despite the precautions I'd taken to make sure I'd find Serena alone, I held my breath until she opened the door. If Laurence had gone to all the trouble to set up a clandestine meeting with Serena, I was betting Vonetta didn't know anything about it. Considering how hard she'd tried to keep me from talking to Serena that night in the ladies' room, I wasn't sure how I'd explain my visit if Vonetta came to the door, or how I'd get past her for the answers I needed.

When the door finally opened, I found Serena wearing a faded terry cloth robe, which she clutched together with one hand. Her eyes were swollen from sleep, and she smoothed the back of her hand across one cheek, dimpled by the pattern of whatever she'd been lying on. She frowned when she saw me. "What are you doing here?"

"We need to talk."

"I don't think so." She stepped back and would have shut the door in my face if I hadn't moved in front of it and stopped it from latching. This isn't a technique I'd recommend. When a fast-moving door meets flesh and bone, flesh hurts.

Serena glared at me as the door bounced open again. "What the hell do you think you're doing?"

I resisted the urge to rub the spot where the door had made contact. "I just need a few minutes," I said. "A friend of mine is in trouble, and I need your help."

"What friend?"

"Richie Bellieu." She grabbed the door again, and I steeled myself for another encounter. "I know he arranged a private meeting with you. Lunch. Today. To talk about your mother. And don't tell me he didn't. I can tell when Richie's lying, and he's not."

Serena didn't slam the door, but she didn't let go of it either. "I don't know what you're talking about. Now move."

"What did Laurence want to talk to you about?"

"How would I know?"

"I'm guessing you know because he tried to talk to you on his own, but you refused to meet with him. That's when he asked Richie for help."

"Well, that just shows what you know," Serena snarled. "I barely even knew Laurence. He had no reason to talk to me."

"Really? That's strange. It sure seemed like you knew him the night of the company meeting. Why did he automatically assume that you were the one who stole his music?"

"I don't know."

She stared right at me, trying to look as if she was telling the truth, but her eyes twitched rapidly, and I was pretty sure she was lying. I don't think she could feel it, and the movement was subtle enough that I'd have missed it if I hadn't been standing so close. No wonder her mother had always been able to tell when she was trying to hide something.

"Whatever it was," I said, ignoring her answer, "Vonetta knew about it. That's why she tried to fire Laurence, isn't it?"

Serena had been about to shove the door against me again, but that made her pause. "What are you talking about?"

"You didn't know about that?"

Serena shook her head.

"Before that meeting, your mother was thrilled to have Laurence as musical director for the production. Less than an hour after the meeting, I heard her threaten him." I could sense her weakening, so I pulled out the big guns. "Twenty-four hours later, he was dead."

Her eyes grew wide with shock. "You can't think Mama killed him?"

"I don't know what to think. That's why I'm here."

Serena chewed her lip for a few seconds, then stepped away from the door and waved us inside. "You can come in, but you can't stay long. Mama's coming home for lunch in about an hour, and I need to get everything ready."

I'd take whatever I could get. "Fine," I said, leading Max around the door and into the vestibule. "I'll be quick."

A long hallway stretched the length of the house to the kitchen at the back and branched upstairs to the bedrooms. The parlor opened off to the right, and it was into this room that Serena led the two of us.

This wasn't my first time in Vonetta's house, but I hadn't been here since Serena and I were teenagers. Not much had changed in that time. The same green couch sat in front of the bay window, the same easy chairs flanked the fireplace. I was pretty sure she even had the same floor lamps and coffee table. In fact, the only concession to the new millennium was the familiar white box with gold trim sitting in the center of the coffee table. Even that could have come from decades past, if not for the big red hearts pasted all over it.

It wasn't until I'd settled into one of the wingback chairs that I realized the box wasn't the right size for the caramels Vonetta had purchased on her visit to Divinity. Were these the chocolates Geoffrey Manwaring had ordered for Laurence's lady friend? It was on the tip of my tongue to ask, but I decided to check the store's records instead. No sense pissing off Serena unless I had to.

Serena dropped heavily into one chair and curled her legs beneath her. "This is such an ugly mess. I don't know what to do. Mama keeps telling me that everything's going to be all right, but I had no idea she'd tried to fire Laurence—" She broke off with a shake of her head.

"It's going to get worse before it gets better," I predicted. "I don't know whether the police are aware of your mother's argument with Laurence, but they're bound to find out. Why do you think she threatened him? What did he do to upset her?"

Serena glanced at me out of the corner of her eye. "What did she say?"

I debated how much to tell her. I didn't want to feed her information that would color her answers, but I *had* barged in uninvited. I probably owed her something. "She told him to get the hell out of her theater, and she said something about him not caring who he hurt. I'm pretty sure she was talking about you, Serena. It's the only thing that would explain such an abrupt change of heart."

"No offense, Abby, but it's really none of your business."

"None taken," I assured her. "Look, I know you don't want to air the family's dirty laundry. I understand that. But Richie Bellieu is a good friend, and I've known you and your mother a long time. I don't want to see anyone hurt. That's why I'm here."

Serena slid an unhappy smile at me. "I know." She shifted in her seat, this way and that, finally sticking one leg out from beneath the robe and kicking it gently. "But you're asking about stuff that's personal. I can't talk about it."

"Once the police find out about your mom's argument with Laurence, you're going to have to talk about it. She's obviously trying to protect you, and the police will want to know why. They might even decide she's covering for you."

Her head shot up and her eyes filled with panic. "I didn't kill him. My mother knows that."

"How does she know, Serena?"

"She knows *me*." The leg started to move faster. "Laurence Nichols was a bastard. Anybody who spent more than five minutes around him knew that. He probably deserved to die for the things he did to people. But *I* didn't kill him, and neither did my mother."

"Then you have nothing to worry about," I said. "Just tell the police where you were when he was killed. If there's somebody who can back up your story, you won't need to worry. Your mother, though . . . She was the first one to find him. I'm the closest thing she has to an alibi, but even I can't swear to how long she was in the auditorium before I got there."

"But she's innocent. And so am I. I only saw him once."

I studied her expression for a long time, looking for signs of guile or deception. I'm not an expert in body language, but I'd learned a lot in my previous life as a corporate attorney and I was pretty sure she was telling the truth. I just didn't see any reason to let her know that.

"I'd like to believe you," I said, "but if you're so innocent, why lie about the meeting Richie arranged?"

Her foot bounced faster still. "What makes you so sure I'm lying?"

Besides all the obvious "tells"? Gee, I wonder. "I hate to break it to you, Serena, but you're not a very good liar. I know I'm asking you to talk about something you'd rather not discuss, but I can't believe you're so determined to keep whatever your secret is that you'd let an innocent man pay for your silence."

"I'm glad you're trying to help him," she said, "but why do you need to dig into my past to do it?"

"Because I have to understand Laurence to figure out what happened to him, and I don't know what part your past plays in his death."

"It doesn't play any part." She stood and walked to the fireplace. She kept her back to me, but I sensed that she was weakening, so I bit my tongue and waited for her to speak. "It was all so long ago," she said after a lengthy silence. "It can't possibly be related."

"If your mother didn't threaten Laurence because of you, tell me why she did threaten him."

She closed her eyes and her head drooped. "It was because of me," she said so quietly I almost missed it. "It had to be."

Finally! "What did he do to you?"

She turned slowly, and the pain on her face made my breath catch. "I met him after you left for college. I was just a kid. Eighteen, maybe nineteen. He was so handsome. Well, you know. He wasn't really famous yet, but he was on his way. And he had that charisma. I was fascinated."

"A lot of us were, just from seeing him on TV."

Serena returned to her chair and curled up again. "He had this way of looking at me . . . I don't know how to describe it, but he made me feel as if I was the only person in the room. I would have done anything he wanted me to do back then."

"I think a lot of women have been in that boat," I said. "I know I have been, especially when I was younger."

Gratitude tinged the sad smile on her face. "Thanks, but you don't know how bad it was. My mom knew there was somebody, but I wouldn't tell her who it was. We fought all the time. I mean, she's great. You know she is. But she can be kind of controlling at times. She saw me slipping away from her, and she grabbed on with both hands. I guess she thought that if she held on tight enough, she could save me."

I'd never been a parent, but I'd seen my brother fight similar battles with his kids. Not on a big scale yet, but even so, he'd never gotten the results he was after. I wondered if any parent ever did. "Let me guess," I said. "It didn't work."

Serena let out a brittle laugh and shook her head. "Not even close. I fought her. I rebelled. And eventually, I ran away."

"That's when you left Paradise?"

She nodded. "It didn't feel like Paradise at the time. It felt like a prison, and I was determined to show my mother that she couldn't call the shots for me."

"Where does Laurence fit in all of this?"

"He and I left together. I was convinced he was my one great love, so where else would I want to be?"

I remembered feeling that way about Roger. My one and only. My soul mate. *Gag.* The worst part about remembering all that youthful romanticism was realizing that my nieces were heading straight into it. I'd give anything if they could get through it with fewer injuries than I had.

But we weren't talking about me, or about Dana and Danielle. I dragged my attention back to Serena and asked, "So your mother still didn't know who you were seeing?"

"Oh, hell no. Laurence's dream was to make it big, and back then the Playhouse was about as big as you could get in this part of the world. I wouldn't have hurt his chances of success for anything."

"But she knows now?"

"Now, yes. I told her the whole story the other night."

I sat for a while, absorbing what she'd just told me, but it didn't quite add up. "That was over twenty years ago," I said. "And you're obviously all right, so it's not as if there was any permanent damage."

Serena's eyes met mine again and the pain was back. "There's no damage you can see."

"Did he hurt you?"

"He didn't beat me or anything like that," she said. "But I was pregnant when we left. I thought he'd be so thrilled, you know? But it was a different world then, and he freaked out. He didn't mind sleeping with me but he wasn't about to marry me, and he sure as hell didn't want a kid with me. He thought it would hurt his chances of being America's favorite, and that's what he was determined to become. If all those conservative Midwest folks had found out that he was sleeping with a black woman . . ." She broke off with a sigh of resignation. "I'm okay with it now, but it hurt like hell then."

"I'm sure it did—on several levels. What happened to the baby?"

"Laurence forced me to have an abortion." She held up a hand, anticipating an argument from me. "I was young. He just had to look at me the right way, and I felt as if I had no choice. I *did* argue with him about the baby. I didn't want to do it. Mama had drilled the idea that life is sacred into me, and having that abortion felt like murder. But I was so desperate for him to love me, I did it anyway."

I didn't know what to say to that, so I did the smart thing and kept my mouth shut.

"Something went wrong with the operation," Serena said, "and I nearly died. Obviously, I survived, but I'll never be able to have kids of my own."

This was a pain I could identify with. I didn't let myself think about my own childless state often, but it was always like a sword in my heart when I did. I leaned across the space between us and put my hand on hers. "I'm so sorry."

She nodded without looking at me. "It's my own fault."

"You did what you thought was best at the time," I said.
"That's all anybody can ever do."

"Yeah, maybe."

"So your mother found out that Laurence was responsible
for killing her unborn grandchild." And Vonetta *would* have
seen it that way. "And she also realized that it was his fault
she almost lost you."

"Yeah." She smiled sadly. "And you know Mama. I think
she was more disappointed when she realized that she
wouldn't ever have grandkids than I was over never having
kids of my own—and that's saying something. When she
found out that it was Laurence who had pushed me into the
abortion, she freaked."

"And that's why she tried to fire him."

"It has to be."

"Is that why she's trying to keep you from talking to
people?"

"I think so. She's kind of touchy about her reputation,
you know? She's worked so hard to fit in, and it wasn't easy
when she first came to town. She was the first African Amer-
ican in Paradise, and a lot of people were skeptical of her—
especially since she was a single mother. She's convinced
that if this gets out, people will think the worst of her, and
that would devastate her."

"It's a different world than it was back then," I said.

"You know that, and so do I. Mama? Not so much." Serena glanced at the clock on the mantel and her mood
changed abruptly. She bolted to her feet, a ball of tension
again. "I'm not even dressed, and she'll be home in less
than half an hour. If you don't leave now, I'll never get anything done."

I still had questions without answers, but I knew a whole
lot more than I had when I got there. I let her usher me to the
door. On the porch, Max stretched in the midday sun and
yawned contentedly. I felt chilled to the bone. Considering
their history, I wondered what Laurence had been planning
to say to Serena when he got her alone. And I wondered why

he'd ordered Vonetta to ban Serena from the theater at the
same time he'd been busy making arrangements to see her
alone. Something about that didn't feel right to me, but I
didn't know if it was because Serena had left something out,
or because Laurence had been a nasty human being who'd
been very good at fooling other people.

Chapter 15

"I don't have time for this, Abby. And neither, I'm sure, do you." Vonetta stood and came out from behind her desk, a deep scowl lining her normally smooth face.

I'd come straight to the Playhouse after my visit with Serena, hoping I could convince Vonetta to tell the police about her history with Laurence. Not only would revealing the truth help Richie by forcing Nate to acknowledge that other people had issues with Laurence, but when the truth came out—and it would—it would look a whole lot better for both Vonetta and Serena if they'd been honest about it from the beginning.

Apparently considering the conversation over, Vonetta gathered a stack of papers from her desk and swept from her office. I trailed her into the box office, determined to stay until she talked to me. "You don't have time *not* to talk to me," I insisted. "This isn't going to go away just because you want it to."

She pushed the Power button on the copy machine and shot a look at me over her shoulder. "I didn't do anything wrong, and I refuse to behave as if I did. Go back to the candy store. The police will conduct their investigation and realize that Laurence's death was an accident. Let's not turn it into something more."

I wished I could agree, but I didn't. "Closing your eyes to the truth won't make it disappear. You know it's only a matter of time before the police find out about Serena."

Vonetta's head whipped around and she pierced me with a stern look. "I don't know what you're talking about."

"Come on, Vonetta. People will remember their argument from the rehearsal. If I know about Serena's relationship with Laurence, the police will figure it out too. You and Serena might have kept it all a big secret, but Laurence didn't seem to think it was as important to hide it as you did."

Her gaze narrowed. "I don't know what you mean."

"I'm talking about Serena and Laurence, and their relationship. The baby. The abortion. It's all going to come out, and it's going to look really bad for you when it does."

She took a deep breath, but the only sign that I'd struck a nerve was the slight flaring of her nostrils. "You're stepping over a line, Abby. Friends don't do that."

Ouch! She knew which buttons to push, that was for sure. But I held my ground. "I'm not trying to offend you," I said, "but I'm really worried about Richie. The police have talked to him twice now, and he's terrified."

"Maybe he has reason to be."

"As a matter of fact, he does, and it's a reason you should understand. Nate Svoboda isn't exactly known for his open mind and free thinking."

She didn't even blink. "That's unfortunate, and I'm sorry Richie's having to go through that, but I don't see why I should let you throw my daughter under the bus to protect him."

"I'm not trying to throw Serena under the bus." I could hear my voice growing shrill with frustration, so I made an effort to pull myself together. "The point is, Serena's history with Laurence is bound to come out. If the two of you tell the police about it first, they won't be able to accuse you of lying to hide it later."

"If Serena's history with Laurence becomes public knowledge, I guess we'll know who felt compelled to share it with the world."

"I don't plan to tell anyone," I assured her.

"Then we don't need to worry. Laurence is the only other person who knew about their . . . relationship, and he wouldn't have told anyone."

"You don't know that for sure," I argued. "It happened a

long time ago. He could have told any number of people about it."

Vonetta lowered her voice to make sure she wouldn't be overheard. "You're forgetting that the reason he murdered my grandchild was to keep his clandestine affair a secret. He didn't want anyone finding out about his relationship with Serena."

"Well, yeah. Twenty years ago. I don't think he was all that worried about it by the time he came back to Paradise."

Vonetta's expression grew as frosty as the ice on the windows. "Serena had nothing to do with Laurence's death. She never even saw him again after that encounter in the rehearsal hall."

The brittleness of her glare made me uncomfortable, but at least I had her attention. "I'm not saying she did, but once the police find out about their past relationship, they're bound to think there's a connection. They're going to ask questions, and somebody will talk."

Vonetta swept her gaze over me once more, then turned back to the copy machine. "Then the police will be wrong."

"Ignoring this won't make it go away," I said again. "Both you and Serena have pretty strong motives for wanting Laurence dead."

Vonetta turned her head slowly to look at me. "You think one of us killed him?"

"I didn't say that. But somebody's bound to dig up the truth about Serena's relationship with him. You'll be doing both of you a favor if you just go to the police and tell them everything."

"No."

I groaned inwardly, wondering how such an intelligent woman could be so damn stubborn. Was she just naive, or was she hiding something? Before I could make an attempt to find out, a harried-looking woman burst through the door carrying a heap of pirate costumes.

"We're going to have to call Esther," she announced. "These costumes are too large for half of the chorus."

"Costumes?" My uneasiness changed direction. They

should have been packing costumes away, not making arrangements for alterations.

Vonetta flicked a glance at the pile of clothing in her arms. "Give her a call. Tell her we need her right away."

The woman disappeared, and I gaped at Vonetta for a few seconds before I could ask, "What are you doing?"

"Working."

"But—" The copier started running, and Vonetta resumed the journey she'd been on when I came in. She left the box office, crossed the lobby, and turned down the long corridor that led to the dressing rooms. Framed pictures of casts from long-forgotten productions stretched the entire length of the hallway, and earlier this year Vonetta had started a second row. Funny, but no matter how many years had passed, I could still tell you exactly which of those pictures I was in. Maybe my stage debut had been more important than I'd let myself believe.

I hurried to catch up with Vonetta, whose stride was almost Amazonian. "You're going to go ahead with the production?"

"Of course. Why wouldn't we?"

"Because Laurence was killed right here in the theater. I assumed you'd shut down."

She glanced over her shoulder as she walked. "The show *must* go on, Abby. Surely you've heard that before. And now I have to start all over and find a new musical director. One that Alexander is willing to work with. That's not going to be easy."

"But the murder was committed here. *On your stage.* One of the cast or crew, or someone connected to one of them, might be a killer."

Vonetta stopped walking and turned to face me. "You're entirely too fanciful, Abby. There's no proof that Laurence's death was deliberate, and unless the police decide beyond a shadow of a doubt that it was, I'm not going to let myself get swept up in emotion. The *accident* happened here, on my stage. It was tragic and untimely, and we're all distressed over it, but I can't think of a finer way to honor Laurence than to go on with the play and dedicate it to his memory."

"What if you're wrong? What if his death wasn't an accident? You could be putting yourself in danger. You could be putting the rest of the cast and crew in danger."

"If you're trying to frighten me, it won't work. Now, if you'll excuse me, I have a lot of work to do." She turned away and tugged open the door to the women's dressing room. "It's funny, isn't it? When I asked you, as a friend, to be in the production, you said you didn't have time. But you certainly seem to have plenty of time to chase shadows."

She let herself inside, and I was left staring at the door as it swished shut behind her.

I was both surprised and a little hurt by the venom in that last comment, but I suppose I deserved it. Turning away, I started back up that long hallway. I'd only made it halfway when a loud crash followed by a shrill scream tore through the air. It took about three seconds to decide that both had come from behind the door Vonetta had just entered. Another three to bolt back down the hall and tear through the door.

The main dressing area with its row of dressing tables and lighted mirrors was cluttered, but empty. A rolling rack of costumes had been shoved up against one wall, and colorful plastic stacking baskets tucked into every available space were filled to overflowing with makeup, hair products, hot rollers, hair straighteners, blow-dryers, and things I didn't recognize. A stack of scripts lay on one of the dressing tables, but Vonetta was nowhere to be seen.

After making sure that she wasn't on the floor behind the costume rack, I hurried into the attached ladies' room. I found Vonetta on the floor, her eyes closed and a trickle of blood on her forehead.

I lunged toward her, our argument forgotten. "Vonetta? Can you hear me?" I touched my fingers to her neck, felt the flutter of a heartbeat, and blinked away tears of relief. "Vonetta, are you all right?"

She didn't move a muscle. Her eyes didn't even twitch. But at least I knew she was alive.

I dug my cell phone from my pocket and checked for a signal. Nope. Not even one bar. I wasn't really surprised. Cell phone service was spotty in Paradise under the best of circumstances. I thought about putting something under Vonetta's head to make her more comfortable, but decided not to move her. I didn't know what had happened, and I didn't want to make an injury I couldn't see worse by moving her.

I got to my feet and headed for the door so I could call for help, but it flew open before I could reach it. Jason Dahl burst into the room, his face a mask of concern. Alexander Pastorelli puffed in behind him, wheezing and out of breath.

Déjà vu.

"Vonetta!" Alexander rushed toward her and knelt at her side. "My God, what happened?"

"I don't know. I was talking to Vonetta in the hall, then she came inside and I started to leave. I heard her scream, so I ran in to see what happened and found her like this. Somebody needs to call 9-1-1."

Alexander's head shot up and he looked at me . . . hard. "You have no idea what happened?"

"None. Why don't you stay with her? I'll go call for help."

"I don't think that's such a good idea," Alexander said, and the look in his eyes left me cold. "You go, Jason. *You* stay here with me."

My legs were shaking so I backed to the sink and perched on the edge of the counter. "You can't seriously think *I* did this. Vonetta's my friend."

"Yeah, well she's my friend, too." As if someone flipped a switch inside him, he went from hard-ass to Mr. Touchy-Feely in the blink of an eye. He brushed Vonetta's cheek with the backs of his fingers and spoke gently. "Vonetta, can you hear me? It's going to be okay. Jason has gone to call for help."

"I didn't do this," I said, more to myself than to him.

"No? Well you'll have a chance to prove it when the police get here."

Great. Just what I needed. More quality time with Nate Svboda. I had a sudden longing to hear Jawarski's voice, but

I refused to let myself call him. A few months ago, he'd expressed some doubt about my feelings for him. He'd asked whether I really liked him, or if I just liked the information he could give me about the case he'd been working on. Ever since then, I'd done my best to avoid talking to him about murder and mayhem. Since I hadn't called to hear his voice before today, I couldn't very well call now.

But oh man, I wished I could.

Chapter 16

❀

I spent the next two hours answering the same questions over and over again. I'd come to the theater to talk to Vonetta. I'd been about to leave when I heard her scream. No, I didn't see anyone else. No I didn't hear anything unusual—except, of course, the scream.

Vonetta had been awake by the time the paramedics arrived, but she hadn't been able to shed any light on her . . . accident, either. She'd walked into the ladies' room and something or someone had hit her from behind, that's all she knew.

The incident raised more questions than it answered. Who would attack Vonetta, and why? Had the spotlight that killed Laurence been meant for her? Or had she seen or heard something when she found Laurence's body that she didn't recognize as being important?

The paramedics' examination hadn't revealed any serious injuries, but they'd loaded her, protests and all, into the ambulance anyway. By the time Nate had finally let me go, reporters had started to gather, and I'd had to run the gauntlet to get away from them. By the time I made it back to Divinity, Karen and Liberty were up to their eyeballs in customers and orders, and I threw myself into the normalcy of caramel and chocolate, lollipops and gummi bears.

I spent the rest of the day trying not to think about what had happened at the Playhouse. It seemed only fair that I make at least a minimal contribution to the effort of getting Divinity through Valentine's Day. Luckily, we were too busy for Karen or Liberty to notice how distracted I was. I made three batches of cherry divinity and manned the phone for a while so Karen and Liberty could catch their breath. In spite of my lack of concentration, the divinity turned out perfectly, which was something of a minor miracle. After packing away the pale pink puffs of candy, I helped Karen and Liberty restock the shelves so we'd be ready to go in the morning. I forgot all about looking for the sales slip Karen had written up for Geoffrey Manwaring until I turned the key in the lock at the end of the day. Promising myself that I'd look for it tomorrow, I climbed the stairs to my apartment.

I was lucky, I guess. Nate and I didn't get along, but we had known each other since we were kids, so he hadn't taken Alexander's accusations seriously. But I didn't delude myself into thinking that the heat was off. I had the feeling Nate would be keeping an eye on me for the next little while.

It had been one helluva day, and I would have liked nothing more than to climb into bed and sleep for hours. But I was too wound up to sleep, too agitated even to sit still. I settled Max in the Jetta, swung past Burger King on my way out of town, and set a course for my brother's house.

I shared my fries with Max as I drove, and I polished off the last of my Whopper with cheese as I pulled off the highway onto my brother's gravel driveway. His truck was in front of the house, and I could see my sister-in-law, Elizabeth, framed in the kitchen window. Lights spilled from almost every window, giving the old two-story farmhouse a warm, welcoming feeling.

The house has belonged to Elizabeth's family for four generations, a fact that I usually find interesting. Tonight it just made me sad. For the first time in a long time, I felt a pang of regret over my life. No husband. No kids. I'd turned my back on my family for so long, I still didn't feel as if I truly belonged here. Thank God for Max. Without him, I'd have been completely alone.

Elizabeth had seen me drive up, and I realized she was watching from the window, waiting for me to get out of the car and come to the door. Shaking off the melancholy, I

climbed out into the cold and made my way along the shov-
eled walk to the front door. I knocked once and let myself
inside. My nieces and nephews were draped all over the
furniture, watching something on TV. The looks on their
faces when they saw me chased away the rest of the clouds.

"Aunt Abby!" Nine-year-old Caleb shot to his feet and
threw his arms around my legs. "I didn't know you were
coming."

I tousled his hair. "You didn't know I was coming? That's
weird. Neither did I!" I waggled my fingers at Dana and
Danielle, who looked pleased to see me but didn't bother
moving, and gave Brody a cool chin jerk, appropriate for
even the most discerning twelve-year-old. "Is your dad
around?"

Brody sat sideways in Wyatt's favorite chair, his back
propped against one of its arms, his legs draped over the
other. He lifted his head slightly and pried his eyes away
from the TV screen. "He's helping Mom with something, I
think. Want me to get him?"

"Thanks, but you look busy. I'll find him." I left the kids
fighting mildly over which of them Max should sit with, and
nosed my way toward the scent of bleach wafting from the
kitchen. I found Elizabeth folding a huge stack of crisp white
T-shirts at the kitchen table. Wearing a pair of sweats and a
T-shirt, her long reddish blond hair pulled into a ponytail,
she looked comfortable and relaxed.

Wyatt's legs protruded from the cupboard under the sink.
I heard a clang followed by a string of words I won't repeat
here. "How in the hell did this happen, Liz? How could you
lose your wedding ring down the drain?"

He sounded angry, but Wyatt often does. It rarely means
anything. I grinned at Elizabeth and nudged the bottom of
my brother's boot with my shoe. "Maybe she tried to grind it
up in the garbage disposal. I wouldn't blame her if she did."

Wyatt lifted his head so he could see and squinted up into
the overhead light. His brown hair was matted to his head in
a severe case of hat hair, and whiskers stubbled his cheeks
and chin. "Funny. What are you doing here?"

"Good to see you, too, Wyatt." I sat at the table with Elizabeth and inhaled the scents of soap and bleach and fabric softener. Homey smells. Comfort smells. For a minute, I wanted my apartment to smell like that. I wanted the sounds of kids and TV floating in from the next room and a husband swearing at pipes under the sink. Could I have something like this with Jawarski? Maybe. But how much of myself was I willing to give up to find out?

Elizabeth got up and pulled a couple of Cokes out of the fridge. She filled two glasses with ice and handed me one along with a bottle. "We heard about the excitement in town. What a mess, huh?"

I poured the Coke over the ice and watched the bubbles rise. "Have you heard about all of it?"

"We heard about Laurence Nichols. Is there something else?"

"Unfortunately. Vonetta was attacked this afternoon. She wasn't seriously hurt, but there's something going on at the Playhouse, and I don't like it."

Wyatt slid out from under the sink and sat up on the floor. "Nate know about the attack on Vonetta?"

I nodded. "Yeah. I got to spend a couple of hours with him this afternoon. For some reason, Alexander Pastorelli decided to accuse me of both attacks."

Wyatt frowned and got to his feet. "Nate didn't take that seriously, did he?"

I shook my head. "He didn't seem to, but he did question me for a while."

My brother pulled a beer from the fridge and carried it to the table. He wiped his hands on a towel and straddled a chair, resting his arms on its back. "You want me to talk to him?"

"Thanks, but no. Actually, I didn't come to whine about myself. I came to see if you know a guy named Doyle Brannigan."

Wyatt opened his beer and took a swallow. "Sure, I know Doyle. What about him?"

"What do you know about him?"

"I don't know. He's a decent guy. Married that friend of yours, didn't he? What was her name?"

"Colleen."

"That's the one." Wyatt took another swig, then put the bottle on the table. "I haven't seen much of him lately, but I used to run into him at least twice a week. Why? You think he has something to do with the stuff going on in town?"

"It's possible." I told them about the night I'd met Doyle and his suspicions about Colleen and Laurence. "I haven't seen him since, but if Laurence's death *wasn't* just a horrible accident, he'd definitely be on my list of suspects."

Elizabeth pulled a T-shirt from a pile in the basket beside her and shook it with a snap. "Do you think Colleen was having an affair with Laurence?"

"I don't know," I said again. "She seemed pretty upset when we found his body, but that's not so suspicious, after all. Seeing a dead body, especially someone you know, is pretty awful. Does Doyle have a temper?"

Wyatt shrugged. "No more than any other guy. He doesn't go around looking for trouble, but he doesn't back down from it either."

"Do you think he might have gone looking for trouble if he suspected his wife of being unfaithful?"

Elizabeth folded the T-shirt with a few sharp moves and sat it on a growing stack. "If he did, who could blame him?"

That response from my normally peacemaking sister-in-law should have surprised me. She's choir director at the Shepherd of the Hills church, for Pete's sake. Not the type you'd expect to encourage violence. But she's also in the process of putting her marriage back together after a particularly stupid move on my brother's part. She knew how it felt to suffer betrayal.

"She denies it," I said, but we both knew how little that meant.

Wyatt considered my question for a minute before he gave me an answer. "I think that if Doyle caught his wife in the act, he might do something about it. But I don't see him whacking somebody over the head with a spotlight just because of a rumor. If there was any truth to it, though, he'd find out. He wouldn't ignore it."

"Do you know where he works? I'd like to talk to him."

Wyatt shook his head. "Like I said, it's been a while. Last I heard, he was working construction for some guy over in Leadville, but I don't know if he still is." He gave me a stern look and added, "I don't suppose you'd listen if I told you to keep your nose out of it?"

I shook my head and grinned. "When have I ever listened to you?"

"Never, but you should."

"I'll consider it," I said, pushing to my feet. "Just as soon as Nate realizes that Richie Bellieu had nothing to do with Laurence Nichols's death."

"Richie." Wyatt scratched at the stubble on his chin and I could see him trying to place the name.

"He's one of the owners of the Silver River Inn."

Elizabeth brightened. "That cute bed-and-breakfast on Silver River Road? I've always wanted to stay there. I think it would be so romantic."

Wyatt's reaction was far different, but predictable. "He one of those funny fellas?" See what I mean? A card-carrying member of the I'm-a-Bigot club, otherwise known as the Loyal Order of the Caribou.

"If you're asking whether he's gay, yes, he is. But that doesn't make him a killer."

Wyatt held up both hands and laughed uneasily. "Hey, I never said it did. Just be careful, Abby. There are some people in this town who aren't real open-minded."

I'd been ready to argue with him, but now I clamped my mouth shut in surprise. It just goes to show, you never can tell about a person. Just when you think you know somebody, they do or say something completely unexpected.

"Thanks," I said when I'd had a chance to regroup. "Is Nate one of them?"

"He's not the worst," Wyatt said, "but it wouldn't break his heart to lock one of 'em away for a few years."

"That's exactly what I'm afraid of. I have to make sure he doesn't get the chance."

Elizabeth added another folded T-shirt to the stack. "Have you thought about going over Nate's head? There must be someone who could keep an eye on him and make sure the investigation is conducted the right way."

"Sure," Wyatt said with a shrug. "But you'll have to go over more than one head to find that guy. Abby has to do business in this town. Best not to make too many waves if there's another way around the problem."

I polished off my Coke and carried my glass to the sink, but the conversation had left me feeling strange, as if I'd been transported back in time a couple of decades or something. Who would have thought that we'd still be tiptoeing around stupid people in the twenty-first century?

Chapter 17

❧

I didn't get the chance to talk to anyone about Laurence Nichols or the attack on Vonetta the next day, but I knew that things were heating up by the number of white SUVs equipped with remote television equipment I saw through my shop window. The news was out.

When I got a few minutes in the afternoon, I called Richie to see how things were going. Two more guests had checked out early, and they'd suffered a rash of cancelled reservations. If things didn't turn around soon, they'd be in serious trouble.

Before hanging up, I warned Richie not to give any interviews. The temptation to set the record straight would be almost overwhelming for a guy like Richie, but there were too many things the press could twist into something ugly. I didn't want that for Richie and Dylan. Besides, as far as I knew, the police still hadn't officially labeled Laurence's death as a murder. Unfortunately, I wasn't sure that Richie could talk about it as an accident. Best not to say anything.

At seven, I locked up, swung past Jawarski's to take in his mail, and headed for the theater. I hadn't seen Vonetta since the paramedics spirited her away, and I wanted to make sure she was really all right. And, okay, I had an ulterior motive for my visit. Whether Laurence's death was an accident or not, someone had attacked Vonetta. The only thing I knew for sure was that "someone" wasn't me.

There had been at least three other people in the building that day, and I hoped one of them had seen or heard something that might help me figure out who was responsible for the attack. Of course, there was a good chance that one of them *was* responsible for the attack. I couldn't lose sight of that, either. I didn't suspect Paisley, but both Jason and Alexander had seemed genuinely shocked to find Vonetta lying on the floor. But if the attacker wasn't one of them, who was it?

As I opened the door into the lobby, piano music floated up from the rehearsal hall and I breathed a sigh of relief. Bad things had been happening, but usually when no one else was around.

I poked my nose into Vonetta's office and found Paisley fussing over her and Vonetta grousing about the unnecessary attention. After asking a few harmless questions to make sure she really was fine, I trotted down to the rehearsal hall to see who was there.

Jason Dahl sat at the baby grand piano, his expression almost dreamy as his fingers moved over the keys. He played well enough, but he was no Laurence Nichols. On the other side of the room, Alexander Pastorelli sat across a small table from Geoffrey Manwaring. Both men looked tense, maybe even a little angry, and my curiosity shifted into high gear.

Thanking my lucky stars for a shot at all three of them at once, I sat in a chair close enough to pick up their conversation if they didn't whisper, and pretended to be fascinated by Jason's music. Unfortunately, I was too far away to pick up more than a word or two. So much for the indirect method.

Jason finished the song he was playing and looked up with a sheepish smile.

Abandoning my efforts at clandestine listening, I left my chair and walked toward the piano, clapping politely. "That was very good. I didn't know you could play."

"I do. A little." He stood quickly and pulled the cover over the keys. "My mom made me and my sister take lessons when we were kids."

"Well, it obviously paid off. But if you don't mind me asking, why are you working as a stagehand instead of putting your talent to good use?"

A flush stained Jason's cheeks. "It's not easy to get a foot in the door," he said with a shy smile. "I'm hoping that if I hang around long enough somebody will give me a chance."

"I'm sure they will. If you have a minute, I wanted to ask you some questions about what happened the other day."

Jason eyed me warily, but he nodded. "Okay, I guess. What do you want to know?"

Our conversation caught Alexander's attention. He looked away from Geoffrey with a scowl. "The kid and I already told the police everything we know."

"So did I," I told him, "but I keep thinking there must be something else. Something one of us heard or saw that we didn't think was important at the time."

"The only thing *I* saw was you, leaning over Vonetta just the same way you were hunched over Laurence the day he died."

"Yeah," I snarled. "Just remember, appearances can be deceiving. How is Laurence's family handling all of this? They must be devastated."

Alexander glanced at Geoffrey in confusion. "Family?"

"I assume he had family somewhere," I said.

Geoffrey crossed his legs with an air of exaggerated patience. "Well, you'd be assuming wrong, then. There's no wife. No kids. He was an only child, and his parents are both dead. Have been for ten years or more."

"Was he seeing anyone?"

"Laurence was always seeing someone. Usually several someones."

"Any particular someones he left behind?"

Geoffrey regarded me through beady eyes narrowed in suspicion. "What business is it of yours?"

"A friend of mine is under suspicion. I'm trying to help him out."

"Who are we talking about? The one who tried to put the moves on Laurence?"

"For the record, Richie did not try to put the moves on Laurence," I snapped.

Geoffrey smirked. "Says you. I know what I know, and

what I know is, your pal Richie was practically stalking Laurence."

"Richie can be a bit overly enthusiastic," I admitted, "but he wasn't *stalking* anyone."

"Cut the kid some slack, Geoff," Alexander said. "He was a fan, that's all."

"That's not what Laurence told me," Manwaring argued.

Alexander barked a laugh. "Yeah, and Laurence was *always* such a truthful son of a bitch. Hell, Geoff, you worked for him for how many years? You ought to know better than anyone else that every word out of his mouth was a damn lie."

This was getting interesting. I motioned for Jason to remain quiet and clamped my own mouth shut so I could see where they would go from here.

Apparently forgetting about me, Geoffrey turned his beady eyes on Alexander. "The man's dead, Alex. Let it go."

"Let it *go*? He practically ruined me in Seattle. How am I supposed to let go of that?"

"It's over now, that's how."

"It'll be over when I get back every penny that son of a bitch took from me."

Geoffrey shot to his feet so fast his chair teetered on two legs, then crashed to the floor with a bang. "He didn't *take* anything from you. You made a bad investment. It happens. Quit blaming Laurence for your own stupidity."

Alexander lunged out of his chair and took a swing, but Geoffrey was too quick for him. Before any of us saw it coming, Manwaring had pinned the older man's arms behind his back. "If you ever take a swing at me again," he growled, "it will be the last thing you ever do." Shoving Alexander into the table, he strode from the room.

I thought about going after him, but the threat he'd just made against Alexander kept my feet glued to the floor. It might have just been big talk, but I wasn't in the mood to find out.

Red-faced and obviously furious, Alexander regained his

balance. I knew he was embarrassed at having been over-
powered in front of Jason and me, but I couldn't just pretend
I hadn't noticed.

"Are you all right?" I asked.

He nodded and shot a withering glare at the door Geoffrey had disappeared through. "I'm fine. But if you're still
trying to figure out who wanted Laurence out of the way,
why don't you ask *him* about the money in Laurence's estate."

"What about it?"

"He just told you Laurence died without any family. I'll
give you three guesses who gets the money now."

Jason pulled his gaze away from the door. "Mr. Manwaring?"

"Bingo. Give the kid a gold star."

"And he owes some of it to you?" I asked.

"He owes at least half of it to me." Alexander brushed
dirt from his sleeves and hitched his pants. He grabbed a
thick file folder from the table and started toward his office.
"Ask him to tell you about our production of *Cabaret* in Seattle sometime. And then throw out 75 percent of what he
tells you as total bullshit."

With that parting shot, he disappeared, leaving Jason and
me alone. "Well," I said with an uneasy laugh, "I think that
went well. Are you sure you want to get into this life? Maybe
you should cut your losses and find a nice, safe job at Home
Depot."

Jason grinned. "Maybe. What do you think that was all
about?"

I shook my head and replayed the last bit of the argument
we'd just witnessed. "Gee, I could be wrong, but I don't
think there's any love lost between those two. I'd really like
to know what happened in Seattle, and why Alexander
blames Laurence for it."

"I don't think you're going to get a straight story out of
either one of them," Jason said.

"Neither do I, but there must be someone who knows
what happened."

"I guess you're right." Jason started to follow Alexander from the room.

"Jason, wait."

He turned back uncertainly. "Yeah?"

"The day Laurence died, you seemed really concerned about Colleen Brannigan. Would you mind telling me why?"

"Well, because she . . . uh . . . she just seemed upset."

"Not because you thought she had a relationship with Laurence?"

His cheeks burned red. "You heard what she said. They were friends."

"But you thought they were more than that, didn't you? Why?"

"I don't know. I mean, yeah, I *did* think that, but I was wrong."

"Maybe. How well do you know Colleen?"

Jason hooked his thumbs in the back pockets of his jeans. "Pretty well, I guess. Why?"

"Have you ever met her husband?"

The kid snorted a laugh. "Yeah. He hangs around her all the time. The day Laurence told her to get rid of him, I thought he was going to lose it, y'know?"

That was news to me. "When did Laurence tell her to do that?"

Jason shook his head as if he was having trouble remembering. "The day before he died maybe? Or the day before that. I'm not sure."

"But you do remember Doyle's reaction. What did he do?"

Jason met my gaze slowly. "I probably shouldn't say anything. I'm sure it looked worse than it was." He took a deep breath and let it out in a rush. "It was a couple of hours later. I was getting some stuff out of the scenery shop and I heard the two of them arguing. Mr. Brannigan was saying all this stuff about Laurence and Colleen, and Laurence was laughing. But not a nice laugh. It was like, 'Yeah? What are you going to do about it?' "

Now we were getting somewhere. "And how did Mr. Brannigan take that?"

"Not well. He got really mad and told Laurence to leave Colleen alone or . . . or it would be the last thing he ever did."

Chapter 18

❦

As soon as I could leave Divinity the next day, I packed Max into the Jetta and aimed for Leadville. Like Paradise, Leadville is an old town settled by miners back in the 1800s. It's not hard to navigate, so it only took me a few minutes to find the address I'd copied from the phone book earlier.

Colleen lived in a two-story Shaker-style house just off Alder Street. A sagging chain link fence encircled a tiny neglected yard; an icy trail the exact width of a snow shovel blade led to the front door. I left Max in the car and followed the trail, crossing my fingers that Doyle wasn't home in the middle of the day.

Colleen came to the door wearing jeans, a peach-colored sweatshirt, and an apron dusted with flour. She brushed a lock of blond hair away from her face with the back of her hand and smiled broadly when she recognized me. "Hey! What are you doing here?"

Leadville was a bit out of my way, so I couldn't just claim to be in the neighborhood. I gave her a watered-down version of the truth. "I had some business nearby. Since I was coming this direction, I looked up your address but I probably should have called—"

She cut me off with a laugh and motioned me inside. As she started to shut the door, she stopped and jerked it open again. "Do you have a dog in the car?"

"That's Max. He goes almost everywhere with me."

"Will he bite me?"

It was my turn to laugh. "Not a chance. If anything, he'd lick you until you fell over."

"Well, then, bring him in. It's too cold to leave him outside."

I hustled back to the Jetta for Max and his traveling water dish, and the two of us followed Colleen into a gleaming kitchen filled with the aroma of ripe bananas. With its simple wooden cabinets and granite counters, the Shaker-style kitchen showed all of the care and pride the house was missing on the outside. Except for the mess on the counter, the kitchen could have been a snapshot in a magazine.

"I hope you don't mind if I finish up here," she said, perching a pair of glasses on her nose. "I'm in the middle of this banana nut bread, and if I stop now I'll never finish."

"Knock yourself out," I said with a grin. I settled Max near the back door and sat at the table where I could watch her work. "It's strange to see you looking so domestic," I said with a laugh. "I still picture you as seventeen and heading for the slopes."

Colleen grinned and attacked the batter with a wooden spoon. "I still ski . . . sometimes. Doyle's not big on skiing, though. He's a certified couch potato, so that kind of slows me down."

Questions bubbled up in my throat, but I didn't want to offend her by asking about Laurence's death the first time Doyle's name came out of her mouth. Telling myself to be patient, I made myself go through the motions. Small talk first. That's how the game was played. "How long have you lived here?"

"Ten years?" She stopped stirring to think about it, then nodded firmly. "Ten years. Eleven in April. What about you? I heard you got divorced. Are you doing okay?"

I nodded. "It was tough at the time, but it's been two years. He's married again. Got a baby. I'm . . ." This was the part where I should say that I was dating Jawarski, but the words still got stuck in my throat at times.

"Dating a cop. I heard." Colleen grinned. "The Paradise

telegraph system is alive and well, my friend. Nothing ever changes."

"Yeah? What else did they tell you?"

"Just that he's ready to make a commitment and you're not. Accurate or not?"

I wagged my hand back and forth and grimaced. "Kinda. Sorta. Not entirely. It's complicated." Which, of course, meant that I didn't want to talk about it.

Colleen accepted that, even if she did look disappointed. "Well, I'm sorry about the divorce. I can't even imagine."

Again, I ignored the impulse to ask her about Doyle. "Your house is terrific. I'll bet you love it here."

She smiled and looked around as if she was seeing the room for the first time. "I do, especially since Doyle and I did all of the work. Mostly Doyle, really. I held the Sheetrock and handed him tools."

"Doyle did this?" This was the third time she'd brought him up, which I took as a sign from the Universe that I didn't have to keep avoiding the subject. "It's beautiful."

"Don't sound so surprised."

"I'm not. Well, okay, I am. I just didn't realize Doyle was so talented."

"He doesn't get all the credit. I designed it. He just did the hard part. I just love the Shaker style, don't you? It's so clean and simple, but elegant in a way."

I'd never given it much thought, but I was quickly becoming a convert. "He's obviously talented. Is this what he does for a living?"

Colleen nodded. "He's been custom-making cabinets for people in the area for six or seven years now. Until last year, he worked for a general contractor, but his side business grew so much last winter, he decided to step out on his own. We're just holding our breath to see if he makes it."

"If this is an example of his work, I'm sure he'll be successful." *If he isn't in prison for manslaughter.*

Colleen's smile grew warmer. "I think so, too. I have a lot of faith in him." She stirred for a minute, her expression growing more pensive as she did. "He didn't exactly make the best impression on you the other night, did he?"

No way I could ignore an opening like that. "He *did* seem pretty upset."

She whipped the spoon around inside the bowl. "I hope you don't think worse of him for that. Doyle can be passionate at times."

Passionate. Volatile. You say potato . . .

"How was he after the cast meeting? Did he calm down?"

The spoon stilled and her smile vanished completely. "What's that supposed to mean?"

Apparently, I'd crossed a line with that question. "I don't mean to sound rude," I assured her. "But he seemed pretty upset with Laurence."

"Yeah, and right before Laurence was killed." Colleen abandoned her bread and gripped the countertop with both hands. "Are you the one who told the police about our conversation?"

Conversation. Argument. I say po-tah-to. "I mentioned it to the detectives." At her outraged cry, I said quickly, "I *had* to Colleen. A man was killed. If I hadn't told them about the things Doyle was saying, I'd have been guilty of withholding information."

"Our conversation was private."

"Hardly—you had that conversation in public. I was standing right there. I couldn't have missed it if I'd tried."

She sniffed and picked up the spoon again, but that was as far as she got with it. "You think my husband killed Laurence?"

"I don't know. I just know Richie didn't."

"What about Vonetta? You saw her. She was covered in blood."

"But there wasn't any spatter. The blood on her came from leaning over him, not from whacking him on the back of the head."

"So you're what? An expert?" She scooped batter into a loaf pan, but the domestic feel was gone. Her eyes were wild, and her snarl almost feral. "You watch *CSI* and suddenly you know all about blood spatter evidence?"

"I didn't say that."

"Well, for your information, Doyle *couldn't* have cut that cable, and he couldn't have killed Laurence. He was at the Avalanche all night."

"*All* night?"

"He was there for a Caribou meeting. He got there at six and he didn't leave until after one."

I hadn't been expecting that, and disappointment hit me hard. "Are you sure?"

"I'm sure." She set the oven temperature and slid the pan into the oven. "You're lucky you're an old friend, Abby. Otherwise I'd tell you to go to hell. My husband did *not* kill Laurence, and I'm furious with you for even suggesting it."

I made a mental note to stop by the Avalanche and find out if Doyle had actually stayed for the entire meeting. "I didn't accuse him," I said. "I only said that he was angry with Laurence."

"He was angry with *me*, not with Laurence."

"Because he thought you two were having an affair." I didn't want to kill our friendship, but I couldn't avoid the next question. "Was he right? Were you having an affair with Laurence Nichols?"

Fire flashed in Colleen's eyes. "That's it, Abby. Go to hell."

"I don't blame you for being angry. I would be, too. But you know the police are going to ask you about all of this."

"Thanks to you."

"If I hadn't told them, someone else would have. For all I know, someone else *did*."

She raked her fingers through her hair, oblivious to the flour she left in their tracks. "Dammit, Abby. You've seen Doyle. He's not the most handsome man in the world, and he doesn't have a lot of self-confidence. When he sees somebody like Laurence—and let's face it, Laurence *was* a good-looking man—he goes a little crazy. But that doesn't mean he'd try to kill the other guy."

"Did he have any reason to be suspicious?"

Her cheeks flamed. "Of *course* not." When I didn't back down, she relented a little. "Okay, so I once had a little crush on Laurence, and he would have gone to bed with me in a heartbeat if I'd said yes. But I love my husband. I would never cheat on him. Never. Doyle blusters a lot, but underneath it all, he knows I'm faithful."

For her sake, I hoped she was right. "Who do you think cut the cable on that light?"

"How would I know?"

"And the attack on Vonetta?"

"That makes even less sense than going after Laurence. You've probably figured out by now that Laurence wasn't the most popular guy around. He had a loyal fan base, but once you got to know him he lost a lot of his charm."

"I've noticed." I decided to give the subject of Doyle a rest. "Do you know anything about a production in Seattle that caused some tension between Laurence and Alexander?"

She tilted her head thoughtfully. "Seattle? Do you have any idea how long ago?"

"No, sorry. But Geoffrey Manwaring and Alexander Pastorelli got into a pretty heated discussion about it yesterday, and I happened to be there."

Colleen rolled her eyes expressively. "Oh. *Geoffrey*. He's a piece of work. He was Laurence's manager for years and years. I'm sure he knows where all the skeletons are buried, and I'm equally certain he never forgets a thing."

"Are you thinking of anything specific?"

She shook her head quickly. "It's just a feeling I get. He's kind of creepy, always lurking, always listening. Sometimes I wondered if Laurence really wanted him around or if he had to keep him around so Geoffrey wouldn't spill his secrets."

"What secrets?"

"I don't know." Colleen turned away to check the bread. "A man like Laurence always has secrets, doesn't he? He was a woman-in-every-town kind of guy."

Was there a note of jealousy in her voice? I couldn't tell. A new idea occurred to me, so I asked, "Do you think Geoffrey was capable of hurting someone if he thought they threatened Laurence in some way?"

"I wouldn't put anything past him. I think he's capable of anything. Why? What are you thinking?"

I didn't feel right talking about Serena's past, so I shrugged. "Nothing really."

I didn't fool her for a minute. "You think Geoffrey hurt Vonetta? But why? Laurence was already dead."

Yeah, but if Alexander was right, his estate was still an issue. People did strange things when money was at stake. "How often did Laurence and Alexander work together?"

"I don't know. Once every few years, I guess. Why?"

"Is there any reason someone might want to keep them from collaborating?"

Colleen leaned on the counter, and I thought some of her anger had faded. "Not that I know of."

"The two of them were close?"

Colleen let out a sharp laugh. "Laurence and Alexander? Who told you that?"

"They weren't friends?"

"They were competitors."

That surprised me. "But why? Alexander's a director. Laurence was a composer."

Colleen came out from behind the counter and sat across from me. "Alexander might be a director, but that doesn't mean that he doesn't have musical talent. Not as much as he thinks he has, but when has the truth ever mattered to a man like Alex? And Laurence was one of the most ambitious people I ever met. He would have steamrolled over Alex to get where he wanted."

Interesting. Alexander claimed that Laurence was a liar, and Colleen made the same claim about Alexander. I wondered if any of these people actually told the truth. "Do you think Laurence wanted to direct this play?"

"I don't know about that. There wasn't a lot of prestige attached. In fact, I was surprised they both agreed to do it, but once Vonetta hooked one, she had the other. I don't think either of them ever turned down an opportunity to work with the other."

"Why? If they weren't friends—?"

She crossed her legs and smiled coldly. "You know what they say—keep your friends close, and your enemies closer."

I thought about Paisley's claim that she'd seen Alexander and Laurence arguing the day before the murder, and I ran through the night of Laurence's death again in my memory. I tried to remember what Alexander had looked like when he came into the theater, but I'd been so focused on Laurence, I hadn't paid attention. And after the attack on Vonetta I'd been too worried about his allegations against me to pay much attention. Now I wondered if he could have been behind both attacks.

Lights swept across the window as a car turned into the driveway, and Colleen's mood changed abruptly. She shot to her feet, a look of raw panic on her face. "That's Doyle. You have to go. If he finds you here asking about Laurence, he'll go ballistic."

Pretty strong reaction for a woman who wasn't having an affair. I still had unanswered questions and some mean-spirited part of me wanted to see whether Doyle would actually go ballistic, or if she just wanted to avoid another argument. But the worry on Colleen's face and a flurry of high school memories won out.

Sometimes I'm too sentimental for my own good.

I grabbed Max's dish and the two of us disappeared out the front door as the kitchen door opened. I hurried to the Jetta, tossing out Max's water as I walked and contenting myself with the knowledge that if Doyle's alibi didn't pan out, I could always come back.

Chapter 19

"No, no, no! On the count of four, move to your *right*. And do it gently! You sound like a herd of elephants. That will never do." Jessica O'Donnell, a petite young woman who looked about fifteen and had the body of a gymnast—all ninety-five pounds of it—clapped her hands as she looked over the ragtag collection of "talent" in the rehearsal hall.

Richie mumbled something under his breath, along with about half the dancers in the room. I had to admire him for showing up *and* for ignoring the speculative glances some people in the cast directed at him. He was stronger than I'd ever realized. I'd told Nate Svboda that I was in the cast when he questioned me after Laurence died, and Vonetta hadn't corrected me. I figured I owed it to her to stick around. Besides, if I was going to be at the theater all the time looking for a way to clear Richie, I might as well have a legitimate excuse.

Rachel swore softly and limped toward a folding chair near the window. I dropped to the floor and tried to find the water bottle I'd lobbed into the corner last time we had a chance to catch our breath.

Outside, a small knot of reporters milled around, waiting for rehearsal to break up so they could try to find someone willing to talk. We'd run the gauntlet on the way inside, and it looked like we'd have to repeat the process when we left.

Alexander had issued an edict when we arrived tonight demanding strict silence with the press. So far, nobody seemed interested in crossing him.

Jessica clapped her hands and bellowed, "Quiet! People! Quiet, please!" in a voice far too large for a girl so small. "I know you're all tired. I know this is a lot to grasp all at once. But this scene is one of the most important in the play. The dance, the mime, is *crucial*. Now please, get back in place."

I found my water bottle and chugged as much as I could before she screeched again.

"Abby? That's your name, isn't it? Do you mind? Everyone's waiting."

Every muscle in my body ached. Dancing—even bad dancing—isn't as easy as it looks. I capped the bottle, struggled to my feet again, and gimped back to my spot on the floor. This had been a mistake. I should have listened to my gut instinct and stayed out of the production. But I was here now, and with my friendship with Vonetta still on shaky ground, being part of the cast might be the only way I could get access to the people I wanted to talk to and the information I wanted to ask them about.

"Are we ready?" Jessica shouted when I'd resumed my position. "All right, then." She turned to Stella Farmer, who sat at the baby grand, waiting for instructions. Stella's a sturdy woman with mint green eyes and strong hands. I've known her since I was a kid, back when her big, frosted hairdo was actually in style. I've never seen her wearing anything but jeans, a man's shirt, untucked, and cowboy boots. Except, of course, when she's at church—and that's only for the occasional funeral.

For years, Stella has been the go-to gal whenever anyone in town needs the piano. She's moderately talented and has the uncanny ability to sight-read anything put in front of her. Which is why she sat at the piano now, ready to sit in for Laurence Nichols.

"From the top?" Jessica said, and Stella started in with a decent rendition of "Stay, We Must Not Lose Our Senses."

"Stop! Everyone stop!" Alexander strode into the room wearing a deep scowl. "I thought you were going to work on the original Nichols piece."

Groans rose up from the cast. We were up, in position,

and ready to move through the steps for the umpteenth time in an hour. I don't think anyone wanted to sit around while Alexander and Jessica argued over which song we were rehearsing.

"Take five, everybody," Jessica called, as if Alexander's order to stop wasn't enough.

The cast had already tromped back to their seats or gone off to take care of business elsewhere in the building. Richie and one of the guys in the chorus disappeared into the foyer. Stella stood beside the piano and arched her back. Rachel pulled off a shoe and scowled at her toes.

I dragged a chair over to sit by her. "I'd forgotten how much of rehearsal is waiting around."

Rachel laughed and wiggled her toes, watching carefully to make sure they all moved. "It's practically *all* waiting. I should have grabbed dinner on my way here. I'm starving."

"I should be at Divinity," I mumbled. "Karen and Liberty are going to wring my neck for getting involved in this."

"Quit worrying. Karen and Liberty are *fine*. I talked to both of them this afternoon. This is the only rehearsal scheduled for this week, and Valentine's Day will be over before you know it. It's not even an issue."

I took another swig of water and stretched my legs. I could hear Jessica and Alexander arguing, I just couldn't hear what they were saying. "What do you suppose that's all about?"

Rachel checked the other foot and shrugged. "Could be just about anything. I get the feeling Alexander is a real control freak. It's his way or the highway."

Jessica's cheeks were flushed with anger. Her arms moved with broad, jerky movements as she spoke. I looked away and met Rachel's gaze. "Who do you think will win this one?"

"I don't know. She's tough, but she's young. I think I'm gonna have to put my money on Alexander." She grabbed her tote bag and began searching inside. She came up with half a roll of Life Savers and offered me one. That's the kind of friend Rachel is.

"I think you might be right," I said. "I wish I could hear what they're saying."

"Move closer."

I grinned and shook my head. "I'm trying to foster the illusion that I'm a regular cast member."

"Good luck with that," Rachel said with a laugh. Jessica's voice rose a level or two, and Rachel leaned back in her chair, smiling contentedly. "Looks like you might be able to eavesdrop after all."

But the argument was over almost before it began. Looking mutinous, Jessica clapped her hands again, glanced around at the diminished cast, and shouted, "Pirates, Daughters, and Voices! Front and center! Now!"

It took a few minutes, but the cast was soon gathered again, and Jessica faced us all wearing a frown so deep, her chin turned white. "We're going to switch," she said. "We're going to work on the original Nichols piece that Alexander has added to this portion of the play."

Richie, who'd come back to the rehearsal hall a few minutes earlier, raised a hand. "Excuse me, Jessica, but we don't have that."

"Of course you do. It was included in your scripts."

"No it wasn't," Richie said. "It went missing before they could make copies."

"I thought Geoffrey was going to have new copies delivered."

"Yeah, well, he didn't," Richie's friend put in. "None of us has seen it yet."

"Son of a bitch!" Alexander's voice bounced off the walls. "That music belongs here, in this production. Laurence wrote it especially for this play. Manwaring has no right to hold on to it."

Richie caught my eye from across the room, but we weren't the only people in the cast who looked startled and confused. "What's going on?" Rachel hissed.

"Apparently, Geoffrey Manwaring never sent Laurence's music like he promised."

"He probably didn't think he needed to since Laurence . . . you know."

"Maybe. But it should have been here the day Laurence died. Did Geoffrey just forget, or did he somehow know Laurence wasn't going to need it?"

Rachel slipped her feet into her shoes and lowered her voice even further "You think he knew something was going to happen to Laurence?"

"I don't know. Maybe. It just seems odd that he didn't follow through. You remember how angry Laurence was when the music turned up missing."

Rachel nodded. "He *was* mad, but even if you're right, how would you ever prove it?"

I shrugged and sat back in my chair. "If Jawarski were here, I'd just tell him about it and let him work his magic. He could get phone records, maybe subpoena a computer for e-mail . . . I got nothin'."

"Then you'll just have to get him to confess," Rachel said with a grin. "That should be easy, right?"

I laughed. "Yeah. Piece of cake." But her joke had hatched a new idea. Jessica and Alexander were still arguing over what to do about the missing music, and they didn't show any signs of letting up. I nudged Rachel and asked, "Did you walk, or did you bring your car?"

"I drove. Why?

"Want to drive over to the Summit Lodge with me? Maybe we can figure out what happened to Laurence's original pieces."

Rachel stared at me as if I'd sprouted a second head. *"Now?"*

"It's better than hanging around here," I said. "I'd walk back and get my car, but if Manwaring *is* a murdering psychopath, I'd rather not show up at his hotel room alone."

Rachel hesitated for only a second, then grabbed her bag and began stuffing her things into it. "Okay, you're on. But only if we can grab something for dinner when we're through there."

That was a condition I could live with. Feeling like kids

skipping school, we ducked out of rehearsal and five minutes later we were speeding toward the mountains on the south end of the valley.

The Summit Lodge is one of three new hotels that have been built in the past few years to accommodate increased tourist traffic. Nestled against the mountains between ski runs and the new golf course, the lodge is an impressive display of varnished wood and polished glass.

We found a parking space near the main entry and scurried inside out of the cold. A fire blazed in a huge open pit in the center of the lobby, and honey-colored wood gleamed all around us, as if management had people working round the clock with furniture polish.

I knew the desk clerks would never give us Geoffrey's room number, so we nosed around until we found a house phone. The scents of garlic and beef swept over us as we searched, and Rachel was so distracted I half expected her to bolt for the hotel's closest restaurant.

After several minutes we found a bank of phones tucked out of sight behind—what else?—a wall of polished wood. I punched the button for the front desk and asked to be put through to Geoffrey Manwaring's room. After a couple of clicks, the connection went through and the phone rang. And rang. And rang. And rang.

After the fourth ring, the call transferred to voice mail. Disappointed, I replaced the receiver. "Well that was a waste of time and gas. There's no answer."

Rachel had already moved on. She dug through her bottomless bag and pulled out a tube of lipstick. "Maybe he's gone to dinner."

"Yeah. Maybe."

"Speaking of which . . . We're eating here."

"Are you kidding? It'll cost a fortune. Jawarski and I came here last year, and they charged fifteen dollars for a burger. And that was on the lunch menu!"

"So?"

"So I'll probably have to sell my car to pay for dinner. Let's go somewhere else."

Rachel slicked on a layer of wine-colored lipstick and dropped the tube in her bag. "I'm not leaving here until whatever I can smell is in my stomach. I'll buy."

I snorted a laugh and followed her back into the lobby. "You're not buying my dinner. There are plenty of great places in town and it'll take us five minutes to get to any one of them. Besides, neither of us is dressed for this place. Let's just go."

Rachel glanced at my sweats and T-shirt with a shrug. "I don't care how we look. If you don't want me to pay for your dinner, you can wait for me in the lobby or you can wait in the car, but I'm not leaving."

I consider myself a reasonably intelligent woman, chiefly because I can recognize an immovable object when I run into it. I could have argued until I was blue in the face. Rachel was not going anywhere. "Fine. Let's go."

We wound our way along a hallway toward the restaurant, flanked by framed shots of local scenery on one side and a long bank of windows that looked out over the valley on the other. It was a beautiful hotel, I wouldn't deny that. It just wasn't forty-dollar chicken beautiful.

A hostess led us through the nearly deserted restaurant toward a table for two tucked in a corner where nobody would see us. I was about to sit when I spotted Geoffrey Manwaring at a table on the other side of the room. "Excuse me," I called after the hostess.

"Yes ma'am?"

Ma'am. I'm not sure I'll ever get used to people calling me that. "We'd like to sit over there, please. One of those tables by the window would be perfect."

I could see the war going on inside her. Say no and offend a customer. Say yes and offend all the others. Luckily, probably because there were only a handful of those "others," she inclined her head and motioned for us to follow her.

"What are you doing?" Rachel demanded as we walked.

I nodded toward my unsuspecting prey. "That's Geoffrey Manwaring. If I'm going to spend twenty dollars for a bowl of soup, I might as well get something extra out of it."

Our hostess seated us at the table directly in front of Geoffrey's. The location couldn't have been more perfect. I smiled, delighted with the turn of events until I opened the menu. The constant assault of beef and garlic on my nostrils had convinced me that I was hungry, too, but steak tonight would mean ramen noodles for the next two weeks. It had better be worth the sacrifice.

After studying the menu for several minutes and trying to make the prices drop by sheer mental power, I decided on a jumbo seafood cocktail (*jumbo* being the operative word) and a Coke for a mere twenty-five bucks. Rachel ordered as if she had money to spare—tomato bisque soup, bone-in rib eye, and a glass of cabernet sauvignon. She squeaked in at just under a hundred dollars, minus tax and tip. A steal at half the price.

While our server was in the back mining the gold dust to sprinkle on each of the dishes, I pasted on a friendly smile and stepped over to Geoffrey's table. "Well, hello. Geoffrey Manwaring, isn't it?"

He looked at me with a blank expression. "It is."

"You probably don't remember me. Abby Shaw. I run the candy shop in town." I held out a hand, which he promptly ignored.

"Ah. Yes." He dabbed a napkin to his tight little mouth and ran a glance over my clothes. "You're the lady who refused to deliver my order."

"We did deliver it," I reminded him.

"Yes. Thanks to the other woman." Apparently, he sensed that I wasn't going to leave, so he linked his hands together on the table and made an effort to hide his irritation. "What can I do for you, Ms. Shaw?"

I took that as an invitation to sit at his table. My mother would have had a fit if she'd seen me. "Well, it's a little thing, really. Rachel and I—that's Rachel right over there— were just at a rehearsal at the Playhouse. The music that Laurence wrote for the production still wasn't there. I'm just wondering if you forgot to order the copies you promised to get?"

What little patience he'd been able to manufacture evaporated while I was speaking. "No, I didn't forget. The music won't be coming. You might as well let the others know."

Not much room for interpretation in that answer. "But I was under the impression that Laurence wrote the music especially for this production. The troupe at the Paradise Playhouse were going to be the first ever to perform it."

Geoffrey motioned for the waiter to bring him another cocktail. "You've been given some bad information. Laurence was in the process of writing his own screenplay. He was also writing the original score. That score is the only unperformed work of his in existence."

What a jerk. I didn't care that we were sitting in a world-class restaurant, or that I looked as if I belonged on the cleaning staff. I hate being lied to. "That's interesting," I said with a cool smile. "I heard Laurence himself talking about that music, so I know you're not telling the truth."

"Do you?" Geoffrey accepted a glass from the server and swallowed half of it in one gulp. "You have something in writing to support your claim? Because I don't. There's no contract. No promise. Nothing."

"Laurence and Vonetta had a verbal agreement."

"Well, that's too bad, isn't it? I don't know anything about a verbal agreement. Now that Larry's gone, his work is going to be worth a small fortune. I'd be an idiot to hand over the last work he ever did to a Podunk operation like the one you've got here."

I could just imagine the reaction this news would get when Vonetta and Alexander found out. "Are you ever going to tell the others that you're backing out of the deal? Or are you just going to let them go on thinking you forgot to send the music?"

"Oh, I'll tell them eventually. But considering the fact that Vonetta tried to weasel out of a legally binding contract with my client, I'm not all that worried about her."

"Maybe you should be."

He laughed softly, and the sound made me so angry I

barely resisted the urge to wipe the smile off his face. "You don't frighten me, candy lady. I've been in this business a long time. You're barely wet behind the ears."

"That's because I was busy practicing law while you were boning up on how to cheat people."

His eyes widened for an instant, but he got over the surprise quickly and laughed again. "Nice try, but I'm not cheating anyone. Like I said, I defy you to find a written agreement promising that music to anyone." He downed the rest of his drink and tossed his napkin onto the table. "In fact, I'll make you a promise. If you produce an agreement, providing it's not a fraud, I'll honor it."

"I'll hold you to it. Now why don't you explain to me how you knew that you didn't need to send the copies of the music to the Playhouse before Laurence died."

Geoffrey's smile faded. "Are you accusing me of having something to do with the death of my best client and closest friend?"

"I'm asking a simple question. You promised Laurence that you'd have the music delivered to the Playhouse the day he died, but you obviously didn't. How did you know he wasn't going to need it?"

Geoffrey sat back in his chair and let out a long-suffering sigh. "After Vonetta tried to terminate their contract—without a valid excuse, I might add—I was kept busy trying to convince Larry not to sue her."

"*He* was going to sue *her*? On what grounds?"

"Breach of contract, what else?"

"Over his participation in this play? Was he crazy, or just vindictive?"

"He was the injured party."

"Not even close," I muttered. "He could probably have bought and sold the Playhouse a dozen times over. Why sue over one little job? I'm sure he wasn't being paid much."

"It was a matter of principle."

I laughed. I couldn't help it. "Somehow I doubt that. Why was he so determined to destroy Vonetta?"

"They had a history."

"I know they did," I said. "But in the version I've heard, he owed her."

Geoffrey's expression grew sober. "You know about that?"

I had no idea if we were talking about the same thing or not, but I nodded. "I do."

"Vonetta told you?"

"Serena did."

Geoffrey laughed through his nose. "Serena. Do you have any idea how angry I was to find out she was here? I checked. I double-checked. She hadn't been back in years. Then Larry and I showed up, and there she was."

"How did Laurence feel about seeing her again?"

"What should he feel? She practically ruined his life. Almost destroyed his career. He was furious."

I wasn't buying it. "How? How did she almost ruin his life?"

Geoffrey looked around to see if anyone could hear us, then leaned across the table and lowered his voice. "She tried to trap him. Got herself pregnant, and then tried to blackmail him into marrying her. Do you have any idea what that would have done to him?"

"A wife and a kid? Yeah. Brutal."

His expression grew somber. "Larry was just getting started in his career. He was a rising star, but that would have sunk him."

"They could have survived," I insisted. "People did."

"Yeah, but very few of them were successful. Laurence Nichols wasn't created to survive. He was born to soar."

"So he insisted that Serena have an abortion, even though she believed that she was killing her unborn child."

Geoffrey's frown etched deep lines around his mouth. "She could have said no."

"She didn't think she could."

"That's not my fault, and it wasn't Larry's."

Men like these gave them all a bad name. "What about other women?"

"What about them? Laurence had 'em, that's for sure. He kept me busy lining 'em up and getting rid of them afterward."

"Was Colleen Brannigan one of them?"

"Colleen?" Geoffrey nodded once. "A long time ago."

"So her husband was right to be jealous of Laurence."

"Not now. At least not from Larry's end. She's a bit long in the tooth these days."

"Yeah, all of forty. Practically decrepit."

"What can I say? He liked 'em younger. She was none too happy when he sent her packing recently, I can tell you that."

That got my interest. "I thought you said it was a long time ago?"

"It was—but there was another flare up a couple of days before he died. I don't know why he suggested her for the job with this production, but I think she saw it as an invitation to reunite. Then she caught him with some twenty-year-old he met at dinner, and went nuts."

"And who did he send the candy to? The twenty–year-old? Colleen? Or was it Serena? Or maybe there was someone else entirely?"

"It wasn't anyone involved in the production," he said firmly. He scribbled his signature on the dinner check and wagged the black leather folder so his server could see that it was ready. "If you want to know who wanted him dead, you don't have to look very far."

"What does that mean? You think Colleen is responsible for his death?"

He shrugged and pushed his chair away from the table. "One of the women in the play did it. I'd make book on it. Now if you'll excuse me, I have things to do."

"Yeah," I said absently. He walked away and I returned to the table where a minuscule glass filled with assorted seafood waited for me. *Jumbo, my ass.* "Sorry about that," I told Rachel. "I didn't expect it to take so long."

"Not a problem." She's that kind of friend, too. "Did you find out what you wanted to know?"

"I don't think so," I said with a glance at Geoffrey's re-treating back. "But I did find out that he has no intention of letting us use the music in the production. He sees dollar signs floating in front of his eyes."

"He looks the type," said my friend, who'd just blown a hundred dollars on dinner. She slathered butter on a roll and pushed the bread basket in my direction. "The question is, did he see those dollar signs before Laurence was killed?"

It was a *very* good question. One I had every intention of answering before I was through.

Chapter 20

My conversation with Geoffrey Manwaring bothered me all the next day. I still hadn't been to the Avalanche to check out Doyle's alibi for myself, but with Valentine's Day just around the corner, work was seriously ramping up. I couldn't skip out again tonight, so I stayed late, melting and pouring and dipping and wrapping until every muscle I hadn't strained learning the dance steps the night before ached from exertion of a different kind.

A few minutes before ten, I climbed the stairs to my apartment, filled Max's dish with kibble, and carried a cold takeout box of crab rangoon into the living room. My apartment is a far cry from the Sacramento condo I once shared with my ex. There's not a stick of furniture that matches any other in the whole place. Everything is secondhand, cast-off from family and friends.

Aunt Grace's old plaid sofa bed holds the place of honor. Uncle Butch's dinged-up coffee table sits in front of it. Near the door is the hideous space-age chair that used to belong to my parents. I sleep on my grandmother's bed and keep my clothes in a dresser that came from the Goodwill. Taken one by one, the pieces are wretched, but together they suit me. Just don't ask me why.

I turned on the television, more to keep me awake until I could finish eating than out of any desire to watch what was on. While I munched, I flipped through channels, searching for something that might hold my interest for a few minutes. When I passed a local channel and realized that their news department was running a story on Laurence Nichols's death. I paused to listen.

Maybe I should have expected it, but the focus on Richie and the repeated mention of him as a "person of interest" in the case made my blood run cold. Even worse was the shot of him leaving the inn with Dylan, doing his best to ignore the questions shouted at him, the flash of the cameras, and the microphones shoved in his face.

If you asked me, Nate was being reckless to turn the media's focus in Richie's direction. There just wasn't enough evidence to support the theory. With very little effort at all, I'd come up with nearly half a dozen suspects, all of whom had stronger motives than Richie for wanting Laurence dead.

I turned the station quickly. If I let myself get worked up about the murder now, I'd never get to sleep. After passing up a couple of reality shows and a news magazine show, I settled on an episode of *Burn Notice* I'd only seen twice and tossed the remote onto the couch beside me. While Michael, Fi, and Sam pulled a scam on some unsuspecting bad guys, I worked on cold crab and cream cheese inside fried wanton wrappers. I'd just popped the last one into my mouth when the phone rang.

I knew instantly that it was Jawarski. Or maybe I should say, I *wanted* it to be Jawarski. I just didn't want Jawarski to know how much I wanted to hear from him. Going this long without hearing from him had made me realize how much I missed him. Not having him around to bounce ideas off of only made it worse. But all of that left me feeling vulnerable, and vulnerable is a problem for me.

"You still up?" he asked when I finally unearthed the cordless phone from beneath the ratty cushions of my plaid couch.

"Yeah. Barely."

"I'm not calling too late, am I?"

His deep voice felt like a warm blanket. I lay down on the couch and let it wrap itself around me. "No, it's not too late. I was just watching TV and having a late dinner. How are things going up there?"

"Good. I went to Ridge's basketball game tonight, and I'm taking both kids to dinner tomorrow night."

He sounded happy. Relaxed. Another reason not to bother him with the murder. "That sounds great. I'm sure they like having you around."

"They seem to, I guess. Cheyenne's been giving her mother some trouble the past few months, but I think it's just the age."

"Thirteen?" I thought back to my own teenage years and grimaced. "I'm sure it is. Most girls that age exist just to give their mothers grief."

Jawarski laughed and I heard something rustle through the phone. "That's what Bree says, too. I'm gonna have to trust the two of you since this is my first experience with a teenage girl."

The warmth I'd been feeling evaporated and a cold, hard jealousy stabbed me at the mention of his ex-wife's name. I didn't know for sure whether he still had feelings for her, or she for him. I didn't even know if the divorce had been her idea or his. But I did know that she'd invited him to Montana, and he'd dropped everything to go.

I sat up and tried to regain my earlier feeling. Comfort. Ease. Trust. "Were you able to get a hotel close to the house?"

He didn't answer at once, and with Jawarski that's a bad sign. "I decided not to get a hotel room," he said after what felt like forever. "Bree offered to let me stay in the guest room so I could spend as much time as possible with the kids."

"You're staying there?" I tried to sound normal, but my voice came out sounding high and tight. "In her house?"

"You're upset."

"No. Yes." Too agitated to sit still, I dropped the take-out box on the coffee table and paced around the living room. "Tell me how I'm supposed to feel about you staying with your ex-wife."

"You're not supposed to feel anything. I'm in the *guest room*, Abby. It's not like I moved back into the bedroom."

My throat grew tight and dry. Somehow, knowing that she still lived in the same house where they'd been a couple made it worse.

Knock it off! I told myself sternly. I hate jealousy, and I hated Roger fiercely for cheating on me and leaving me worried and frightened that it would happen again. "I think it's great that you and the kids can spend so much time together," I said, and I meant it. I just hated everything else that came with it.

"Yeah." A long silence fell between us, and I wondered if he could hear the fear in my voice. "Got a call from Nate Svboda the other day," he said, just as I was about to make an excuse to hang up. "He told me about Nichols."

Terrific. Thank you, Nate. "Why did he call you? Can't he just let you take some time off?"

"He thought I should know. So I'm guessing from that comment you weren't going to tell me?"

"You're on vacation," I said. "I didn't want to interrupt the time you have with the kids."

"Yeah? Well, thanks. So what's going on? Are they making any progress?"

"You think Nate would tell me if they had?"

"Probably not. But you *do* have a way of finding out anyway."

Yeah. One of my dubious skills. "Did Nate tell you that he thinks Richie is the killer?"

Jawarski's voice grew guarded. "He told me about the evidence they've gathered so far. You have to admit, Abby, it doesn't look good."

"Every bit of that evidence is circumstantial," I said firmly.

"Until I can see what they've got, I'll have to take your word for it. I assume you're up to your eyeballs in it."

That comment fell into the plus column. Sure, he was living with his ex-wife for a couple of weeks, but I can overlook a lot for a man who doesn't try to control me. "Richie's my friend," I said. "He's *our* friend. I can't just let Nate lock him up for a crime he didn't commit."

"Give the guy a break, Abby. He's doing his job."

"I think we're going to agree to disagree when it comes to Nate. Richie didn't do it."

"If you have proof that Nate's not doing his job, take it to the chief. Otherwise, be careful, okay? Stay out of his way."

"Not a problem," I promised. In Nate's path was the *last* place I wanted to be. I was about to say something else when a woman's voice floated through the connection.

"Pine? Are you coming?"

My breath caught and my stomach lurched. *'Are you coming?'* Where? How many options could there be at nearly eleven?

"Listen," I said, struggling to sound normal in spite of everything, "I have to be up early in the morning so I should probably—"

"Oh." He cut me off. "Sure. I understand. The kids are waiting to watch a movie anyway."

The kids. And Bree. "You don't want to keep them waiting."

"Right. Listen, I'll call again in a day or two. And Abby?"

"Yeah?"

"I'm not taking Nate's side, you know."

"Oh. Yeah. Right."

"I just worry about you, especially when I'm not there to make sure you're all right."

I wanted to believe him, but the insecurities I'd been battling since the divorce made it damn tough. "I'm fine."

"Okay. Just promise me you'll be careful. I love you. I don't want anything to happen to you."

The air escaped my lungs in a *whoosh*, and for the first time in recent memory I couldn't think of a single thing to say. *I love you?* Was he kidding? What kind of man says a thing like that over the phone? On the heels of being beckoned away from the phone by another woman? An ex-wife? While staying in her house—allegedly in separate bedrooms?

I don't know how long I sat there before I realized that he'd hung up and I was listening to a dial tone. I only know that the conversation had just made everything a whole lot more difficult between us.

Chapter 21

Friday morning dawned gray and dreary. Low-hanging clouds had moved into the valley overnight, bringing with them the threat of another storm. The overcast sky didn't help my mood, already at a low point thanks to the conversation with Jawarski that had left me jittery and confused, and too wound up to sleep.

Jawarski had some nerve saying he loved me, especially under the circumstances. What was I supposed to do with it now that he'd said it? Did he expect me to say it back? That wasn't going to happen until I was absolutely certain I meant it, not one minute before. And I had no intention of saying it until I knew a whole lot more about what was going on with him and his ex.

Unfortunately, going to work didn't do much to relieve the stress. A small cluster of reporters had taken up residence in the parking lot, and they'd dogged me while I took Max for his morning constitutional. Back in the shop, the hearts hanging from the ceiling fluttered each time the heater kicked on, dancing around my head and taunting me with every spin. That only made my mood worse. I tried to find comfort in the soothing smell of chocolate and the rhythm I'd established in the kitchen, but my timing was off this morning. What should have been a smooth series of actions as I rolled nougat centers and dipped them in tempered chocolate felt jerky and unnatural.

I stayed busy until late afternoon, but the first chance I got, I packed up the boxes ready to ship and escaped to the post office. I decided to walk, hoping that the exercise and fresh air would help clear my mind. I had to run the gauntlet of reporters again, but since I had Max with me, it wasn't difficult to get through. After following halfway up the block, they seemed to realize I wasn't going to talk and fell away.

After that, the walk was almost pleasant. The clouds had trapped warm air in the valley, so for the first time in weeks the temperature climbed above the freezing mark. Small trails of water ran from beneath mounds of snow that had been lying in the streets and on the edges of parking lots for weeks.

To my surprise, there was no line at the post office, so I was in and out in less than ten minutes. I wasn't ready to go back to Divinity yet, so I told myself I could take ten more minutes to walk around the block.

After half a block, my mood slowly began to lift. I'd find solutions to every one of my problems, I promised myself. It was only because they'd all hit at once that I felt overwhelmed and out of control. Even my questions about Jawarski and our relationship felt overblown in the clear light of day. He'd be home in a few days, and we'd work everything out. I had nothing to worry about.

I reached the corner and waited for a short line of traffic to pass. As I stepped off the sidewalk, a dark-haired man of about thirty fell into step with me. He wore jeans and a ski jacket, the usual fare for most of Paradise's population, and he had a broad, open face and a friendly smile.

"Nice day, isn't it?" he asked.

I nodded, oddly pleased to be having a conversation—however brief—that had no connection to Valentine's Day, the murder, or Jawarski. "Looks like it's going to snow again. Let's hope we don't get the cold trough with it this time."

"This last one lasted a long time," my companion agreed. "You *know* it's cold when it has to warm up to snow."

With a laugh, I stepped onto the curb on the other side of the street. The beauty of meaningless conversation with a total stranger is that it's so brief. One or two sentences is more than enough. There's no pressure to sound intelligent, or to say the right thing. There are no feelings to consider.

I started to offer one of the socially acceptable conversation enders, like "Have a good one," when I realized that the man beside me wasn't playing by the rules. Instead of walking faster or falling behind, he matched my pace. And when he asked, "You're Abby Shaw, aren't you?" I started growing suspicious.

"Who wants to know?"

Max found something interesting buried beneath an old pile of snow and stopped to investigate.

The man come to a halt and held out a hand. "John Haversham, KZPY News."

Irritated that he'd slipped up on me that way, I ignored the proffered hand. "You're a reporter."

"How could you tell?"

"It's the beady eyes. They give you away. Now, if you'll excuse me, I have things to do."

Grinning as if he was having a great time, he lowered his hand. "Aw, come on. Surely you can spare two minutes."

"For you? Afraid not." I put my head down and tugged on Max's leash, determined to ignore him.

"Hey! Give me a break!" He hurried past me and tried to block my path. "This is the biggest news story of my career. Why don't you just tell me what you know?"

"Not a chance." I brushed past him and kept walking. Max kept an eye on him, but his little stump tail wagged as if he'd found a new best friend. Some attack dog.

Haversham didn't give up. "Detective Svboda named Richie Bellieu as a person of interest in the case. What do you know about him?"

"Nothing I'm going to share with you."

"I thought they said he was a friend of yours. Or did I get that wrong?"

I ground to a halt, and he had to sidestep quickly to avoid plowing into me. "Yeah, he's a friend of mine. And he happens to be innocent, so why don't you leave him alone?"

A pleased grin inched across the reporter's face. He held up both hands, lifting and lowering them alternately as if they were scales. "Gee, I don't know. The police tell me he's a person of interest. The lady from the candy store says he's innocent. Which one should I pay the most attention to?"

Growling in frustration, I took a step away. "If that's your attitude, I have nothing to say. Max, kill."

With a laugh, Haversham grabbed my arm and pulled me around to face him. "Listen, Abby. You're not doing your friend any favors."

Max and I growled at the same time. "Get your hand off me."

Haversham seemed to realize that he'd gone too far. Releasing me, he backed a step away and held up his hands to show both of us that he wasn't a threat. "Sorry. I didn't mean to offend. It's just that I need some answers. There are too many loose pieces to this case. Nothing fits."

"And you want me to help you."

"I was thinking we could help each other. People tell me you have a knack for finding things out. Is that right?"

If he thought I was going to admit that to a reporter, he was nuts. There are laws. "I'm a candymaker," I said. "That's all."

"Okay." Haversham laughed under his breath and shook his head. "You're also in the cast of the play that's in production at the Playhouse, is that right?"

I couldn't see any harm in admitting that. "That's right."

Max had gone back to wagging his tail. *Traitor.*

"How long have you known Richie Bellieu?" Haversham got brave enough to hold out his hand for Max to inspect. When the dog didn't bite it off, Haversham moved it slowly to Max's head and commenced scratching.

Max sat and closed his eyes in ecstasy.

I rolled my eyes in exasperation, and answered Haversham's question. If he'd been in Paradise for longer than ten minutes, he already knew the answer. "A couple of years."

"And Laurence Nichols? How long did you know him?"

"Never met the man."

"You were in the same production, but you never met him? You expect me to believe that?"

"Frankly, I don't care what you believe. But yeah, we

were in the same production and we never met. He died before we could be introduced."

"Got it. How well did Richie Bellieu know him?"

"I have no idea," I said. "Let's go, Max. We're through here."

"My sources tell me that they met recently."

I slanted a glance at him. "See? You don't need me."

"I've been told that Bellieu tried to initiate a romantic relationship with Nichols. Didn't he realize that Nichols was straight?"

What was I supposed to say to that? I wished I'd never said good morning to the creep. "Your sources are wrong," I told him. "Richie Bellieu did not try to initiate a romantic relationship with Laurence Nichols."

"Then what did Nichols do to upset him?"

"What makes you think he was upset?"

"I have a witness who heard Bellieu threaten to kill Nichols."

"No, you don't."

"Yeah, I do." Haversham tried to catch up with me, but I walked faster so I could stay a step ahead. "This witness heard your boy Richie say, and I quote, 'I ought to rip his fucking heart out.' Pardon the language."

I rounded on him, my heart slamming against my rib cage. "Don't be ridiculous. Richie would never say something like that."

"And yet he did. I take it you didn't know?"

I shook my head slowly. "I don't know anything about it. Who told you he said that?"

Haversham perched on the edge of a concrete flower box. "You want me to reveal my source? When you won't even answer a few simple questions? I can't do that. Tit for tat, Ms. Shaw. You give me a little something, I give you a little something back."

I hated bargaining with the devil, but my conscience wouldn't let me walk away from whatever he knew. "Tell me the name of your witness. If it's somebody credible, I'll give you something."

His smile grew a little wider. "I'm going to hold you to that."

"Fine. Who told you about it?"

"My witness is a stagehand named Jason Dahl. You know him?"

I nodded. "Yes." Was it true? Had Jason heard Richie threaten Laurence? I couldn't think of any reason for him to lie, but why hadn't he mentioned it to anyone else?

Or had he? I asked, "Do the police know about this?"

"They do now. Now, what have you got for me?"

I didn't want to tell him anything, but if I went back on my word I'd only create trouble for everyone. "What do you want to know?"

"Laurence Nichols and Serena Cummings. What's the deal between them?"

We were skirting dangerous ground now, and I had no intention of opening my big mouth. "What makes you think there's any 'deal' between them?"

"Again, a source. What can you tell me?"

I gave that some thought. It wouldn't be hard to find out that Laurence had worked with Vonetta all those years ago, so I gave him the version approved for public access. "They knew each other years ago," I said. "They met when he was working on a play for her mother."

"And? Why did she hit him?"

"She hit him? When?"

Haversham rolled his eyes in exasperation. "Do you know *anything* I don't?"

"Probably not. When did she hit him?"

"According to my witness, Laurence cornered her in the back of the theater the day he died."

So, Serena had lied to me when she said she hadn't seen Laurence again.

"I don't know what he said to her," Haversham went on, "but she hauled off and whacked him—or so I'm told. Do you have any idea why?"

What a choice. I could tell him and destroy Serena's trust in me, or I could lie to him and go back on my word. A sudden chill raced through me, but I didn't think it was from the weather.

I wish I could say that revealing the truth about Serena's affair with Laurence and her abortion wouldn't have a negative impact on Vonetta's reputation in town, but what if I was wrong? Attitudes in Paradise have changed a lot in the past forty years, but we're not perfect yet. I could name half a dozen influential people off the top of my head who would use anything—even a decades-old mistake—to prove that people who didn't fit the mold were some kind of moral, emotional, or physical threat to the community. Oh, sure, there are a lot more reasonable people around than idiots, but one idiot can do a whole lot of damage in a short period of time.

"I don't know," I said, willing myself to give nothing away. "I've been trying to find out, but I haven't been able to yet."

Haversham studied my expression for a long time before he pushed away from the empty flower box. "Yeah. Well. You gamble a lot in this business. Sometimes you get lucky. Sometimes you don't." He pointed one finger at me. "But you owe me, Abby. Remember that."

Chapter 22

I walked away from Haversham furious with Richie for forgetting to mention that he'd threatened Laurence. I wondered how much longer Vonetta's secrets were going to stay hidden, and I was more determined than ever to find the killer before those old stories had to be revealed. I checked my watch and decided I could spare a few more minutes away from Divinity. This was as good a time as any to find out if Doyle Brannigan had really been tossing back a few with his fellow Caribou at the time of the murder.

The Avalanche is a small bar tucked neatly behind a dry cleaner and a travel agent. I've been inside before, but only a handful of times. Most of the clientele is in the over-fifty crowd, and you're more likely to find truck drivers and ranchers bellied up to the bar than upwardly mobile professionals.

A *U*-shaped bar takes up one side of the building. A bandstand and dance floor take up the other half. It was still too early for the after work crowd, but already a local garage band plucked out tired versions of old country favorites. The only people who appeared to be listening were the bartender and one drunk young woman who danced alone in front of the stage.

I ran a glance over the bar's patrons, noticed a familiar figure, and hitched myself onto a stool next to my Uncle Whit. He's a big man who's always been able to hold his own in any situation. When I was a kid, his bulk came from muscle. That wasn't the case any longer.

He crushed out a cigarette and squinted at me through

the smoke. "Hey, princess! What brings you here?" His grav-elly voice, carved over the years by way too many cigarettes, sounded like music to my ears. When I didn't answer im-mediately, his obvious delight at seeing me faded quickly and his squint turned suspicious. "Your aunt Becky didn't send you, did she?"

I leaned up to kiss his weathered cheek and ordered a margarita—frozen, with salt—from the hovering bartender. "Relax," I said with a grin. "Your wife didn't send me. You're perfectly safe."

Whit wagged his gray head from side to side. "I doubt that. That old woman's always sending people out to spy on me. She sent your cousin Bea in here after me last week."

I barely suppressed a groan. I've had my share of run-ins with Bea, and I wouldn't wish an encounter with her on my worst enemy. Aunt Becky must have been feeling pretty desperate to skip her own kids and send Bea to drag Uncle Whit home. I sympathized with her, but Uncle Whit looked so forlorn, I actually felt sorry for him. Yeah, he drinks more than he should, and he smokes like a chimney. He's made my Aunt Becky's life interesting, and not always in pleasant ways, but he has a heart of gold and he'd help anyone who needed it. "Well, I hope you sent her packing."

The band finished one song and started another. Whit shook a fresh cigarette from the pack in front of him. "Bea means well, even if she does sometimes come across like some biddy from the Salvation Army."

I laughed and nudged him with my shoulder. "You shouldn't say things like that about Bea, even if they are true."

Whit grinned at me like we were grand conspirators and struck a match. He inhaled greedily, sucking in the very thing that's probably going to kill him. "I don't know what happened with that girl, but I blame her mother."

I bit my lip and ducked my head to hide my smile. Bea's mother, Aunt Evelyn, is a nice lady and I do love her. Really. But she *is* a bit of a cold fish, and she never has fit in with the family like the other in-laws. "Well, I didn't come to check up on you," I assured him again. "I'm here for a totally different reason."

His wise old eyes narrowed behind another plume of smoke. "Something to do with the way that young fella died?"

I never could get anything past him. "Yeah," I said. "Something about the way Laurence Nichols died." My margarita appeared, and Uncle Whit and I haggled for a few minutes over who was going to pay for it. He's not a wealthy man, but he has a lot of pride, so I eventually let him win. I'd find a way to get him back, anyway.

I took a mouthful of slush, making sure I got just the right amount of salt with it. "Were you in here on Monday night?" It wasn't really a question. Uncle Whit was at the Avalanche every night, but just about everyone in the family pretended not to know that.

"The night of the accident?" I waited while Whit pretended to give that some thought. "I think I was for a little while. Why?"

"Any chance you were here between eight thirty and midnight?"

"Sure. It was a Caribou meeting. I got here a little after six and stayed until Wyatt came by. That was probably about one." Most people don't know that Wyatt frequently stops by to drive uncle Whit home. It's not something Wyatt ever talks about, but it's proof that behind his gruff exterior he has a heart of gold. The rest of the family is so grateful he gets Whit home safely, we all pretend not to know what he's doing.

"You know a guy named Doyle Brannigan?"

Uncle Whit perked up at that. "Sure I know him. He's a Brother Caribou."

"Did you see him in here that night?"

Whit thought again, and this time I thought his confusion was probably genuine. After six most nights, he lives in a state of perpetual fog. "We're talking about the night that guy got himself killed, right?"

I nodded and sucked up more margarita. "Did you see him?"

"He was here," Whit said slowly. "Bought a round of drinks, as I recall."

Making sure he'd be remembered? Clever. "How long did he stay?"

Whit took a long pull on the beer in his hand and signaled for another. "He was here until the end."

That's about what I expected to hear. "Did he ever leave your sight? Maybe to visit the men's room or make a phone call?"

Whit flicked ash, missed the ashtray, and brushed it off the bar with his hand. "You askin' if maybe he could have slipped out and done the deed?"

"Something like that."

"I suppose it's possible, but not very likely. Monday night was a big night. Had our monthly business meeting and the dartboard championships. If Doyle had left, he'd 'a had to walk right past me 'cuz I was sittin' right over there." He closed one eye and pointed with his cigarette toward a seat near the entrance.

"What about the back way? Could he have gone out without anyone knowing?"

Uncle Whit sucked something from a tooth and looked toward the back of the bar. "You looked out the back way lately?"

"Not lately."

"Nobody's goin' out that way, girl. It's been blocked for the past two years." Concern flashed through his eyes, and he dropped his voice and leaned closer. "Just don't tell nobody. The fire marshal would shut this place down in a heartbeat if word was to get out."

"This place hasn't inspected in that long?"

Whit lifted one burly shoulder. "Sure it's been inspected." He winked, as if to say I knew how things worked, and I guess I did. Junior Evans, the bar's owner, was a loyal member of the Caribou and so was the fire marshal. Everyone knows the Caribou take care of their own.

"There's no other way out of here?"

"Not that I know about." Uncle Whit took another pull on his beer. "You can't seriously think Doyle killed that fella."

"I seriously think he's one of half a dozen people who might have," I said with a rueful grin. "All I know is that Richie Bellieu is innocent, so if it wasn't Richie, and it wasn't Doyle, who was it?"

Whit crushed out his second cigarette and plucked a stray bit of tobacco from his tongue. "Who's gonna get something now that the man's dead?"

"His manager. He's already circling like a vulture over Laurence's estate." I drummed my fingers on the bar while I gave that question some more thought. "Doyle gets his wife back."

Whit shook his grizzled head again. "Couldn't 'a been him, sweetheart. I told ya, he was here all night."

"Alexander Pastorelli wins their long-standing rivalry, and he's pretty bitter about something he invested in that he blames Laurence for. I don't know if that would be enough to drive him to murder, but Alexander *is* the last man standing."

"How about women?" Uncle Whit asked. "Lord love 'em, they're usually at the root of a man's sorrows."

I mentally cataloged Vonetta, Serena, and Colleen. "Could be," I said around another mouthful of slush. "Somebody he screwed over in the past?"

Uncle Whit nodded. "Or an ex-girlfriend who didn't like the way things ended? Anybody like that hanging around?"

"Yeah, probably. Laurence Nichols wasn't a very nice person." I propped my chin in my hands. "I've found lots of people who hated him, even people who had pretty good reasons for wanting him out of the way. But I still don't see how someone could have committed murder by cutting the safety cable on that spotlight—unless the murderer is the luckiest person on the face of the earth."

"Maybe it wasn't murder."

"Then why attack Vonetta? And if Vonetta does know something she shouldn't, why hasn't whoever it was attacked again? Nothing about this makes any sense."

Uncle Whit put a hand on my shoulder and squeezed. "Cheer up, pumpkin. Somebody out there knows what you're looking for, and one of these days they'll talk."

Maybe so, but I wasn't going to hold my breath. Even if Uncle Whit *was* right, would the truth come out soon enough to help Richie?

Buoyed by the margarita and time spent with Uncle Whit, I hurried back to Divinity. I spent the rest of that evening and all the next day restocking the rapidly dwindling display of Valentine's Day candy bouquets. I filled half a dozen vases with chocolate roses or heart-shaped lollipops, added silk greenery and baby's breath, and arranged the vases on the display case just inside the front door. When I'd finished with those, I dragged a dozen baskets from the supply cupboard and filled each with homemade fudge, brittle, cherry divinity, and other assorted candies.

Though the death of Laurence Nichols was always rolling around inside my head, I forced myself to stay at Divinity. There would be time later to ask Richie about Jason's claim that he'd threatened to kill Laurence.

Elizabeth and the girls showed up promptly at ten Saturday morning, and I put them to work making sure that Karen and Liberty had everything they needed. The shop was crowded with six of us working, but we managed to stay out of each others' way for the most part.

Karen organized the others into an assembly line of sorts, while I gathered a hodgepodge of the most popular candy bars we stocked and arranged them in baskets, wagons, bowls, hat boxes, and teacups. When the clock finally crept around to seven, I'd scrunched so much ribbon into decorative bows, my hands were cramped and aching. It took almost an hour to serve the customers who were still browsing, but at last Liberty flipped over the sign on the door to Closed, and I gave myself permission to knock off for the evening.

After a quick shower and a change of clothes, Max and I headed out for his evening walk. Now that the workday was behind me, I found myself at loose ends. I hadn't heard from

Jawarski since the conversation that had ended badly, and every day my mood grew a little worse. He and I had spent so much time together, I'd almost forgotten how to get through a Saturday night on my own.

He was due back in a few days, and I still didn't know how to react when he got here. Did I love him? I felt almost obligated to tell him that I did, but what if I didn't mean it?

Did I trust him? Was I ready to make a commitment, or was it still too great a risk? My head hurt just thinking about it.

I'd been planning to grab some takeout and eat in my apartment, but the realization that I'd become so accustomed to having Jawarski around changed my mind. The weather had stayed relatively warm all day, and as I pondered my options a few lazy flakes of snow drifted toward the ground. They melted as soon as they touched the ground, but it wouldn't be long before the temperature dropped and they began to stick.

I'd dressed warmly, and my boots could handle the snow, but I didn't want to leave Max out in the weather for long. He's too spoiled for that. I decided on the Lotus Blossum, a restaurant that serves Thai and Vietnamese cuisine. Critics give it high marks, but it's still casual enough for jeans and my favorite Denver Nuggets sweatshirt. The jewelry store next door was closed, so I settled Max in its recessed doorway for shelter from the storm and stepped inside the restaurant where the rich scents of garlic, curry, and chili wrapped themselves around me. I inhaled greedily and congratulated myself on making a brilliant choice.

I've eaten there enough to know a few of the waitstaff by name. Dak-Ho led me to a small table near the front window, where I could see if Max needed me. Dak's Korean, not Thai *or* Vietnamese, but nobody's keeping track. We spent a few seconds on small talk while I ordered an egg roll, sautéed lemon grass and chili chicken, and my favorite, Thai tea.

Dak hurried off with my order, and I took stock of my surroundings for the first time. Most of the other diners were couples, either dining alone or with friends. A few months ago, I'd have shrugged off the flicker of discomfort at being alone in a crowd. Tonight, it bothered me.

In the months after my divorce, I'd worked hard to stop feeling uncomfortable dining alone, and I wasn't happy to find that I felt uneasy and exposed—two emotions that had gained a foothold while I was hanging out with Jawarski.

Determined to shake off the negative emotion, I unwrapped a set of disposable chopsticks. Opened the napkin packet and set out the silverware rolled inside. Sipped ice water and tried to ignore the amorous adventures of the couple closest to me. The waitstaff hustled in and out of the kitchen, carrying trays of food, delivering drinks, checking on diners to make sure they had everything they needed.

Dak-Ho hustled past me carrying a loaded tray, assured me that my tea would be out in a moment, and hurried to the other side of the dining room. As he bustled away again, I recognized Jason Dahl sitting across the way, and I was seized by a sudden profound need to ask him about the threat he claimed he'd heard Richie make against Laurence.

I hesitated just long enough to make sure that Jason was alone, then crossed the room and slid into the chair across from him just as he lifted a spring roll dripping peanut sauce to his mouth.

"Hey Jason."

"Abby?" A glob of peanut sauce dropped to the table. "What's up?"

"Just grabbing a quick bite. I saw you over here and decided to say hello."

He smiled uncertainly and lowered the spring roll to the small white plate in front of him. "Are you alone? Do you want to join me?"

I waved off the invitation almost before he finished issuing it. "No, thanks. I don't want to intrude." I smiled warmly. "I just wanted to ask you about something. I ran into a reporter this afternoon who claimed that he'd been talking to you. His name's John Haversham and he's with KZPY."

Jason had finally managed a bite, so he nodded as he chewed. "Yeah, I talked to him. Why?"

"He says that you heard Richie threaten Laurence. Is that true?"

Jason froze for an instant, then nodded slowly. "Yeah. I did. Why?"

Disappointment made my heart heavy. I hadn't realized how much I hoped Jason would tell me that Haversham was a big, fat liar . . . until he didn't. "Would you mind telling me about it?"

"About what? Richie?"

"Yeah. What was going on when you heard him threaten Laurence, and what did he say?"

Jason put down his spring roll again and wiped his mouth with his napkin. "Okay, sure. He was coming out of the auditorium. I was working on a backdrop. I don't know what happened or anything. I just know that he was furious about something. He said something like he ought to rip out his fucking heart."

"How did you know he was talking about Laurence?"

"Because I saw Laurence go in there a few minutes earlier."

"Maybe Laurence wasn't the only person in there," I suggested.

Jason considered that, then shook his head. "Naw, I'm pretty sure he was. He told me he was meeting somebody in there and asked me to keep an eye out. I got the impression he didn't want Vonetta to know."

"Did Laurence say who he was meeting?"

Jason shook his head again. "No, but I assumed it was a woman. It usually was."

"Did you notice when Richie arrived?"

"Nope. I assumed that he went in through one of the other doors. Either that, or he was already in there. Hey! Maybe that's when he cut through the safety cable on the light. I never thought of that before."

"Richie didn't cut that cable," I said automatically.

"If you say so."

"I do. How difficult would it be for someone to climb up into the rigging and cut the cable?"

"Not that hard. The Playhouse is pretty small, so it's not as if they'd have to go up two or three stories. All it would take is a few minutes alone and a ladder."

"That's what I was afraid of. Where did you learn all this stuff?"

Jason grinned. "Would you believe high school? My sister was in the drama department, and I had to catch a ride home with her after school so I started hanging out around the kids on the stage crew."

"There's one other thing that's been bothering me," I said. "How hard do you think it would be for someone to use a spotlight as a murder weapon?"

"As a murder weapon?" Jason picked up his second spring roll and dipped it into the sauce. "I don't see how it could be done. For the light to fall just right and hit someone in the exact spot that would cause death? It's like a one in a million chance."

Unfortunately, that's exactly what I thought.

Dak surged out of the kitchen with my Thai tea. He caught my eye and jerked his head, first toward my table, then toward Jason's. Jason noticed him and asked again, "You sure you don't want to join me? It's no intrusion. Really."

"Thanks, but no," I said, and got to my feet. "I had a long day at work, and I'd be lousy company." Besides, I had plenty to chew on. No matter how many questions I asked, the answers just kept taking me around in circles. Doyle, Colleen, Geoffrey, Vonetta, Serena. I cycled around and around, over and over, but I still wasn't any closer to the solution.

Chapter 23

❦

The storm was just beginning in earnest as I finished dinner. Every muscle in my body ached with weariness, but my mind was too wound up for sleep. Still hoping I could clear my head, I walked through town slowly, enjoying the brisk air and the feel of snowflakes on my face. I'd always felt safe walking in town, even at night. Our low crime rate is one of the best things about Paradise, but even that is changing.

On impulse, I walked past the Playhouse. Many of the businesses in town were closed up tight, but since most of the cast and crew are working their real jobs during the day, night's when a lot of the work is done in semiprofessional theater. When I saw lights still burning in the lobby and Vonetta's Buick in its usual parking space, I decided sleep could wait.

I kicked the snow off my boots and brushed all the flakes I could from Max's coat before stepping into the lobby. The scent of freshly cut wood filled the air, and country music blaring from a stereo in the distance mingled with the muffled sound of hammering and the high whine of an electric saw. The crew must be working on scenery.

When the saw fell silent, I heard the low hum of conversation coming from the rehearsal hall. The level of activity tonight was a far cry from the deserted theater I'd stepped into on Monday night.

I checked Vonetta's office first, but the door was wide open, and I could tell at a glance that she wasn't inside. To my surprise, I felt a niggling worry spring to life. After all, last time I'd gone looking for her, I found her onstage with a dead man. Logic told me that history wouldn't repeat itself, but that didn't stop the feeling of dread from rising up in my throat.

"Here we go again, boy," I muttered to Max as I led him toward the drone of voices in the rehearsal hall.

He seemed to understand—at least I told myself he did. Sometimes you have to create your own support system.

Vonetta wasn't there, either, but at least this time the rehearsal hall wasn't empty. The two women who'd been so enraptured by Laurence the night of the mandatory meeting were sitting at a prop table, running lines. Alexander sat a few feet away, pretending to work on a stack of papers in a file folder and watching the women from the corner of his eye.

One was young and thin, no more than twenty-five I guessed, with long, dark hair and wide, expressive eyes. The other looked a bit older, in her early thirties maybe. Her shoulder-length blond hair had been seriously overprocessed, and boredom was written all over her face.

I couldn't tell if Alexander was paying attention to their acting techniques, or if he was interested in them for some other reason. Everyone said that Laurence had played the field extensively, but no one had mentioned Alexander as his rival when it came to women. Now I wondered if the two men had ever been interested in the same women, even fought over one or two . . .

The dark-haired actress flubbed a line and dissolved into laughter. The blond waited with exaggerated patience for her to regain control. A smile, more fatherly than lecherous, curved Alexander's lips. But when he glanced away from the women and noticed me, the smile disappeared. A bland expression replaced it faster than I could blink, which made me rethink the whole fatherly thing.

"Abby," he said, his voice as bland as his face. "What can I do for you?"

I could have given him a long list of things, but I didn't think he'd be willing to comply. I wasn't even sure why I'd come to the theater, except I was pretty sure this was where the answers to my questions were. "I'm looking for Vonetta," I said, grabbing the first thing that popped into my head. "Have you seen her?"

"She's not here. I believe she went to dinner."

The brunette nodded. "Yeah, she did. She left a while ago, so she should be back soon."

Great. Now what excuse could I give for hanging around?

The brunette at the table took care of that for me. "Hey, aren't you in the cast?"

I tried not to look overly grateful. "That's right. I'll be playing Isabel."

She lunged out of her chair and pumped my hand. "That's cool. I'm Jody." She nodded toward her companion. "That's Hannah. We're voices."

They were also the two people who'd been standing closest to Laurence when he'd discovered that his music was missing. I had no idea if they'd seen or heard anything important, or even if the missing music was connected to Laurence's death, but talking to them suddenly seemed like a good idea. "So you'll be in the sound booth on stage, speaking for the rest of us, right? Are either of you Isabel's voice?"

Hannah slid a disinterested glance at me through a veil of strawlike bangs. "I'm Edith's voice. She's doing Kate." The look she gave Max was a little less bored. "I'm not sure you can have your dog in here."

"It's okay," I assured her. "He's been here before. He goes everywhere with me." I found an empty chair and dragged it toward the table.

Hannah looked away, a slight curl on her lip. *Darn.* There went my dreams of becoming Best Friends Forever.

I spotted a short stack of scripts on the windowsill, so I grabbed one and plunked myself into the chair. "What scene are you working on? Do you mind if I join you?"

"Of course not," Jody assured me.

Hannah lifted one shoulder in a slow-motion shrug. "Knock yourself out."

She was going to be a barrel of laughs over the next few

weeks. I could tell already. "Is this your first production at the Playhouse?"

Jody shook her head. "I've been in five before this one, usually in the chorus. This is the biggest part I've had. Hannah's been in a few plays, too, haven't you?"

"A few." Those eyes climbed slowly to my face and stopped there. "You?" I wondered if she was always this friendly, or if she had something against me.

"This is my second, and my first was . . . a while ago. To tell you the truth, I'm surprised that we're still going into rehearsal. I thought for sure Laurence's death would derail the play."

Alexander spoke for the first time in several minutes. "An obvious newcomer to the theater," he said with a cool smile. "Everyone knows the show must go on."

I refused to let him discourage me. I turned my script to the page with my entrance on it and smiled up at him. "That's what Vonetta said, too."

Jody agreed. "The accident was freaky, but . . . well, you know. Accidents happen. I'm sure Laurence would have wanted us to go on with the show."

"Yeah. Probably. Didn't I see the two of you talking to Laurence the night of the meeting?"

Jody blushed. "Yeah. We were so excited to work with him. It's still hard to believe that he's gone."

"Did you know him well?"

"No." That gem came from Hannah. She didn't elaborate.

Jody looked embarrassed by her friend's response. "Not really. We just met him, like, that day."

"Creepy," Hannah said without looking up. I wondered whether she meant Laurence or the falling spotlight.

"Let's not get sidetracked, ladies," Alexander said. "Talking about Laurence's tragic accident isn't helping anyone."

Color flooded Jody's cheeks. She ducked her head and mumbled, "Sorry."

Hannah didn't even blink. "Whatever."

It might not be helping him, but he wasn't my concern. "I

wonder what happened to that music," I said. "Laurence must have been beside himself."

Hannah's gaze dropped to the script in front of her. "He wasn't happy, that's for sure."

"Did he have any idea who took it?"

"I thought Serena did," Jody said, her brow creased with confusion.

"She said she didn't," I reminded her. "I just wondered if he suspected anyone else."

Hannah's unblinking stare stayed glued to my face. "How would either of us know that?"

"Well, the two of you *were* right there by the piano, and you could hear everything that was going on."

Jody's frown deepened. "Are you accusing one of us of taking it?"

"Not at all," I said, quickly. "I'm just wondering if either of you saw or heard anything unusual that night."

Jody shook her head. "I didn't really notice anything besides that Richie guy throwing himself at Laurence. It was embarrassing, if you ask me."

I'm not sure how it was even possible, but Hannah's expression grew even less animated. "You're just saying that because of all the talk. He didn't do anything different than anyone else that night."

Maybe we *could* be Best Friends Forever after all.

Alexander spoke up again. "I really must insist, ladies. No more talk about the accident *or* about the missing music."

I wondered why he was so anxious to keep us from talking. Was he only concerned about the production, or did he have something to hide?

Jody dropped her gaze back to her script, but she looked at Hannah from beneath furrowed brows and whispered, "You have to admit, everybody knows that gay guys are, like, major drama queens. He probably wigged out when Laurence turned him down."

Jody, on the other hand, was off my BFF list permanently.

"That's nothing but an old, tired stereotype," I whispered

back. "And for the record, Richie was not interested in Laurence in that way."

Hannah looked more interested than she had since I walked through the door. "Are you a friend of his or something?"

"A very good friend. There's no way he cut the safety cable on that spotlight. But someone did, and I'm trying to find out who."

Hannah slid a glance at Alexander and dropped her voice a notch. "If you ask me, it was probably Serena."

She sounded so definite, my pulse stuttered. "Why do you say that?"

"Because she hated him. I mean, she *seriously* hated him."

Jody's mouth formed a little *O* of surprise. "How do you know *that*?"

"I overheard them talking."

"When?" The word snapped out of my mouth with more force than I'd intended, so I tried softening it with a BFF-type smile. "I mean, before or after the meeting?"

"The day after. I was in the ladies room. They were in the women's dressing room." Hannah leaned in even closer and dropped her voice another notch. "I think Laurence kind of chased her in there, and she was furious. She told him to get the hell away from her."

Doubt clouded Jody's expression. "Are you sure?" Because as we all knew, no woman in the history of the world had ever been able to resist Laurence Nichols.

Hannah slid a quelling look at her. At least it would have quelled me. "He said they needed to talk, and she said 'Over your dead body'."

I wanted to make sure I'd heard right. "Over *your* dead body?"

"Exactly. And a few hours later, he was dead."

Alexander shot out of his seat and came to stand at the head of our small table. "I'm not going to say this again. I *won't* have all this pointless speculation about Laurence's unfortunate death. Do you understand?"

Jody squirmed in her seat, obviously distraught at having angered him. Hannah rolled an unimpressed glance in his direction. "It's a free country, Alexander. We can talk about it if we want to."

"Not while you're in my production." Anger turned his face a mottled red. "Either let it go, or you're out of here. All three of you."

That sent Jody over the edge. "Shut *up*, Hannah. Please. I've worked too hard to get here. Don't screw it up for me."

Hannah might have argued with Alexander, but Jody's distress got to her. She sank down in her chair and the expression of boredom slid back over her face. "Fine. Have it your way."

I still had a dozen questions to ask, but the conversation was over . . . for now, anyway. I bit back my disappointment and tried to concentrate on the script in front of me. For the first time in days, I felt as if I'd made a little headway. Obviously Serena had lied to me about not seeing Laurence again, and that made me wonder what else she'd lied about.

I was determined to find out.

Chapter 24

I woke up early on Sunday morning, threw on a clean pair of jeans and my favorite sweater, and gulped coffee as Max and I drove toward the Silver River Inn. Last night's snowstorm had blown out of the valley just before sunrise, and a foot of fresh, sparkling powder covered everything in all directions. That made the drive slow going, but the steady scrape of snow shovels mixed with the drone of snowblower engines and the rumble of snowplows resounded as Paradise dug out from the storm.

A storm of a different sort was brewing inside me. The longer I thought about Richie hiding something from me, the angrier I got. I'd been busting my hump all week, trying to clear him of suspicion, and the whole time he'd been conveniently leaving out important details, like the fact that he'd threatened to rip Laurence's heart out a few hours before Laurence died. Call me crazy, but that seemed like an important detail to omit.

I'm firm believer in energy, the kind every person gives off. The kind that warns people in advance when you're in a foul mood so they can steer clear. My energy this morning must have been off the charts because I found a parking space right in front of the inn. Even cars must have been able to feel my irritation, and that realization made me feel powerful.

Of course, there was an alternative explanation as well. There always is. But I didn't want to believe that Dylan and Richie had lost so much business there were places to park in front of the inn on a busy snow day in the middle of ski season.

I picked up on a few other subtle clues as Max and I negotiated the stairs that led to the inn's main entrance. Like the fact that the reporters were still hanging around, but they were all inside their SUVs with their heaters running, which meant they weren't expecting to get an interview any second. And the fact that several inches of fresh powder lay undisturbed on the stairs. And the fact that the inn's front door wouldn't open when I tried it. I couldn't remember the last time the door had been locked when I'd come to see Dylan and Richie.

A couple of car doors slammed, and a wave of reporters came after me. I was in no mood, so I turned around and shouted, "Come one step closer, and I'm letting my dog loose."

I didn't dare look to see whether Max was cooperating by looking fierce or wagging his tail in anticipation of a new game. All that mattered was that my bluff worked. The thundering herds stopped in the middle of the street, consulted with each other for a few seconds, and then turned away. I made a mental note to buy Max his very own Whopper and tried the door again.

Maybe they'd just locked up to keep the reporters out, but it still made my stomach knot. Even if we cleared Richie right that minute, would they be able to rebound from this? Or would they lose the inn? Maybe even leave Paradise?

I tried to shake off the negative thinking. If they moved on, at least they had each other. But I don't have that many close friends, and I didn't want to lose the few I had. I rang the bell, and after a few minutes Dylan opened the door and ushered me inside.

"Sorry for the wait. With all those reporters hanging around, we've been a little cautious."

"And with good reason," I said. I hugged him quickly and tried to kick the snow off my shoes. I finally gave up the battle and left them at the door. "How are you holding up?" I asked as I followed Dylan into the kitchen.

"As well as can be expected for a couple of guys about to lose everything. How about you?"

"You're not going to lose everything," I told him firmly. "We're going to clear Richie of all suspicion, and when we're finished the inn will be doing better than ever."

Dylan tossed a grateful smile in my direction and lifted the coffeepot. "You interested?"

"Absolutely."

"I just put a breakfast casserole into the oven. You're welcome to join us."

"Sounds perfect," I said. "But I didn't come here for you to feed me."

"Humor me," he said, and made a valiant effort to grin. "We don't have anyone else to cook for."

"You got it. So where's Richie?"

"In bed, feeling sorry for himself. Why don't you go on in? He might actually pull the covers off his head for you."

"He seemed fine at rehearsal the other night. What happened?"

"The last of our reservations for Valentine's Day canceled. On the plus side, we'll have the entire inn to ourselves. It should be wildly romantic."

He was trying so hard, I made myself laugh. but it wasn't easy. "Let me know when the casserole's out of the oven," I said. "I'm famished."

I followed a winding corridor created by several additions to the original structure to the master suite and knocked on the door. "Richie? It's Abby. Can I come in?" He didn't answer immediately, so I played my ace in the hole. "Max is with me."

The muffled sound of rustling bedding came through the door, followed by a quiet, "You can come in, I guess. But warn Max that I look like dog shit."

"I don't think he cares," I said as I turned the knob. "I know I don't."

Max saw his friend and bounded onto the bed, nudging and licking and wagging with excitement. Richie sat like a lump in a pair of boxers, his expression maudlin. Usually, Richie takes great pains with his appearance, so the five o'clock shadow, matted hair, and dark circles under his eyes had me worried.

I perched on the foot of the bed and tried to catch his eye. "Dylan's making breakfast, and he's invited us to stay for it. How about getting dressed and coming into the kitchen so we can talk?"

"I'm not hungry."

"I understand that, but you need to keep up your strength. None of this is going to be any easier if you let yourself get run-down."

Richie slid a look at me. "Eating an egg isn't going to suddenly make it all better."

I'm as sympathetic as the next guy, but his attitude—on top of the fact that he'd conveniently forgotten to tell me some important stuff—was seriously pissing me off. "Neither will lying in bed all day feeling sorry for yourself. Get up. Put on your robe, at least, and come into the kitchen."

His head shot up and he gaped at me as if I'd just ordered him to wear mismatched socks. "I'm in pain here, Abby. This is a very difficult time, and I don't need you getting all bitchy with me."

Ooo-kay. So that's how we were going to play it? "I'll make a note of that. Why don't you make a note of the fact that when a friend sticks her neck out to help you, it's a good idea to tell her the truth?"

His eyes flashed with anger, but at least he was awake now. "I *have* told you the truth. I can't believe you'd even suggest that I haven't."

"The whole truth?"

"Absolutely." He put an arm around Max and pulled him close. Like I said before, sometimes you gotta create your own support system. "Who told you I was lying? I would never do that to you."

"It's not so much an out-and-out lie as an error of omission. Why didn't you tell me that you threatened Laurence?"

Richie's mouth opened and closed a couple of times before he managed to gasp out, "It's a lie. I never threatened him."

"You never said you ought to 'tear his fucking heart out'?"

The blood drained from Richie's face and his shoulders slumped again. "Well, yeah, I said that, but I didn't say it *to* him, and I certainly didn't mean it."

"Somehow, I don't think the police are going to care that you weren't looking Laurence in the eye at the time. Why didn't you tell me?"

"Because it didn't mean anything. I was just . . . pissed. That's all."

"Oh. Just *pissed*. That makes all the difference." Okay, so that was a touch sarcastic, but really! "What were you pissed about?"

"I can't tell you."

I gaped at him. "You'd better tell me if you want my help."

Richie got to his feet and ran a hand along the back of his neck. "I would if I could, but I can't. It's not my story to tell."

So there was a third person involved. That could be good news, or it could be bad. "Fine. Whose story is it?"

"I can't tell you that, either."

I let out a sigh of frustration. "Are you kidding me? I thought you understood how bad your situation is. If somebody can help explain why you came storming out of the auditorium threatening to kill Laurence Nichols, you need to tell me who it was."

Richie met my gaze with bloodshot eyes. "You think I don't know how bad things look? Well, I do. I get it, okay? Dylan and I could lose everything. We're already on the downward spiral. I don't have a lot left, but I do have my honor. I need to hang on to that, if nothing else."

"Whoever it is will understand. If we can't clear you of suspicion, you could end up in prison. For a long time. Maybe forever. You owe it to yourself and to Dylan to do whatever you can to save yourself."

Richie shook his head. "How can Dylan respect me if I go back on my word just because I hit a road bump?"

"This is more than a road bump, Richie. This is—"

"I said no, and I meant it Abby. There's nothing more to talk about."

Abby's head meets immovable object—again. I fell back on the bed and closed my eyes, trying to think of something I could say that would change his mind. "Well, it has to be someone involved in the play," I said, thinking aloud.

"What are you doing?"

"Trying to figure out who you're talking about. Maybe whoever it is will talk to me."

"Leave it alone, Abby."

I ignored him. "And it has to be someone who was at the theater that day. If I can't find the call sheet, I'm sure Vonetta will tell me. That will at least help narrow it down."

"I said back off."

"And it has to be someone with a connection to Laurence. Someone who doesn't want that connection made pub—" I cut myself off and sat up straight. "It's Serena, isn't it?"

Richie went perfectly still and we stared at each other for a full minute, both trying to guess how much the other knew before we said anything more.

"It *is* her, isn't it?"

"You know about the—?"

I nodded. "She told me about it when I went to see her after Laurence died."

All the air left Richie's lungs in a *whoosh*, and he dropped heavily onto the bed. "She swore me to secrecy."

"I didn't even realize you knew her that well," I said.

"Well, she didn't actually confide in me on purpose. I overheard their conversation completely by accident. Laurence was such a jerk to her, and she was so upset I couldn't just sneak out and pretend I hadn't heard it."

"Okay, so now I know who it was. Tell me about their conversation. What did they say?"

Richie raked his fingers through his hair in an effort to tame it. It didn't work, but I took that as a sign that he was starting to feel better. "Okay. Well . . . I was looking for some stuff that I'd left in the sound booth earlier. I found it and was just getting ready to leave when Serena came into the auditorium."

"She didn't see you?"

He shook his head. "I turned the lights off when I left the booth, so I was in the shadows, I guess. I would have said something, but Laurence came in right behind her, and after the little dustup we had over lunch, I decided to just stay where I was. I didn't want him to accuse me of trying to molest him or something."

"Good call."

Richie's lips twitched. "Yeah. Well. Anyway, she told Laurence to get away from her, and he said something smarmy, like 'Oh, come on baby, don't be like that,' and she called him a bastard, and he laughed at her and said, 'I don't know why you're so angry. That whole thing happened years ago. Why don't we just let bygones be bygones?' and that's when she got really upset."

"He tried to sweep it all under the rug?"

Richie nodded. "Like it wasn't even important. She said that he'd ruined her life, and he said, 'Hey, it was you or me, babe. Every man for himself,' and she said, 'Well, you certainly looked out for *your*self,' and he said, 'Don't be so melodramatic. It's not as if we were going to be together forever,'' and then she tried to slap him, but he caught her wrist and I think he hurt her, and he said, 'Hey, we both knew how it was, and if you think about it, I probably saved you a whole lot of trouble. At least you didn't have to do the whole single mother on welfare thing, right?'"

Just when I thought Nichols couldn't sink any lower in my estimation. "What a heartless creep."

"You can say that again. Anyway, Serena hauled off and smacked him, and he laughed, and she told him to stay away from her, and he said he was here for the duration, and they'd be seeing lots and lots of each other, and he said it in such a lecherous, disgusting way I wanted to smack him myself." Richie paused to suck in a breath. "And anyway, he finally left, and she was crying, and I just *had* to say something to her, and she told me the *whole* story . . ." He shrugged and exhaled again. "And that's it. It just really upset me, you know? I used to think Laurence Nichols was this great guy, and I was so excited to meet him. . . ."

I finished for him. "And he turned out to be a self-absorbed homophobe. Disappointing, I know. But that's going to be the thing that saves you, Richie. Remember that.

He looked up hopefully. "Really? You know a way to clear me?"

Oops. I felt like a jerk for offering hope when I wasn't sure I could deliver. "Not yet, but I will. I promise."

Yeah, I know. It was a rash promise, and I was foolish to make it. But my back was against the wall. And besides, it seemed like a good idea at the time.

Chapter 25

I stayed at the inn just long enough to eat breakfast, then hightailed it back to Divinity in time to meet Elizabeth and the twins. While Karen and Liberty waited on customers, Elizabeth stuffed strawberry lollipops into bags and the girls tied each one with a red bow. Orders kept piling up, and even with my sister-in-law and nieces helping, it was all we could do to keep up with demand. No matter how fast I churned out fresh candy, it disappeared before I had more ready to replace it.

I ordered dinner for the entire crew—two Gut Buster Specials and a Hawaiian Paradise from Black Jack Pizza. Extra cheese bread since Wyatt and my nephews were making deliveries and post office runs for me. There isn't enough cheese bread in all of Paradise to satisfy those three, but I made an effort.

Wyatt took the kids home early since they had school the next day, but I stayed until nearly midnight with Karen, Liberty, and Elizabeth trying to get a jump on Monday's orders. By the time I finally locked the doors and climbed the stairs to my apartment, I was so tired I could hardly keep my eyes open. Unfortunately, I was even more hungry than tired, so I hauled the leftover pizza home with me.

Three more days, I told myself as I dragged one foot after the other. After that, business would slow down again, and life would get back to normal. Jawarski would come home, and my imagination would stop conjuring images of him deciding he couldn't live without his ex-wife. I'd figure out how I felt about him and find the courage to actually put it into words. And all would be right with my world.

I doubted that any of us were as eager for that as poor Max. He met me at the door, his entire body wagging with excitement that I was home. I felt so guilty for ignoring him all day, I divided the leftover pizza between us and even warmed his slightly in the microwave before giving it to him.

It's the little things.

Still battling guilt pangs, I sat beside him on the living room floor. Halfway down, I realized that I'd made a mistake, but it was too late to reverse direction. I'm not completely out of shape, but I'm also not twenty-five anymore. My forty-year-old muscles seized up as I sat, and froze solid the instant my butt hit the floor.

"You might have to help me, buddy," I told Max as I slid his plate in front of him. "Otherwise, we're going to spend the night right here."

Max is pretty spoiled, so I knew he wouldn't like that any more than I did. He wolfed down his pizza with gusto and began to eye mine—just more proof that I'm more indulgent with him than I should be.

"Oh no, you don't," I warned him. "I earned this. I need this. You don't get it."

He licked his lips and his eyes tracked the slice as I lifted it to my mouth and returned it to the plate. I managed to remain resolute until I reached the crust, which was no longer soft, warm, or edible. I tossed him the uneaten bit just as the phone shrilled into the silence of the room.

My heart skipped a beat, and I nearly choked on my pizza. Phone calls in the middle of the night are never good news. While I know that midnight doesn't qualify as "middle of the night" to some people, I'm usually in bed by then, especially when I have to work the next day.

A bit panicked, I looked around frantically for the handset. One of these days I *have* to get more organized.

The good news was I found the phone wedged into the

cushions of the couch so I could grab it from where I sat. The bad news? It had been off the charger for at least three days, and I expected it to start flashing Low Battery any second.

I punched the On button, praying that nobody I loved had been in an accident or had a heart attack. "Hello?"

"Hey, slick. Did I wake you up?"

Jawarski. My heart did its usual tap dance, but with the anticipation came a slow-moving feeling of dread. What if he wanted me to respond to his ill-timed "I love you"? I didn't have the energy, either mental of physical, to deal with "us" tonight.

"Not yet," I said. "I just left the shop about twenty minutes ago."

"I tried to call around eleven. When you didn't answer, I figured you were still working. Either that or you had a hot date." He laughed, but I thought I sensed a question in there somewhere.

If and when I made some kind of commitment to this relationship, it would have to be on my terms. Otherwise, it would be meaningless. I dodged the silent question and told myself I'd figure out what I felt after I got some sleep. "Yeah, well, it's been busy."

"I remember how it was last year." His voice was low and soft, and the reminder that we'd been through this season together once felt uncomfortably intimate. "You holding up okay?"

"I'm sitting on the floor eating pizza with Max. What does that tell you?"

Jawarski laughed. "Sounds like you're doing just fine, then. Listen, I've been meaning to talk to you about Valentine's Day."

I felt myself tensing. *Not tonight.* Not when I was tired enough to sleep sitting up. "Do you mind if we talk about that later? I'm exhausted tonight."

"I suppose not, but—"

"Tomorrow," I said. "Just let me grab a few hours' sleep first."

I could almost hear Jawarski's frown over the phone, but he didn't argue. "Sure. What's going on with the case?"

Happy to talk about anything but the two of us, I filled him in on everything I'd learned so far. I hesitated over telling him about Serena and Laurence, but if this thing between us was real, didn't I have to trust him?

"I don't get it," he said when I'd finished. "Why is keeping all of that quiet so important to Vonetta?"

"Because she's worked really hard to make her place in this town. She's been battling racial prejudice her entire life, and people are always quick to think the worst because of who she is. And because some people don't believe in second chances."

"The old guard might give her trouble," Jawarski agreed, "but there are plenty of people who would understand. Besides, it was all a long time ago."

"Yeah, but Vonetta just found out about it. She knew about the abortion, and she knew Serena couldn't have kids as a result, but she never knew about Laurence's part in it until he came back to town."

"Sounds like a motive to me."

Was it? I didn't want to believe that Vonetta could do something like that, but Jawarski might be right. Look at the way she'd acted with me, and all I'd done was talk to Serena. Laurence had been a much greater threat than I was.

I scraped another mushroom from the pizza and downed it. My butt was beginning to ache from sitting on the hard floor, so I dragged myself onto the couch and from there to my feet. "I suppose either one of them could have snapped," I said. "But is either of them skilled enough at whatever to predict how that spotlight would fall if they cut the safety cable?"

"The spotlight was a diversion," Jawarski said. "I got a call this afternoon after the autopsy results came back. Laurence didn't die from the blow to his head. He died from potassium cyanide poisoning."

I dropped my pizza, and Max lunged for it. "He *what*?"

"He was poisoned. He ingested enough potassium cyanide

to lose consciousness before he could call for help and died almost immediately."

"So it really was murder." I sank onto the couch cushions again. "Now all we have to do is figure out who bought the poison? Can it be that easy?"

Jawarski laughed. "I'm afraid not. It's not common, but there was a supply at the theater. Apparently, they use it when the want to make plaster look like gold."

"So anyone at the theater could have gotten to it?"

"That's what I'm told."

"That doesn't help Richie much, does it?"

"Unfortunately, no," Jawarski said. "How are he and Dylan holding up?"

"Shaky. They've lost every reservation they had for Valentine's Day, and when I went over there this morning the inn was empty. Not a single guest anywhere."

Jawarski whistled softly. "In the middle of ski season? That's not good. Maybe some unsuspecting person from out of town with a pressing need to slalom will check in."

"We can only hope." I carried the phone into the kitchen and dug around in the fridge until I found a can of Pepsi buried under the leftovers. "Meanwhile, I'm no closer to figuring out who killed Laurence. Did Nate tell you if they're considering any other suspects? Or are they completely focused on Richie?"

"They're doing their jobs, Abby. Have a little faith. They'll get it right. Svboda's a decent cop. He knows the job."

"And *I* know *him*. Just do me a favor. Don't tell him about Serena and Laurence. That's just between us for now."

"You're asking me to withhold information that may be material to a murder investigation?"

"I'm asking you, as my . . . friend . . . to keep it quiet. At least until we know for sure whether it had any bearing on the murder."

"I'm a police officer, Abby. I have responsibilities."

"Yeah, but you're not on duty. You're not even in the jurisdiction."

"That doesn't matter. I can't just take the job off like a coat. I'm a cop now, today, this minute, not just a cop tomorrow when I get back to town. It doesn't work that way."

Jawarski and I have these discussions all the time. Usually, I'm not bothered by the sounds of frustration or irritation in his voice, but that's when we're face-to-face. Communication loses a lot in translation over the phone, and it's even worse through e-mail or—shudder—text messaging. Suddenly, I needed to be in the room with Jawarski, looking into his eyes, watching him half smile even while making noises that indicated deep annoyance. The noises by themselves were a little frightening.

So frightening, I changed the subject and spared us both. "So when are you leaving there? It will have to be soon if you're going to be back by Wednesday."

"Yeah. About that."

That didn't sound promising. My appetite faded abruptly and cold dread sat like a stone beneath my heart. "About what?"

"I'm going to be delayed a couple of days. Cheyenne's got the flu, and she doesn't want me to leave. Bree's working part-time now, so it'll be good if I can stay here with Chey while she's out of school."

"Oh." It was all I could manage. Even that word felt heavy and hard to get out.

"She's got a fever. Last night, we even talked about taking her to the emergency room."

We. That nasty, jealous part of me lifted her head and smiled knowingly. I tried to shove her back down, but she put up a fight. "Is she doing better tonight?"

"A bit, but she's still pretty sick. I can't leave until I know she's going to be okay."

My rational side understood, and even applauded his decision. If I'd had children of my own, I'd want their father to do the same thing. Every kid deserves to be loved that much. I gave my irrational side another shove and hoped Jawarski couldn't hear her in my voice. "No, of course not. I'm sure Cheyenne will feel a lot better having you there."

"She seems to," he said. "I have to admit, it does my old ego good. Anyway, I talked to the chief tonight, and I'm cleared from duty for the rest of the week. I may not need to stay that long, but you never know."

"Take your time," I urged. "We'll be here when you get back."

We spent another minute or two saying good-bye, and this time Jawarski avoided the *L* word like he would the plague. I should have been pleased, but as I tossed the rest of my pizza to Max and scuffed down the hall to get ready for bed, I realized that I was anything but. I didn't want to feel pressured into saying that I loved him, but now that *he'd* said it once, I was going to notice every time he didn't say it in the future.

I burrowed under the blankets and tried not to think about Jawarski, Laurence, or Richie. But I had a feeling that sleep would be a long time coming.

Chapter 26

The rapidly approaching holiday made it impossible to slip away the next day, but the first chance I got after closing, I headed straight for the Playhouse. I was sure that the police had already confiscated the poison, but now that I knew for certain that someone had killed Laurence on purpose, I was more determined than ever to figure out who the killer was. It would have been bad enough for Richie to be convicted of manslaughter. First degree murder was another story, entirely.

The fact that the potassium cyanide had been sitting on a shelf just begging to be used opened the doors wide open on the suspect list. I didn't have to figure out who was capable of calculating the trajectory of a wildly swinging spotlight and shoving Laurence into its path at precisely the right moment. I didn't have to figure out who was strong enough or agile enough to crawl around inside the fly system to cut the safety cable. I just had to find someone capable of opening a jar.

Easy, right? Like taking candy from a baby.

Vonetta and Alexander were in a meeting with the sound crew when I got there, so I decided to look around a little on my own. I was sure the police had gone through Laurence's office already, but there might be a few interesting things lying around that could give me some idea. A little gilt statue tucked conveniently inside someone's coat pocket or an electroplating set left in an open duffel bag—*something* to point me toward the last person who'd dipped into the potassium cyanide. Maybe I'd take a quick look at Alexander's office while I was at it . . . since he was otherwise occupied, and all.

I had no idea what excuse I'd give if someone asked what I was doing. I counted on myself to be clearheaded and brilliant enough to come up with something if I needed to. Crossing my fingers that the back rooms of the theater were either deserted or bustling with activity, I cut through the rehearsal hall and tried to look as if I had something important to do. It didn't matter to me which, as long as I could slip in and out of rooms, workstations, and offices without anyone taking notice.

I checked the call-board to see who was scheduled to be in the theater and breathed a sigh of relief when I saw that the only thing scheduled that evening was the meeting in Vonetta's office. That didn't mean no one else was there, but chances were good that I'd have time to look around.

Calculating that I had about fifteen minutes to call my own, I hurried toward the shop area. I checked the prop shop first, reckoning that if the potassium cyanide had been used to turn cheap props into gold, it was a good place to start. I found a couple of plaster rocks, the façade of a mountain cabin, some pirate-wear, and an eye patch, but nothing that screamed "property of a murderer."

I nosed around through the paint shop, the lighting shop, and the sound shop, but everything I found looked innocent to me. Knowing that I was running out of time, I abandoned the shop area and headed for Laurence's office. I had one hand on the doorknob when the sound of furtive footsteps reached me from somewhere nearby.

My heart shot into my throat, and instinctively I ducked behind the long rack of costumes pushed up against the wall. A second later, Colleen Brannigan came around the corner. With a silent laugh at my own foolishness, I started to climb out from behind the rack when Colleen paused and tilted her head to listen. She glanced over her shoulder, as if she worried that someone might see her, and I decided to stay right where I was.

Hoping she wouldn't notice me hiding, I shrank deeper

into the shadows. My arm brushed a spider web, and I fought to suppress a shudder. I'm not afraid of much, but spiders are right up there on the top of my short list. I closed my eyes and tried to calm the rapid-fire beating of my heart. Told myself I wasn't trapped in a dusty old corner that had been left to the spiders for too long.

Dust rose up from something I touched and tickled my nose. I held my breath and willed the sensation away, but it was no use. The battle to avoid sneezing made my eyes water, and I was breathing so loud, it was a miracle Colleen didn't hear me.

She crept toward the small room that had been Laurence's office and let herself in the door. All those high school memories made it hard to think of her as a possible murderer, but now, here she was, sneaking around like . . . well, like me. Only I didn't think she was there to clear someone else's name.

After glancing around once more to make sure she wasn't being watched, she disappeared inside the room and closed the door behind her. I dashed out from behind the wardrobe rack and brushed wildly at my clothes and hair to make sure I hadn't brought any crawling friends with me.

Once I was reasonably sure that I was alone, I tiptoed across the prop room and put my ear to the door. I heard drawers opening and closing, and paper rustling as Colleen searched for something. From the sounds of it, she was conducting a pretty frantic search, too. But what was she looking for?

I considered knocking on the door, but if I interrupted her before she was finished, she'd only lie again. I'd have a much better chance of learning the truth if I let her find it first.

I made myself comfortable on a rolled-up rug and waited for about ten minutes until the door opened. Colleen inched outside, pulled the door shut with a soft click, and turned. When she saw me sitting there, she gasped and one hand flew to her chest. She recovered quickly, and laughed as if I hadn't just caught her rifling through a dead man's office.

"My gosh, Abby, you scared me half to death. What are you doing?"

"Waiting for you."

"For me? Why?"

I stood and put myself at eye level with her. "What were you looking for in there?"

"In there?" She bought a second by glancing over her shoulder at the office door. "Oh, Laurence's office? Vonetta asked me to look for his copy of the script." She looked down at her empty hands and back up at me. "It wasn't there."

"Really? Vonetta sent you to look? Then why were you hiding?"

The smile slipped from her face, and she tried to step around me. "I wasn't hiding."

"I saw you go inside, Colleen. I sat here while you ransacked the office. You weren't looking for a script."

"You don't know that."

"You're right, I don't. But Vonetta does. Should we ask her?"

Colleen's shoulders slumped and resignation darted across her face. "No, let's not."

That's what I thought. "You want to tell me about it?"

"Not particularly."

"Then let me guess. Laurence had something of yours and you want it back. What was it? Pictures?"

Her eyes flashed fire. "Why don't you mind your own business?"

"This *is* my business," I said. "I don't like it when people frame my friends for murder."

"I didn't kill Laurence," she snarled, "and I would *never* frame an innocent person."

"Then what are you looking for?"

She glared at me for a long time. Maybe she could tell that I wasn't going to back down. Maybe she sensed my desperation to clear Richie. Whichever, she let out a sigh heavy with resignation and said, "Letters. I wrote them years ago. I thought they were gone until I took this job and found out Laurence still had them."

I didn't know whether to be disappointed in her or happy to find someone else with a motive. "So Doyle is right. You and Laurence *were* lovers."

"Yes, but a long time ago. Ten years. Doyle and I were going through a rough patch. I was young and unhappy, and Doyle seemed so dull and ordinary . . . I was convinced I'd made a mistake marrying him."

"So you did cheat on him."

Her head drooped. "Laurence and I were in a production together. He was everything Doyle wasn't. Young. Handsome. Exciting. He'd just booked a job as a producer on a production in Seattle and that seemed so exotic to me—" She broke off and flushed with embarrassment. "I know. It sounds silly now. And it didn't take long to figure out that I wasn't the only woman he was seeing, or that he didn't really care about me. I ended the affair after about six weeks, but it lasted long enough to give him ammunition."

"He was threatening to share the letters with Doyle?"

She nodded miserably. "I begged him not to, but he was such a bastard, he wouldn't listen."

"What did he want for them?"

"That's just it. He didn't want anything. He just wanted to make me miserable. It would have given him great pleasure to rip my marriage apart."

"Why would he do that if he didn't care about you?"

"Because Laurence didn't like losing. It wasn't that he cared so much about me, but he did care about being the winner, and he was very protective of his reputation. He had to be the one who called the shots, and he never forgave me for dumping him. If I'd been patient a few more weeks, he would probably have tossed me aside, and that would have been that."

I wasn't so sure about that. Any man who'd hang onto love letters that had no sentimental value for ten years was probably much more ruthless than she gave him credit for. "Did you find them?"

She shook her head again. "I don't know where they are. If the police find them before I do, Doyle will leave me."

"If it's been ten years—"

"Doyle will understand?" Colleen cut me off with a harsh laugh. "Get real, Abby. Would *you* understand?"

She had me there. "No, I probably wouldn't."

"I didn't kill him, Abby. I swear it on everything that's important to me. But now that he's dead, I want those letters before someone else finds them. I can't let Doyle find out *now*. It would ruin everything. Promise me you won't say anything to anyone. Please."

What could I say to that? We'd been friends once, and I wanted to believe that she was telling me the truth. Did she love Doyle? I thought she did. Yeah, maybe he deserved to know the truth. But after this long, what good would revealing it do?

"I won't say a word," I promised. "As long as you're telling the truth, and those letters aren't connected to the murder. If you're lying to me, all bets are off."

I hoped I wouldn't regret my decision, but I couldn't help thinking that Colleen had bigger things to worry about than my mouth. If she and Laurence had been lovers once, chances were Geoffrey Manwaring knew about their relationship. And I was pretty sure he had the letters she was looking for, and if he did, there was no telling what he'd do.

Chapter 27

❦

I didn't think much about the murder for the next two days. Hearts and candy took all my attention and every waking hour. Luckily, I didn't have much time to think about anything else either, including the fact that I would be spending Valentine's Day alone after the shop closed. When the thought did cross my mind—which was inevitable, considering the nature of the holiday and the looks Karen and Liberty gave me when they thought I wasn't looking—I consoled myself with the fact that I had Max. He's warm, attentive, and completely devoted. Who could ask for anything more?

Karen and Liberty drove me crazy, chattering under their breath about their holiday plans with Sergio and Rutger whenever they thought I couldn't hear them. I did my best to ignore their conversations, but I wasn't sure which were worse: the whispers, or the sudden silence when they realized I'd come up behind them.

Wyatt came by after work both days and helped with all the grunt work behind the scenes, while I helped wait on the last few frantic customers who raced through the front door in a mad search for that perfect gift. One that looked as if they'd put hours of thought into their choice. And yes, you're right. They were mostly men.

By evening on Valentine's Day, business finally began to slow down. Wyatt left. Walk-in traffic slowed to a trickle, and I sent Karen and Liberty home so they could enjoy their own romantic evenings. Bone-weary and, frankly, tired of people, I closed up the shop at eight and climbed the stairs to my apartment.

My date was waiting for me at the kitchen door, ears perked, tail wagging, and bits of wicker clinging to his nose and mouth. In the living room, I found the remains of a basket that had once held a handful of magazines. The magazines themselves were mostly intact, even if several of them had teeth marks in the corners and two were missing their covers.

Okay, so Max isn't perfect. But at least he doesn't shack up with his ex-wife under the pretense of checking on his kids. Was I bitter? Hurt? Angry? Yes, to all of the above. Did I really think Jawarski was playing around with Bree behind my back? I wasn't sure. Did I trust him? Apparently not. Or maybe it was myself I didn't trust. Roger had been carrying on with Bimbette for a long time before I caught him, and that was the problem.

I should have known. I should have seen signs. I'm sure I *did* see signs. But I'd ignored them. And now I was terrified that if I let myself fall in love again, I'd become complacent again, and I'd miss something vital to my peace of mind. As a result, I was suspicious of everything.

I hated feeling that way, but I couldn't just flip a switch and feel something else.

Grumbling under my breath, I picked up the tattered magazines and swept up the bits of wicker scattered all over the apartment. I dumped the trash into the can and sat on the couch to discuss dinner plans with Max. He'd grown bored with my cleanup efforts and had turned his attention to something more interesting. All I'm going to say is that it involved licking.

On second thought, maybe Max wasn't the ideal partner. I'd have to work on that switch-flipping idea.

I wasn't in the mood for fast food, but I wasn't up to having dinner solo at any of Paradise's restaurants. Not tonight. I could call for pizza or Chinese delivery, but I couldn't face the possibility of looking pathetic to the delivery person. I was far too hungry to go to bed without putting something in my stomach, and my kitchen was bare, so that left Burger King.

Yeah, I know a Whopper alone has enough fat and calories for a full day's supply, but I didn't care. Those are what make it such terrific comfort food. Max and I hurried down the stairs, climbed into the Jetta, and set off for the north end of the valley. Paradise might be growing, but so far we've managed to keep fast-food restaurants and chain stores from reaching the downtown business area. You can find either if you want them badly enough, but you'll have to drive to do it.

I wasn't the only person in Paradise without a date. At least a date willing to spend more than twenty bucks on the evening. The line at Burger King wrapped around the building—lots of folks otherwise occupied on a night meant for love.

Waiting in the exhaust-filled procession left me way too much time to think, and my thoughts wandered about wildly. By the time I shoved money through one window and had food shoved into my car through another, I'd decided against going home to eat in my empty apartment. Instead I pointed the Jetta toward Jawarski's house.

I told myself that I was only going to take in his mail and make sure everything was still secure, but I found myself wondering if he had any pictures of Bree hanging around— you know, for the kids. Or not.

It was crazy. I knew it was, even while I was gathering his mail and slipping on the ice that had formed on the driveway. I told myself to get a life as I turned the key in the lock, and again when I flipped on the light in the kitchen. I even managed to wolf down the Whopper and fries and toss the trash before I walked into the living room and started snooping.

Let me set the record straight by saying that I would *kill* Jawarski if I found him nosing around through my stuff. I'd end our relationship *right now* if I found out he suspected me of cheating on him. And I do not consider myself a crazy person—usually.

But the fact that I considered for one minute digging through his things so I could see his ex-wife just proves that I was in the grip of a major bout of insanity. Fueled, I'm sure, by all the hearts and romance talk I'd been forced to endure for the past few days. Believe me, it would have driven anyone over the edge.

I scanned the bookcase on the first floor and found only three rows of paperbacks with words like *Ops* and *Conspiracy* and *Prey* in the titles. I was halfway to the second when my cell phone chirped. I dug it out of my pocket, checked the caller ID, and froze. I waited so long to answer, I thought I might have missed the call, but I finally flipped the phone open and croaked, "Hello?"

"Happy Valentine's Day." Jawarski's voice sounded warm and intimate, and I felt about an inch tall.

I turned around and sank onto a step, confusing Max in the process. He nudged past me and found his way to the bathroom where the seat was up. I could tell, even from a distance.

"Thanks." My throat was tight with embarrassment, but I managed, I think, to sound almost normal. "Same to you."

"Miss me?"

I thought about saying no, but I was in his house, digging through his stuff, looking for a photo that would either set my mind at ease or make me even crazier. "Yeah," I admitted. "I do."

"Hey, listen, I'm sorry I can't be there tonight. I really wanted to do something great, just the two of us."

"I'm sorry, too," I said, and the honesty made my stomach hurt. "But you're there with the kids. That should be fun if Cheyenne's feeling better." You have to understand that I'm not against honesty. I'm just against opening myself up for heartache. And lowering my defenses for this guy would open me up in a big way. I'd been fighting it for almost two years, and look where that had gotten me.

"She's a lot better," he said. "I should be able to leave soon."

Soon. I closed my eyes, hoping that not looking at his apartment would let me pretend to be somewhere else. "That's good to hear."

"So what are you doing tonight without me?"

"I'm . . . uh. I'm at your place, actually. Bringing in the mail."

"Really? So what are you wearing?"

I laughed in spite of my discomfort. "Trust me, you don't want to know. It's been a rough few days."

"I'm sorry to hear that. Are you going out with friends . . . or anything?"

I nearly swallowed my tongue. It almost sounded as if *he* was jealous. "No, I picked up a burger and fries on the way here. When I leave, I'm going home. Max and I will probably catch some TV before bed. How's that for exciting?"

"You're disappointed."

"About what?"

"I should be there. We should be heading out somewhere romantic. Seeing what the evening brings. Maybe even talking about a romantic breakfast in the morning."

I'd been railing against the whole Valentine's Day idea for days, but suddenly the thought of a romantic dinner didn't sound so bad. Of course, I'm also a notorious chicken, so the idea of dinner *and* breakfast was a lot less scary when he was nine hundred miles away.

"It's fine," I told him. "I'm not disappointed. You're where you need to be."

"You're sure?"

"I'm sure."

And I was. When we hung up a few minutes later, I walked down the stairs and out the door. My insecurities might rise up to bite me again one of these days, but at least for tonight they were under control.

I gave Karen the day after Valentine's Day off. She'd worked hard, and she deserved a day to recuperate. While

Liberty restocked shelves, I spent the day gleefully pulling down hearts from the walls and ceilings, paying bills, and planning candy production for the next few days.

The call-board at the Playhouse had me scheduled for a run-through of the script with the entire cast that evening, so whenever Liberty wasn't chattering about her romantic evening with Rutger—dinner at Gigi, drinks and dancing afterward—I thought about the murder. Unfortunately, I didn't come up with anything useful. Alexander's rivalry with Laurence hadn't produced anything interesting. I believed Colleen's story. And Serena's. Uncle Whit backed up Doyle's alibi, and I was convinced that Richie was innocent.

That left Vonetta. And a cast of about twenty people. And a stage crew of at least that many, none of whom had any reason I knew of to want Laurence out of the way. I wondered if the police had anything more concrete than I did, and wished Jawarski was home so I could ask. Of course, that wasn't the only reason I wished Jawarski home, but that's enough about *that*.

Business was so slow, I let Liberty go home early, and then locked up promptly at seven. Max and I set off a few minutes later. We took the stairs that cut through the middle of the block downhill to Ski Jump and grabbed two Philly steak sandwiches and coffee at the deli. With food in hand, we cut through the narrow slip of land between Walgreens and the travel agency on our way to the Playhouse.

After settling Max in the box office with one sandwich and a bowl of water, I hurried to the rehearsal hall where the rest of the cast was already gathered. I'd expected to walk in late, so I was surprised to find that the read-through hadn't started. A few people milled about the room aimlessly. Others sat on folding chairs in a loose semicircle, contributing to the low buzz of conversation.

Richie sat on a seat at one of the tables, talking quietly to Rachel. I nodded to Paisley and Serena, who were both on the other side of the room, and slid onto an empty chair between Rachel and Richie. "I can't believe I made it in time,"

I said as I shook off my jacket. "I was sure you'd have started already."

Richie looked pretty scaled down that night in black jeans, black T-shirt, a short white denim jacket, and classic black and white Chucks. I was so glad to see him up and dressed, my heart did a little skip-hop. But Rachel was ready for her close-up in black slacks, a black turtleneck, a plum leather jacket, and stiletto boots. Sitting between them, I felt like a plate of yesterday's leftovers. It's a good thing I like them both so much, or I'd have to find other friends.

Rachel rolled her head toward Alexander, who was answering questions for a couple of cast members. "He's so pissed. We should have started at least fifteen minutes ago, but Colleen's not here yet."

Considering everything that had happened around the Playhouse lately, the news made me uneasy. "Has anyone heard from her?"

"She's here somewhere," Richie said. "She came in right behind me. She's just not *here*."

That made me feel a little better, but it didn't completely erase my concern. "Has anyone gone to look for her?"

Rachel shook her head. "Alexander goes ballistic when anyone tries to leave the room. He says we all have to be here when she finally decides to join us."

I got to my feet again. "Well, I'm not just going to sit here. Something could be wrong." I took off for the door that led to the shop area.

Richie scrambled after me. "I'm coming with you."

Alexander bellowed as we darted from the room, but we both ignored him. I couldn't just sit around doing nothing while Colleen was missing.

Richie's not exactly fighting material, and normally I wouldn't expect him to be of much use if a vicious killer was lurking somewhere in the bowels of the building. But I was ridiculously glad not to go searching for Colleen on my own, and with his life and his future on the line, he had added incentive to be tough.

As it turned out, it took about thirty seconds to find Colleen—laid out on the floor near her workstation in the shop area. Jason knelt beside her, gently patting her face as he tried to rouse her.

My heart shot straight into my throat when I saw them. "What happened? Is she all right?"

Jason glanced back at me, panic written all over his face. "I don't know. She's breathing, but she was like this when I found her."

Richie dug his cell phone from a pocket. "I'll call the paramedics."

"I think she's coming around. Maybe we should find out what happened first." Jason focused his attention on Colleen as her eyelids fluttered, then slowly opened. She answered a few questions, insisted that she was fine, and Jason helped her sit, using a nearby box as support.

I tried to be patient, but I was dying to know what had happened. If she'd been attacked, we were losing precious seconds while her attacker got away. I hunkered down in front of her and said, "We're going to call an ambulance, but while we're waiting for them, do you feel up to answering a few questions?"

Colleen started to shake her head, but almost immediately winced in pain and stopped moving. "Don't call. I'm fine."

"You could be hurt," I told her.

"I'm *fine*," she said again. "If you call the paramedics, Doyle will hear about it, and that will upset him."

Point taken. "Okay, but I want you to promise that if you notice any side effects, you'll have someone take you to a clinic."

She closed her eyes briefly and inched her head downward. "Of course."

It wasn't the ideal situation, but she was sitting up and talking, and she seemed lucid, so I wouldn't pressure her into anything that might cause problems in her marriage. "Can you tell me what happened?

"I wish I knew." She touched the back of her head gingerly and glanced at her fingertips as she pulled her hand away. "No blood," she said with a sigh of relief. "Thank heaven for small favors." She shifted to make herself more comfortable. "I came back here to get my prompt script before the meeting. I heard a noise, and before I could turn around to see what it was, somebody hit me. That's all I know."

Jason looked outraged. "This is the third attack on someone in this production. What's going on around here? Is somebody trying to shut us down, or what? Are any of us safe?"

"I wouldn't worry too much," I reassured him. "The attacks do seem random, but I don't think they are."

"Why not?"

"It's just a feeling I have." In an effort to keep his mind occupied with something more productive, I suggested, "Could you find something for Colleen to drink? There should be water in the green room."

He stood uncertainly, but he finally grabbed Colleen's mug from her table and started away. That ought to keep him busy for three or four minutes.

"When you think you can stand, we should probably make sure nothing's missing," I told Colleen.

Panic flooded her face. "Is my prompt script there? We can't do anything without it, and there's no way I could re-create it."

Richie hurried toward her makeshift desk. "What does it look like?"

"It's a three-ring binder, about this thick." Colleen held up her fingers to illustrate. "It has everything in it—all my notes on blocking, and the cues for lights and sound. If that's missing, it will be a disaster."

Richie lunged at something on the table's far corner and held up a thick binder. "Is this it?"

Colleen looked so relieved, I thought she might cry. "Yes! Thank you." She held out her hands and cradled it against her chest, but her smile faded quickly. "Who would do something like this? What did *I* do?"

"Good question. Can you think of anything you've said

or done in the past few days that might make someone want to hurt you?"

"I don't think so."

"Have you seen anything that felt unusual to you? Overheard a conversation you weren't meant to hear? *Anything*?"

She shook her head as Jason loped back into the room with a bottle of water. He held it out to her, and she took it with trembling hands.

His eyes latched onto her hands. "You're shaking. I think we should call your husband."

"No!" She must have realized how strident her response sounded because she forced a smile. "My husband is busy. I don't want to disturb him."

"But if you're hurt—"

Colleen uncapped the bottle and sipped, but the look on her face made it clear she wasn't happy with him for pushing. "Back off, Jason. I don't need you worrying about me."

Her response surprised me, but then, she had just been hit on the head, and she was in obvious pain.

"I'm just trying to help," Jason said.

"Well, I don't need your help. Frankly, the way you're always hovering gives me the creeps. Now would you *please* just back off?"

Jason stepped back, hands in the air as if she'd pulled a gun on him. "I just thought—"

"Well, *don't* think," Colleen snarled. "You're a stagehand. *I'm* the stage manager. And I don't need you to make yourself feel important by sticking your nose into things that are none of your business."

Jason fell back a step. He looked so wounded, I felt sorry for him.

Richie did, too, I could tell by the look on his face. He took Jason by the shoulders and led him away from the desk. "I know you're trying to help," he said quietly, "but she's really upset. Laurence's death has us all jumpy. I think maybe you should just, you know, give her some space. Once Abby figures out who really killed Laurence, we'll all be able to get back to normal."

"Isn't that dangerous?" Jason squeaked.

"It might be," I admitted. "But what's the alternative? I can't just sit back and let someone frame Richie for murder. If this keeps up, Vonetta will have to shut down the production, and then she'll suffer, too. And sniping at each other isn't going to help anybody. Let's just try to hang on for a couple of days, until I can figure out who's behind this."

Jason bobbed his head. "I need this job, too, you guys. I don't want the production shut down."

Colleen rolled her eyes. "No one wants the production to shut down. And that's all the more reason not to make a big deal out of what just happened to me. If those people out there find out there's been another attack, I'm afraid we'll lose most of them to panic."

Richie folded his arms across his chest and scowled at all three of us. I could see the argument play out on his face—concern for his castmates at war with his instinct for survival. His fear of the potential danger at odds with his need to find some normalcy in his world again.

"Fine," he said at last. "We'll just tell them the prompt script was missing. That should explain why we've been back here so long."

"What should explain?"

I think Alexander's voice startled us all, but maybe me most of all. I whipped around and found Vonetta and Geoffrey a few feet behind him. Luckily, the rest of the cast had stayed in the rehearsal hall so we could still avoid mass panic, but I wondered how long they'd been standing there, and how much they'd overheard. And, of course, I wondered which of them had thumped Colleen on the back of the head.

Chapter 28

Four hours later, I collapsed onto a folding metal chair with a groan. Colleen sat next to me and stuck her feet out in front of her as the last few cast members straggled out the doors.

"How are you feeling?" I asked when we were finally alone. It had been a grueling read-through, thanks to Alexander's foul mood. He'd been anything but patient as we ran through the script, snapping at every mistake, yelling at every missed cue. He'd stormed back and forth along the length of the table, peering over shoulders and making us all so nervous half of the cast members could barely get through their lines.

When we finally reached the last scene of the second act, the cast evacuated so quickly it might have been comical if the whole situation hadn't been so frustrating. Empty soda bottles lay abandoned on the table, along with wrappers from fast food and snacks people had brought in with them. The room looked as if someone had thrown a party for a bunch of five-year-olds.

"I'm fine," Colleen assured me. "Really. I have a slight headache, but it's nothing that a few Tylenol can't handle. I'll just tidy up a bit and head home. I'm sure I'll be back to normal by tomorrow."

Exhausted from the week I'd had, I stuffed the notes I'd made into my script and picked up Max's leash. "You're not seriously going to clean up after those people. They're all adults. Make them do it when they come in tomorrow."

Colleen laughed and got to her feet. "I'm not going to

leave this mess for Vonetta to find in the morning. It'll only take a few minutes."

I thought she was being optimistic, but I made myself get up so I could help her. "Fine, but I draw the line at doing windows. If I stay much later, I'll fall asleep standing up."

Colleen waved me back toward the chair. "You don't have to help."

"Oh, yes I do. My mother raised me better than to sit here while you do all the work. I'll grab a garbage bag out of the supply closet."

"OK," she called after me, "and then I'll give you a lift home."

Old habits die hard, and one of mine is resisting any offer of help. "It's only a few blocks."

Colleen cut me off before I could even finish. "Don't be silly. It's nearly eleven, and it's probably ten below zero out. There's no reason for you to walk, and *my* mother raised me better than to send a friend off into the night when I have a perfectly good car."

We worked quickly, gathering trash, wiping away crumbs, and straightening chairs. Fifteen minutes later, Colleen stepped back and surveyed our handiwork. "Perfect. I'll just grab my purse and keys, and we'll get out of here."

The Playhouse seemed deserted as we hurried through the shop area to Colleen's workstation, but my imagination was out in full force. I thought I saw movement in every shadow and heard scuffling sounds every time one of us took a step. After making sure the lights were out in the back of the house, we cut through the auditorium to the box office, unchained Max, and stepped out into the bitter cold.

Colleen paused to lock the door behind us, and I shivered in a brutal gust of wind that subtracted at least ten degrees from the temperature. I huddled into my coat as I followed Colleen down the sidewalk. She turned down a narrow alley, deeply shadowed and much longer than I remembered it being. Way down at the other end, it opened into a parking lot that served a handful of businesses, including the Playhouse and a new coffee shop that appeared to be closed for the evening.

Colleen and I walked quickly, barely speaking except to mutter about the wind and the cold. As we reached the end of the alley, the dimly lit parking lot stretched out in front of us. It was nearly empty except for Colleen's 4Runner in the far corner and a couple of other cars that had been sitting long enough to have thick frost on their windows.

We took only a few steps toward the 4Runner when Max stopped walking and growled low in his throat. His ears perked straight up, which is never a good sign. Instantly alert, I glanced at the deserted buildings that surrounded us and, more importantly, at all the unlit spaces between them. All that empty space suddenly felt ominous and Max's agitation made my nerves twitch.

The dog's hackles rose. He strained at his leash, and I argued with myself about the wisdom of letting him go. If someone was out there and meant us harm, Max might protect us. On the other hand, he might just take off at a dead run, the way he sometimes did. I was in no mood to chase him through town.

"What is it, boy?" I asked softly. "Is somebody out there?"

"I don't like the sound of this," Colleen whispered. The panic on her face was as clear as my own must have been. "Come on. Let's go."

She didn't have to tell me twice. I tugged on Max's leash and we ran toward her car. She'd parked at the far end of the small parking lot, in a corner swathed in menacing shadows. Tonight, the gloom wasn't half as threatening as whatever had Max upset. I ran as fast as I dared, nearly losing my footing twice on icy patches I couldn't see. The parking lot wasn't big, but my lungs burned even before I reached the end of the row. The result of sucking in so much cold air, I guess. And a serious lack of running on a regular—or even an irregular—basis.

Colleen aimed her key chain at the 4Runner and the lights flashed as the locks switched. While Colleen raced for the driver's side, I urged Max into the backseat, shut the door, and reached for the front door. As my fingers brushed the door handle, something hard and heavy slammed into the back of my head and neck. Pain shot up the back of my head and down my spine. My knees buckled, and I staggered beneath the impact.

Max went crazy inside the car, barking, growling, and clawing at the door and window. I tried to grab the door, but whatever it was hit me again. I felt the air leave my lungs, and felt myself drop like a sack of sugar to the ground. My forehead hit the pavement, and pain splintered into a million pieces. Clouds filled my vision. The shadowy figures of feet and legs moved away, but I couldn't tell whether my attacker was heading toward Colleen or away from us both.

Desperate to warn Colleen, I tried to shout, but the words caught in my throat. I willed myself to stand, but my arms wouldn't work, and my legs felt useless.

The sound of a scuffle reached me a few seconds later. A cry; the clatter of something heavy being thrown away; the sound of footsteps running in the opposite direction. He was gone, and I was alive.

But what about Colleen?

I lay there for a long time, trying to regain my equilibrium. When I could speak again, I called out for Colleen but she didn't answer. Twice, I tried to sit up, but my stomach lurched and I broke out in a cold sweat each time I lifted my head. Spots danced in front of my eyes, and I knew that the slightest exertion would make me pass out. In this cold, losing consciousness could be deadly, so I lay down on the icy ground and closed my eyes, hoping the dizziness would go away soon.

Max was still going crazy inside the 4Runner. His claws raking across the glass and his high-pitched whine were the only things I could hear. At least he'd stopped growling. I took that as a good sign.

At last, the dizziness began to pass and I dragged myself upright. Even then, I had to sit very still for a minute or two before I dared move again.

Standing was still more than I could handle, so I inched on all fours across the frozen ground and prayed that Colleen wasn't dead. I found her unconscious and bleeding from the nose and a long scratch on her face, but her heartbeat felt strong, and her breathing seemed steady.

Weak with relief, I leaned against the 4Runner and thanked anyone who might be listening that we'd both survived the attack. In that moment, it was enough.

Shivering in the cold, I cranked up the heater and held my hands over the defrost vents. A few minutes earlier, Colleen had pulled the 4Runner into the middle of the parking lot. From there we could see anyone approaching us long before they reached us. Maybe the attacker wouldn't come back, but I hadn't expected him to strike Colleen twice in one night, either.

I rubbed my hands together and huddled in my seat, keeping one eye on Colleen for signs of shock while we waited for the police to arrive. She hadn't argued with me about reporting this attack, but I knew she was dreading explaining what happened to Doyle. I sympathized, but this guy was becoming bolder all the time. Ignoring him wasn't going to make him go away.

Nate Svboda showed up about five minutes after the first officers arrived on the scene. He got out of his SUV, planted his fists on his hips, and looked around while a uniformed officer caught him up on the case. After a few minutes, he swaggered toward us, his face cold and hard and disapproving.

He opened my door and ran a look over first Colleen, then me. Neither that look nor the first words out of his mouth make me feel better. "So . . . you just can't keep your nose where it belongs, I see."

Every muscle in my body ached, and a whole lot of other parts as well. I wanted to give my statement and go home, not necessarily in that order. But my head was pounding too hard to give much attitude in return. "Maybe it's escaped your notice," I said, wincing with every word, "but we're the victims here. We were attacked, probably by the same person who killed Laurence Nichols."

Nate leaned against the door and shook his head. "So I hear. What'd you do to make him come after you?"

"We walked out of the building," I said. "I know, I know. I should have known better. Now will you please take our statements so we can go home?"

"Sure." He pulled a toothpick from his pocket, shoved it into his mouth, and spent some time getting it situated just right. "Jackson'll take your statements in just a minute," he said when he was comfortable again. "In the meantime, why don't you tell me what happened."

I told him the whole story, from the minute we left the Playhouse until we dialed 9-1-1. His scowl grew deeper with every new development, until I swear, the corners of his mouth were touching his chin.

"You get a look at the person who did this?" he asked when I finished talking.

"Unfortunately, no."

He glanced at Colleen, and she shook her head. "I didn't see a thing. He was so quick, I didn't even hear him coming."

"Male or female? Can you tell me that?"

"Male," I said, surprised at my certainty.

"That's what I think, too," Colleen put in. "He was strong. Really strong."

"Maybe, but whoever it was also had the element of surprise." Nate rubbed his chin and glanced at the narrow space between the Playhouse and the coffee shop. A couple of uniformed officers were going over the area with flashlights, but I didn't expect them to turn up much in the way of evidence. "You think that's where he came from?"

"It has to be," I said. "It's the only way he could have reached us without us noticing him. The parking lot was empty except for a couple of other cars."

Nate nodded thoughtfully. "Anything happen tonight that might have prompted the attack?"

I made eye contact with Colleen and silently urged her to

tell him about the first attack. If she didn't, I would. I think she knew that. Reluctantly, she nodded. "I think the same person attacked me before the cast read-through."

Nate's eyebrows winged upward in surprise. "Twice in one night?"

"It looks that way," I said.

"Sounds like you're lucky to be alive. Got any idea why this guy's after you?"

A shudder shook her. "No. It doesn't make any sense at all. I have no idea why anyone would want to hurt me."

Nate shifted the toothpick in his mouth and fixed on me next. "What about you, Abby? You got any ideas?"

"No, but there has to be *some* connection. What other plays have you worked on with Laurence?" I asked Colleen.

She looked surprised by the question. "I don't know. A few."

"Start with the most recent," Nate suggested.

It was my turn to be surprised. I think it was the first time in history he's acted as if any of my ideas had merit.

"There was a production at a theater in Vail a couple of years ago." Colleen sounded hesitant at first, but she rapidly warmed up to the idea. "It was *1776*. Laurence was musical director, I was assistant director."

That made me sit up and take notice. "*Two* years ago? I thought you hadn't seen him in ten years."

"I never said that," Colleen corrected me. "We worked together two or three times, we just didn't have much to do with one another. During the production in Vail, he was involved with someone and that took up a lot of his time."

I was pretty sure that wasn't the impression she'd given me the last time we talked about this, but I wasn't going to quibble. All I wanted was the truth. If Nate could get it and let me hang around to listen, more power to him.

"Anyone else from this group work on that one with you?" he asked.

Colleen brushed a lock of hair away from her forehead. "A couple of people from the cast look familiar. I don't know their names, but I can find out for you."

"Do that." Nate motioned for one of the uniformed officers to join us and take notes. "Anything unusual happen with that play?"

"Not that I remember."

"Okay." The toothpick shifted again. "What about before that?"

Colleen wobbled a little and leaned against the 4Runner to steady herself. "We worked together in Breckenridge a couple of years before that. He was in a lead role. I was casting director."

"Same questions," Nate prompted. "Anybody else from this group work on that one? Anything unusual happen?"

Colleen had to think about it for a minute. "Nobody that I can think of, but we did borrow some props from Vonetta. It was a production of *The Civil War*, and she ended up consulting on some of the scenes. She was there for a couple of weeks, I think."

My heart beat a little faster. For the first time since Laurence's murder, a couple of pieces actually fit together.

"Anybody else?"

Colleen shook her head. "I don't think so. I don't remember. And nothing unusual happened while we were in production, but one of the girls in the chorus found out she was pregnant right before our run ended, and I heard a few months later that another one committed suicide."

"How long afterward?" I asked. "Could it have been connected to the play in some way?"

"Oh no." Colleen looked shocked that I'd even suggest it. "It was months afterward, and I only heard about it through a friend I ran into somewhere. It had nothing to do with us."

"And the next one?" Nate prodded.

"Eight years ago. *Cinderella* in Estes Park. I don't remember anyone else being involved. This is a wild-goose chase." Nate didn't respond except to ask, "That the last one?"

Colleen started to nod, but stopped herself and flashed a look at me filled with misery. "Ten years ago in Aspen. *How to Succeed in Business without Really Trying.* Nobody else from this group involved, and nothing unusual." Nate checked with the officer to make sure he had everything written down, then released him to go back to whatever he'd been doing. "Doesn't seem like much to go on," he said, "but keep thinking." He actually patted her shoulder like a real person. "If you come up with anything, let me know."

"I will," Colleen promised, but I knew she'd never tell Nate about the real connection she had with Laurence. Nate would have felt honor-bound to tell Doyle. I knew Colleen would do almost anything to prevent that, but I also wondered whether Doyle had already put the pieces together. Because two attacks on the same person in one night . . . Well, that felt kind of personal to me.

Chapter 29

I called in sick the next day. The police had kept us in the parking lot until almost one A.M. taking our statements, and Nate had insisted that we go to an all-night clinic—the closest thing Paradise has to an emergency room—to make sure we were all right. He'd also dropped Max off at Karen's so he wouldn't be left in the cold while we were getting treatment, which was a thoughtfulness that surprised me. I wasn't surprised, however, to learn that he'd called Doyle to drive Colleen home, though I knew it worried her.

By the time Doyle drove off with Colleen and Officer Jackson retrieved Max from Karen's and helped me up the stairs to my apartment, the sun was already coming up. Too cold and tired to care about much, I crawled into bed still wearing my jeans and sweater and vowed to sleep all day.

I didn't manage to sleep *all* day, but thanks to the magic of the painkillers I'd been given at the clinic, I slept until the medicine wore off later that morning. Even before I opened my eyes, I knew I was in for a rough day. Pain throbbed from the back of my head to the spot behind my eyes, and the soreness in every other part of my body almost made me cry when I accidentally moved one leg.

Max inched up on the bed and looked me over. He was so concerned, I managed to get one arm working well enough to scratch between his ears. Poor guy. He'd tried to warn me. It wasn't his fault I hadn't paid attention.

I swallowed another pain pill and dragged my aching body into the bathroom. Against my better judgment, I checked my reflection in the mirror and winced. Bruises had formed beneath my eyes and on my left cheek. I was pretty sure I saw some on my neck, too, but I couldn't move my head to check. My head felt as if it had been split like a ripe melon, and my vision wasn't clear by a long shot.

Moving slowly, I managed to strip off my clothes and turn on the shower. Climbing into the tub and pulling the curtain shut behind me took a little longer. The hot water felt good at first, but when I turned to let the spray hit my back, I could have sworn the water evaporated and a thousand burning needles took its place.

I let out a cry that brought Max to his feet, and turned away from the water as quickly as I could. It just wasn't fast enough. I fumbled the water off and pushed the curtain open again, but by that time tears were streaming down my face. I just wasn't sure whether they were brought on by pain, fear, or anger at the person who'd attacked us.

As I stood there, trying to regain control over my emotions, a knock sounded on my front door. I was tired of wallowing in self-pity, so I shouted, "Just a minute," and hustled as quickly as I could to my bedroom. I tugged on an old pair of sweats that I found on my closet floor and pulled a soft old sweatshirt over my head, then hurried into the living room and threw open the front door.

Vonetta stood on my landing, looking as regal as ever in a long leather coat with matching hat, gloves, and scarf. "I heard what happened," she said. "May I come in?"

She'd barely said two words to me in days, so I didn't know what to expect. I nodded and stepped aside to let her in. After closing the door on the cold, I motioned her toward my sagging old couch. She sat at one end. I perched on the other.

Once there, I didn't know what to say to her. Had she come to yell at me for asking questions, or was she here as a friend? Almost as soon as I sat down, I was on my feet again and aiming for the kitchen. "Can I get you something to drink? I could put on a pot of Chocolate Mudslide or—"

She waved me back toward my seat. "Nothing for me,

thank you." And when I didn't disappear into the kitchen to make some for myself, "Sit down, please."

I returned to the couch and sat gingerly. I tried not to cringe, but judging from the frown that creased Vonetta's face, I knew I'd failed. "The police told me what happened, Abby. I came by to tell you how sorry I am. And, of course, to see if there's anything I can do for you."

"Why should you be sorry?" I asked. "You didn't do this."

"No, but I still feel responsible. Maybe if I'd been more careful this could have been prevented."

I sat back cautiously, testing the pressure of the couch against my back before I relaxed. It hurt, but the pain medication must have been working because the discomfort was bearable. "Why?" I asked. "What do you know that you haven't told me?"

"Nothing. You know about Serena's past."

I nodded. "She told me about the baby, and about the abortion. I'm sorry Vonetta, I know it must have hurt."

Vonetta nodded miserably. "I know I was rude to you, but I didn't want anyone else to find out. It wasn't personal. It's just all too painful for her, and it's too fresh for me. I can't talk about it yet." She crossed her legs carefully and smoothed her hands across her lap. "Laurence was a dreadful man, Abby. I didn't kill him. I want you to know that. But I'm not sorry he's dead."

I fell silent for a minute and let that hang in the space between us. It seemed so odd to hear Vonetta talking like that in her cultured, controlled voice I needed to process, I guess. "Tell me about the play you worked on with Laurence and Colleen in Breckenridge," I said at last.

She pulled back in surprise. "What play?"

"*The Civil War*. Colleen said that you loaned the theater some props and that you consulted for a couple of weeks."

"Gracious! I'd forgotten all about that. I really wasn't involved in that production. What makes you bring that up now?"

"There has to be a connection between the people who

have been attacked. You. Laurence. Colleen. So far, that's the only common thread I've been able to find."

"And you," Vonetta said. "Don't leave yourself off that list."

I lifted one shoulder carefully. "I think the attacker went after me because he knows I'm trying to catch him. The rest of you are a different story. Do you remember anything about that group of people? Anyone who was different, maybe? Did something happen that someone might be holding a grudge over?"

Vonetta's lips curved gently. "Against Laurence? I'm sure there was something. But Colleen and me? I don't know what it could be. I consulted on a couple of scenes. She was casting director, if I remember correctly. We had nothing to do with one another."

"There must be something," I argued. "Something that ties the three of you to the murderer. Otherwise, these are all just random acts of violence, and I don't believe that."

"What else could they be? There *is* no connection. Besides, every attack is different. The police said that Laurence wasn't just hit, he was poisoned. You're obviously hurt, and so is Colleen. I'm walking around with barely a scratch, and thank goodness none of us has been fed potassium cyanide."

She was right, but I still couldn't shake the idea that there was a connection. I just hadn't found it yet. And I had more questions to ask before she left. "I understand that Geoffrey Manwaring is refusing to let you use the music Laurence wrote for this production."

Vonetta rolled her eyes in exasperation. "Geoffrey's as miserable as Laurence was. I'm not a bit surprised that he's hanging on to those pieces to see what he can get for them."

"And is it definite? He inherits Laurence's estate?"

"As far as I know. The two of them worked together for years. I think he's the only person Laurence ever met he didn't alienate. They're two of a kind, that's for sure."

"So you're not upset about the music?"

Vonetta laughed softly. "I didn't say that. I'm just not surprised."

"Do you think Geoffrey could have killed Laurence to get his hands on the money?"

She tilted her head to one side, as if she hadn't considered that idea before. "Anything's possible. He's certainly capable of it. But unless the rumors are *very* well hidden, he's done quite well over the years. To the best of my knowledge, he didn't need the money. Without a desperate need, I just don't think he would have killed his only friend to get it."

Vonetta got to her feet and smiled down at me. "I don't want to keep you up. I just needed to see for myself that you're all right. And you might as well know that we're shutting down the production."

"Can you do that and survive? Financially, I mean."

She nodded. "I have insurance. It's not the greatest, and we're going to take a substantial hit, but we should be able to keep our heads above water if we're careful. Now rest so you can heal. Is there anything I can get you?"

I started to shake my head, but that only made the pain move forward further still. "No. I'm fine. I just need to sleep, I think."

Vonetta brushed a kiss to my cheek and walked to the door. "I want you to call if you need anything," she said, sounding more like herself than she had since she arrived. She paused with one hand on the doorknob and locked eyes with me. "Promise?"

"Sure." I'd made that promise before, but I'd never meant it. Unfortunately, I doubted I could get down the stairs and out the door on my own today. If I wanted anything to eat or drink, I was going to have to ask for help. And that wasn't all. I hadn't been able to take Max outside all day. So far, he'd been good about holding it, but sooner or later he was going to need a walk. Difficult as it was for me to let someone do things for me, for once I might be forced to make an exception.

Chapter 30

My back and neck were a little less sore by the next morning, but the bruises on my face and neck hadn't faded. If anything, they were darker and angrier than ever. There wasn't enough makeup in all of Paradise to cover the bruises and minimize the swelling.

Liberty came upstairs throughout the day to take Max for his walks, and Karen kept a watchful eye on the inventory in the store. Divinity was known for having fresh candy made daily, but I thought that staying out of sight for a few more days might be better for business than letting customers see a giant grape working in the kitchen.

Wyatt and Elizabeth stopped by that evening bearing a huge plate of cheese enchiladas, rice, and beans. Oh, and food for themselves, too. Wyatt even produced a six-pack. I knew I shouldn't have a beer on top of the pain medication but, let's face it, Mexican food is just not meant to be eaten without alcohol.

While I tried to find a comfortable way to sit at the table, Elizabeth bustled around the kitchen, gathering everything civilized people use when they eat. I didn't want to disappoint her, so I scooped an enchilada, rice, and beans onto the plate she gave me and pretended that I wouldn't rather eat straight out of the Styrofoam box.

Wyatt heaped his plate with smothered burritos and dug in. "You look like a Mack truck hit you," he said around a mouthful. "Any idea who did this to you?"

I shook my head gently. It didn't hurt quite so much tonight, but I wasn't sure whether that was because of the pain meds or the beer. "I didn't get a good look at him. In fact, I didn't get a look at all—except for his shoes, and I could barely see those."

Elizabeth spooned salsa onto a crisp taco and pushed the bowl to the center of the table. "You don't have any idea what kind of shoes he wore?"

"No, unfortunately." I filled my mouth with enchilada and closed my eyes in ecstasy over the spicy, cheesy goodness. When I could speak again, I admitted, "I'm not even absolutely certain the attacker was a man."

Glancing up sharply, Elizabeth said, "You think it could have been a woman?"

"I can't completely rule a woman out."

Wyatt pulled a longneck bottle from the six-pack and cranked it open. "Oh, come on, sis. You know who did it."

"No. No, I don't. As far as I can tell, nobody has a motive for any of the things that have been happening."

"You might not know his motive, but I'd say skipping town is a pretty good indicator that the director—what's his name? Allen Pastaroni?—did it."

My heart skipped a beat or two. "Alexander Pastorelli? He skipped town? When?"

"Nate says they went to talk to him about the attack, see where he was last night, that sort of thing. Funny thing, he wasn't anywhere to be found."

Elizabeth sent Wyatt the same kind of look she gave the boys when they were acting out. "Don't make it sound so mysterious, Wyatt. He checked out of his hotel early this afternoon, that's all. It's not as if he slipped off in the dead of night."

"Oh." A dull disappointment settled over me again. "We shouldn't be surprised, I guess. Vonetta closed down the production today."

"We shouldn't be surprised about that, either," Wyatt said as he forked up some rice. "If you ask me, it was way past time for her to cut her losses and walk away. Three people attacked? One dead? Time to give up."

"I suppose so," I said. "Alexander didn't waste any time getting out of town, did he?"

"No, he didn't." Elizabeth got up to grab the salt and pepper and carried them back to the table. "I guess we're a little too small-town for him these days."

"We've been too small for him for years," Wyatt muttered. "You ask me, he got too big for his britches a long time ago."

I didn't say anything to that, and neither did Elizabeth. My leaving town for the university had long been a bone of contention between my brother and me. It wasn't just me, either. Any time someone left Paradise to search for a bigger, broader life, Wyatt took offense. It was an argument we'd had too often, and one I didn't want to have again.

Keeping quiet isn't easy for me, but I'm learning. I concentrated on shoveling food into my mouth until Wyatt spoke again. "You don't think it was him?"

I glanced up and reached for the square of paper towel masquerading as a napkin by my plate. "Who? Alexander?"

"Yeah. The director. You're attacked one night, and he takes off the next day. Don't you think that sounds a bit fishy?"

He had a point. More importantly, he was trying to help. "What did Nate say?"

Wyatt's eyebrows scrunched together over the bridge of his nose. "You care about what Nate thinks? You musta been hit harder than I thought."

I grinned. "I didn't say *that*. I just wondered what his theory was. Does *he* think Alexander is the killer?"

Wyatt mopped chili verde from his mustache and leaned back in his chair. "No, he doesn't. He's still putting his money on Richie."

Elizabeth barked a disbelieving laugh. "He thinks Richie attacked Abby last night? Did he say that?"

"Didn't have to. I know how Nate thinks. He checked out the director fella's hotel room, but that's *all* he did. If it was me, I'd-a gone after Pastorelli. Caught up with him and asked him about last night. Nate didn't do that. Just chalked it up to the play closing and went back to the station."

I lowered my fork to the table and eyed my brother care-fully. As long as I could remember, he'd stuck up for Nate whenever I objected to something he'd done. This was the second time in a week he'd said something negative about his buddy. I wondered what was going on with them, but I decided not to ask. Another time, maybe. "Does anyone know where Alexander went?"

"Beats me," Wyatt said with a shrug. "Coulda gone home, I guess. Or off to New York so he could become a big Broadway . . . whatever."

"Well, he's gone now," Elizabeth said. "If he's the one responsible for what's been going on around here, he might just get away with murder."

"He will as long as Nate's in charge of the case," I muttered. "I suppose we'll never know what drove him to do it."

"Probably not," Elizabeth agreed.

Wyatt's only response was a low growl.

"Does that bother you?" I asked him.

"Hell, yes." He put his bottle back on the table with a bang. "Son of a bitch attacked my sister. I want his ass in jail where it belongs."

I wasn't sure which surprised me more, Wyatt's dissatis-faction with Nate or his defense of me. I know he loves me— that's never been a serious question. But our relationship hasn't always been easy, and I haven't always been sure that he *likes* me.

I nudged him with my shoulder. Pain shot up my neck, but I ignored it. It didn't seem to matter so much right then.

"Until Nate can find him and lock him up for good," Wyatt said, "I want you to be careful. Don't go out alone, okay?"

"Wyatt—"

"I'm serious, Abby. For once, don't argue with me."

"I'll be careful," I said, "but I can't promise that I won't go out alone. I live alone, remember? Besides, like you said, Alexander's probably long gone. I'm sure I'll be fine."

And I believed that I was. It just goes to show how wrong you can be.

I was still too sore the next morning to work and too bruised to put myself on display in the shop, so I spent the day lying around the house. I watched a few daytime talk shows, but that got real old, real fast. I tried reading, but I'd read every book on my shelves at least twice. The first time someone knocked on my door, I raced toward it eagerly. But when I checked the peephole and saw John Haversham standing on my porch, I decided Regis and Kelly weren't so bad after all. I ignored him and went back to the TV.

The second time Haversham came by, around noon, I avoided him again. And the three calls he made to my home number also went unanswered.

I'm sure some people would consider the attack on Colleen and me newsworthy, and I might even talk to him when I wasn't so loopy from the pain medication. But not now.

When I needed a break, I called Colleen to check on her. She was sore and bruised, as well, but Doyle was taking time off work to stay with her and she didn't sound concerned about having him around, so I told myself not to worry. I tried Jawarski's cell phone twice, but he didn't answer either time. I even called the police station for an update on the investigation into the attack, but all I got for my trouble was a brisk assurance from Nate that they were working on it.

Finally, just after sunset, I decided I couldn't stay locked up in my apartment any longer. Haversham or not, I needed fresh air. I needed to see people and eat food that hadn't been delivered by friends or family. And I needed some nice, thick foundation to help disguise the bruises on my face so I could go back to work. I couldn't take another day of this.

I wasn't up to walking with Max tugging at the leash, so I waited until Liberty came to get him, then slipped into boots with traction and a hoodie so I could hide my bruises and avoid the stares of curious passersby. After tucking a couple of twenties into my pocket, I made my way down the stairs and set a course for Walgreens.

A stiff wind had blown into the valley during the afternoon, and I shivered in the cold. The fresh air didn't clear my head completely, but it did chase away some of the clouds that had been hovering in my brain since the attack. I probably wouldn't feel normal again until the medication left my system.

Determined not to let the weather drive me back indoors just yet, I pushed through the rising wind. I'm not a fan of foundation and other heavy makeup, but at the rate my bruises were fading it would be weeks before I dared show my face. If I had to wait that long, I'd need intense therapy. Lots of it.

Inside the drug store, I pushed a cart resolutely toward the cosmetics aisle. I'm not a complete novice when it comes to makeup, but I stopped obsessing about my appearance when I divorced Roger and came home to Paradise. That's not to say that I don't want to look good, just that I don't feel the need to plaster my face with chemicals to do it. Give me a little eye shadow, some blush, and lip gloss and I'm good.

When I reached the pain killer aisle, I decided on a quick detour. I'd walked away from the clinic with enough pain medication to last for a few more days, but I couldn't work if I was taking it. Just as I started down the aisle, a hand brushed my shoulder. I cried out in surprise and spun around quickly.

"Did I startle you?" Paisley asked. "I'm sorry."

Relieved to see a friendly face, I managed a weak smile. "Sorry. I'm a bit jumpy, I guess."

"I'm not surprised. Being attacked the way you were. It's horrible." She studied my face and grimaced. "Gee, he didn't mess around, did he?"

If I hadn't known how bad I looked, I might have been hurt by her reaction. "No, he didn't."

"Are you okay? I mean other than the bruises and all? You're not seriously hurt?"

I shook my head. "No, I'm not. Just sore."

"Thank goodness for small favors. Do the police know who did it?"

"Not yet. But I think the fact that Alexander disappeared early the next morning says something."

"Alexander?" Paisley's mouth fell open in stunned silence. "You think *he* attacked you?"

"I think it's a strong possibility."

Paisley shook her head in disbelief. "That's just unbelievable. He seems so . . . normal."

"Yeah, well, a lot of criminals do." My stomach growled so loudly, I knew she could hear it. Guess I was hungrier than I thought. I was also weaker than I'd expected, and I knew my outing wouldn't be a long one. I mumbled something about talking to Paisley later and started away.

She came with me. "Did you say that Alexander's gone?" When I nodded, she frowned and asked, "Are you sure about that?"

"Nate told Wyatt and Elizabeth that Alexander had checked out of his hotel. Why? Have you seen him?"

"No. In fact, he wasn't at the theater today, but—" Paisley broke off with a shake of her head. "Nate has to be wrong. All of Alexander's stuff is still at the Playhouse. I can't imagine him leaving town without it."

I put the small bottle of ibuprofen back on the shelf and picked up the economy-sized bottle. "You're sure he left things behind?"

"Positive. Vonetta was complaining just this morning that he left his day planner in the rehearsal room again. And when I took it back to his office, all of his pictures were still on the desk."

I wheeled the cart slowly away from the painkillers and toward the makeup aisle. "I can't imagine him leaving those pictures behind," I said as we walked. "But I guess it's possible that he forgot them."

Paisley cut a questioning glance at me. "No. There's no way. Either he ran off and left them on purpose, or he didn't leave by choice."

Frowning thoughtfully, I stopped in front of the makeup display and studied the choices spread out in front of me. But my mind wasn't on the makeup any longer. "If he scurried off in the night, that could mean that he's the one who attacked us. And if not . . ."

"Then maybe he's another victim."

I didn't want to think about that possibility, but Paisley had a point. I wanted to believe that Alexander was the one who'd attacked Colleen and me, and I wanted to believe that the attacks and the murder were related, but assuming anything might be a mistake. "Is that where his day planner is now? In his office?"

Paisley nodded. "Why? Do you want to look at it?"

"If I can. Is Vonetta there now?"

"She went home about an hour ago," Paisley said, "but that's okay. We can go anyway." She pulled a key from her pocket and dangled it on her finger.

"Vonetta gave you a key?"

"I was part of the production team. I needed it for when she couldn't be there, and I haven't given it back yet. What do you say? Do you want to go?"

Forget the makeup. A chance to look through the theater without other people hovering was too good to pass up. I grabbed the ibuprofen from the cart and hurried to the cash register.

The wind had grown stronger in just the few minutes I'd been inside. We'd probably have snow by morning, but tonight bits of garbage and twigs blew down the streets and made it hard to see. I kept my head down and waited for a couple of cars to pass, then followed Paisley across the street to the Playhouse.

While she fumbled with the key in the lock, I stood on the sidewalk feeling a bit like a burglar. I didn't know how Vonetta would react if she learned that we were here without her, but I didn't have time to worry about that. Liberty would be back with Max any minute, so I promised myself that I'd look through Alexander's office quickly and get back home.

I felt a bit uneasy going into the Playhouse after hours

without Max, but if someone had helped Alexander disappear, his pictures and day planner might soon follow. If he had gone away on his own, they might hold a clue nobody had noticed yet. I didn't want to miss this opportunity.

After what felt like forever, Paisley finally got the key to work and we stepped inside. "Lock it again," I said when it looked as if she was going to walk away. "I don't want anybody sneaking in behind us."

Every building has its noises, and the Playhouse is no exception. But an unfamiliar building can sound downright freaky when it's deserted. Especially one where there's been a murder. Cutting through the auditorium or walking backstage would be the quickest routes to Alexander's office, but I wasn't in any hurry. I would have made myself get up on that stage for the play, but walking into the auditorium in the dark . . . it wasn't going to happen.

I jerked my head toward the rehearsal hall, and Paisley trailed me down the long hall. Judging from the look on her face, she wasn't any more eager to cut corners than I was. All around us boards creaked and walls popped as the building adjusted to the lowering temperature outside.

"This place is creepy when nobody's around, isn't it?" She spoke barely above a whisper, but her voice sounded unnaturally loud, and I realized that I was straining to hear anything out of the ordinary. A footstep. A hush of movement.

My heart hammered in my chest. Every groaning board, each gust of wind made me almost jump out of my skin. The attack had terrified me, and I was skittish as a result. And I sure wasn't eager to repeat the experience.

Inside the rehearsal hall, I fumbled for the lights. When I finally found the switch, I flipped on all four panels to chase the shadows from every corner, but Paisley grabbed my arm and whispered, "Don't turn them on. We don't want anyone to know we're in here snooping around."

My stomach dropped and an icy finger traced a line up my spine. I really didn't want to walk through the darkened Playhouse with only a few emergency lights to show me the way, but I wanted to alert the killer even less. Reluctantly, I turned off the lights again and took a couple of deep breaths to slow the pounding of my heart.

What if Alexander wasn't the killer? What if the real killer was here, hiding somewhere, waiting for another chance to finish the job he'd started? And, by the way, what was I doing, prowling around a deserted theater with only Paisley for protection?

I'd completely ignored Wyatt's warning, which is what I do, but I was putting Paisley in jeopardy. If I'd been thinking clearly, I never would have decided to sneak around like this. I blame the painkillers.

We inched through the shop area and finally reached the small room that had been serving as Alexander's office. I motioned Paisley inside, shut the door, and turned on the overhead light. "Nobody will be able to see the light with the door closed," I told her before she could protest.

Paisley was right, Alexander's possessions were all over the room. The cluster of pictures and the day planner on the desk. A sweater on a hook near the door. A pair of boots below that. His copy of the script, beginning to show signs of use. A digital camera on a shelf.

"See what I mean?" Paisley asked, hands on hips as she gazed around the office.

I really hoped that he'd run after the attack, but I had to agree. "It *does* seem odd that he left so much behind."

"Yeah. Wouldn't you think he'd at least take the camera? And the sweater. He could have taken those without making anyone suspicious."

But I was focused on something else. "If the boots are still here, that meant that he was wearing his street shoes when he left."

"Does that mean something?"

A gust of wind blew something against the side of the building. I swallowed my nervousness and said, "Maybe. Doesn't it seem odd? I mean, if you were going to hide between a couple of buildings in the middle of February waiting to attack somebody, wouldn't you put on boots first?"

"I might."

I shook my head quickly, ignoring the stab of pain in my neck. "You'd have to. Otherwise, the snow would make the bottoms of your shoes wet and you wouldn't have any traction. That's not a chance you'd take if you wanted to catch someone off guard and kill them, is it?"

"Maybe he didn't want to kill you. Maybe he just wanted to frighten you."

"Yeah. Maybe." I sat in Alexander's chair and opened his day planner, and Paisley's thoughtful expression morphed into eagerness.

"What are we looking for?"

"I don't know," I admitted. "Anything unusual." I checked the front of the planner first and found more pictures of Alexander with minor celebrities—most of whom looked familiar, but none of whom I knew by name. I found several credit cards and a few receipts. Nothing suspicious in any of those, at least not that I could see, although it seemed really odd that Alexander would leave the credit cards behind.

I leafed quickly through pages in the day planner. I found a few notations, but nothing out of the ordinary. A couple of doctor's appointments, some phone numbers, but that was about it. I didn't expect to find a notation to "buy potassium cyanide," but I was hoping for something that would tie the case up in a big red bow for me.

After a few minutes I sat the planner aside and moved on to the pictures on the desk. While Paisley rummaged through the desk drawers, I glanced at each photograph briefly, then removed the backs of the frames to see if there was anything incriminating there. It was a stretch, but since I had no idea what I was looking for, I might as well be thorough.

I was about halfway through the row when a face in one of the pictures caught my attention. Alexander stood in front of a group of people, proudly pointing toward the marquee. Laurence Nichols was in the picture with him, beaming at the camera with that charismatic smile that had captivated his fans. Between them stood two young women. I didn't think either of them could have been older than twenty. Alexander had an arm slung around the shoulders of a pretty brunette. Laurence clutched a grinning blonde to him, one hand on her butt in a gesture that seemed both provocative and possessive. But it wasn't any of those faces that caught my eye. It was a young man standing at the edge of a crowd behind them that made me look twice.

He couldn't have been more than fifteen or sixteen. A kid. But the look of hatred on his face froze everything inside me. "Look at this," I said, holding out the frame to Paisley. "Is that kid in the back who I think it is?"

She took the photograph and studied it for a minute. When she found the kid, her eyes snapped up to meet mine. "Jason Dahl?"

"It's him, isn't it?"

"If it's not, it's his twin brother." She handed the picture back to me. "I didn't realize he knew Alexander and Laurence. He never mentioned it."

"No, he didn't, did he?" My mind was racing as bits and pieces of the past few days came back to me. Jason had been there immediately after the murder, and also after every attack. He was young and strong, and he had easy access to anything Vonetta had here in the theater.

Who was he looking at with such hatred in the photograph? Alexander or Laurence? Jason had been carrying around a bitter hatred of one of them for the past . . . what? Seven or eight years, I calculated.

Eight years. What had Colleen said about the play she and Laurence worked on eight years earlier? One of the young women in the chorus had found out she was pregnant right before the play wrapped. Another had committed suicide a few months later.

I had a feeling I was looking at both of those young women right that minute.

Chapter 31

My heart was thumping so loudly, I could hardly hear myself think. Of everyone involved in the play, Jason was the last person I would have suspected of killing Laurence. He'd seemed so innocent, so eager to please.

This was it. This was the connection. But how did Jason factor in? Colleen would be able to tell me.

"Where's the nearest phone?" I asked as I shot to my feet.

"In the box office."

"Good. I need you to do something for me. I don't want to stay here much longer, but I need a photocopy of this picture. And can you find Colleen's number? Call her and ask about the two young women in Breckenridge. Ask her what they looked like, and ask her which one got pregnant, and which one took her own life. Got that?"

Paisley bobbed her head. "Yeah. Okay. What about you?"

"I'll finish going through the desk, just in case there's something we've missed. We can meet up front in five minutes." Liberty would be wondering where I was, and I didn't want to make her worry, but I didn't want to abandon the search now that we were here.

Keeping one eye on the passing time, I dug through desk drawers and checked two drawers of a file cabinet, but if there were any other clues in that room, I didn't know what they were.

I was contemplating whether to move on to Laurence's office or call it quits when I heard someone moving around outside the door. Probably just Paisley, I told myself, and returned a stack of folders to the filing cabinet.

From the corner of my eye, I saw the doorknob turn. I opened my mouth to tell Paisley that we needed to leave when it hit me that something was wrong. The doorknob *was* turning, but slowly. Too slowly. And I knew with a sudden, awful certainty that the person on the other side *wasn't* Paisley.

My stomach lurched and I swear my heart stopped beating for a full minute. I looked around frantically for a place to hide, but I was too late. The door opened and Jason appeared in front of me, and I thought I might be sick.

When he saw me, he laughed with relief. "Abby? You scared me half to death! What are you doing here?" He seemed so boyish and innocent, I wondered if I'd only imagined the raw hatred in the picture.

"*I* scared *you*? You're the one who was skulking around out there. Why didn't you just open the door?"

"I thought you were Alexander." He came into the room and closed the door behind him. "Paisley told me that he's the one who attacked you, so when I saw the light under the door, I figured he'd come back. I didn't want him to get away again."

He looked almost embarrassed by the mistake, and my confusion deepened. Was I wrong?

"I appreciate the effort," I said with a grateful smile. "Next time, though, it might be better for you to call the police."

Jason tilted his head to one side and looked past me to the photographs on the desk. Would he notice that the one with him in it was gone?

He hitched his thumbs into his pockets and hung his head, but some of his boyishness faded. "Look at that. People are already starting to take Alexander's stuff. I guess nothing's safe, is it?"

My breath caught in my throat and my hand began to tremble, but I fought to control my physical reaction so he wouldn't know that I suspected him. "Has Alexander really left town, then?"

Jason shrugged. "How would I know? I'm just a stagehand. He doesn't confide in me." Even his voice had changed.

It sounded harsh now. Clipped and angry. But he hadn't completely abandoned his masquerade, and that gave me hope. If I could just get out of this office. If I could just get to the lobby. If I could just get out of the theater, everything would be all right.

"Right," I said. "Well, then, I should probably get going."

Jason gave me an odd look, but he nodded and said, "Why are you here, anyway?"

What excuse could I give for sneaking around in the theater in the middle of the night? "I'm helping Paisley," I said when I couldn't think of anything else.

Right in front of my eyes, the innocent young man slipped away and someone older and more confident took his place. "With what?"

"This and that." Something he'd said earlier suddenly snapped into place and my mouth went dry. *Paisley told me that Alexander is the one who attacked you.* But when had Paisley told him that? I'd only told her a few minutes ago. Doing my best to sound normal, I said, "Speaking of Paisley, I'd better find her. I'm sure she's wondering what happened to me by now."

Jason's brows knit and he shook his head sadly. "Oh, I don't think so. Paisley's not worried about much of anything right now."

My blood turned to sludge in my veins. What did that mean? Had he hurt her . . . or worse?

"Did she leave without me?" I started toward the door, praying he wouldn't stop me.

He stepped into my path and gave me a look filled with sadness. "No, she didn't leave. She's in the box office, right where I found her."

I tried not to panic. "Is she hurt?"

Jason shrugged. "I don't know. That depends on how much she knows."

What was I supposed to say to that? I was having trouble breathing, so I concentrated on pulling air into my lungs and pushing it out again. "Paisley doesn't know anything," I said when I could speak again. "She's just making some copies for me."

"Of Alexander's pictures? What do you need those for?"

Could I make him think I still suspected Alexander? I doubted it. All of my instincts urged me to stall for time, but I didn't hold out much hope that anyone would come to help. Liberty might eventually get worried when I didn't come back to my apartment. She might even call the police, but what would Nate do if she did? Probably nothing. At best, he'd drive by the theater, see that it was dark, and move on. Face it, nobody knew where I was. Nobody was coming to help. I was on my own.

Keeping one eye on me the whole time, Jason backed to the door, opened it, and grabbed a length of rope that he'd probably brought with him. Seeing it made my spirits lift. If he were about to kill me, why tie me up? I had to believe that he intended to keep me around—at least for a little while. There was a chance I could survive.

"Why couldn't you have left things alone? Why did you have to keep poking around and trying to figure out who killed Laurence?"

I couldn't see any harm in admitting the truth. "The police suspected a friend of mine, but I knew he didn't kill Laurence."

"Richie?" Jason looked almost sorry. "He's a nice guy. I didn't want to let him take the blame, but I'm not going to prison. Not for killing Laurence Nichols. I did the world a favor, and anyone who knew that son of a bitch would agree."

"You've hated him for a long time, haven't you?"

Jason nodded. "You have no idea how much."

"Who was she? A girlfriend?"

He said nothing for a long time, then finally, "My sister. Tess."

"And she committed suicide?"

"He lied to her. He used her. He made her believe he loved her, and then he just tossed her away like yesterday's trash. And for *that* she gave up her life. Hell yes, I hated him. Put your hands out in front of you, please."

Please? Hysterical laughter bubbled up in my throat, but I swallowed it and held my hands out as instructed. Some long-forgotten warning shot through my head, and I left some room between my wrists so he couldn't bind them tight.

He caught on to my trick and forced my wrists together roughly. "I don't want to do this, Abby. Don't make it more difficult than it already is."

Was he serious? What did he want me to do, apologize for the inconvenience? My body ached all over from the attack in the parking lot, and every jerk, every shove, every bite of the rope threatened to bring on the tears.

My mind raced through possibilities as he finished cinching my wrists together and began binding me to the chair with a second piece of rope, but there wasn't much I could do. Even if there had been a butcher knife sitting right in front of me, I wouldn't have been able to grab it.

I should never have left home without Max. I should never have come to the Playhouse without letting someone know what I was doing. I'd been *attacked*. Viciously. I should have known better.

Stop it! I told myself firmly. It didn't matter how I got here, what mattered was getting away. That's what I needed to think about.

I searched the foggy recesses of my brain for the last thing Jason had said, and latched onto it. "If you hated Laurence so much, why did you wait so long to come after him?"

Jason pulled the rope around my stomach so tight I thought I might throw up. "I was too young at first. I didn't think I could do it. But my mom got sick after Tess died, and she just never got better. Depression, they said. They pumped her full of pills for a few years and tried getting her to talk about what bothered her, but none of it did any good. She just wasted away."

"I'm sorry," I said, and I genuinely meant it. He'd suffered a double tragedy, and he'd blamed it all on Laurence. "So you found out where he was going to be working, and you applied for a job?"

Satisfied that I wouldn't be able to move my upper body, Jason moved on to my lower half. He tied a knot around one ankle and lashed my leg to the chair. "Naw. I didn't go looking for him or anything. I got the job here a couple of months ago. I was trying hard to move on with my life. And then one day, there he was. I couldn't believe it."

"Did he know who you were?"

Jason shook his head and yanked the rope hard. "He didn't even remember my sister. I asked him about her. He couldn't even remember her name."

"He was a jerk," I said. "And he treated women shamefully. He left a path of destruction behind him everywhere he went. But killing him wasn't the right way to deal with it, Jason. And what about the rest of us? Why did you attack Vonetta? And Colleen? And me?"

He tied the knot tight and stood. "You just got in the way. The others were partly responsible for Tess and my mom."

"How?"

"Colleen talked Tess into trying out for that part. She's the one who brought that ass into our lives."

"And Vonetta?"

Jason turned toward the door. "She told Tess to go out with him. Kept saying what a nice guy Laurence was. Convinced Tess that she'd be all right with him, in spite of their age difference."

"But she had no way of knowing what Laurence was really like. Not then!"

"Didn't she?"

I could tell he didn't believe me. "Neither of them would make the same mistakes now," I assured him. "Laurence has hurt them both. And what about Alexander? What have you done to him?"

Jason ignored me and disappeared into the shop area and returned with a roll of duct tape and a box cutter. "Now here's what I want you to do," he said. "I'm going to put this on your mouth, and then I'm going to leave for a little while."

He wound the tape around my head, covering my mouth.

The bruises from the attack burned as the tape stuck to them, and I cried out in protest. He ignored me and kept wrapping until it felt as if my entire head was on fire.

"I want you to stay right here until I get back," he said, surveying his handiwork. "If you do, I'll let you live when I leave here. If you don't . . ." He held the box cutter to his throat and made a slashing motion, then shut the door and left me alone.

His footsteps faded away almost immediately, and I got to work. He'd left my nose clear, so I could breathe, but the tape around my mouth made me feel as if I'd suffocate any minute. Using every muscle I could, I tried to scoot the chair closer to the desk. I'd noticed a pair of scissors in one of the drawers earlier. I wasn't naive enough to believe that he'd let me live after all of this. My only hope lay in finding a way to escape.

If I could reach the scissors, and open the blades, and position myself just so, I might be able to cut through the rope. The chair scraped across the floor inch by inch, the noise so loud each time I moved, I was sure Jason would hear it and come back to finish me off. Pain seared my head and neck, and lashed repeatedly through my forehead until I thought I'd pass out from that alone.

At last, I moved close enough to touch the drawer with my fingertips. I struggled for a long time, trying to get a finger under the notch in the drawer long enough to work it open, but my hands were at the wrong angle, and the ropes dug painfully into my wrists when I strained too far in either direction.

Frantic now, I looked around for something else I could use to free myself. I'd been trapped inside a burning building a few months earlier, and the panic of that morning came back to me as I struggled to free myself.

Finally, with no alternative in sight, I shoved the chair backward and rubbed the ropes against the corner of the desk. It wasn't nearly sharp enough to cut anything, but I had to do something. I couldn't just sit here and wait for Jason to get back.

After only a few minutes, my shoulders and arms ached from the effort of moving my hands up and down. Sweat trickled down my back and dripped into my eyes. I had no idea whether I was making progress or not, but it didn't matter. Too soon, I heard footsteps approaching the office again, and I knew my time was up.

Chapter 32

I barely had time to register the footsteps when the door flew open and Paisley scurried inside. I've never been so glad to see anyone in my life. A bright red mark showed on one cheek, and she limped slightly, but she was alive and she'd come back to save me. Every mean thought I've ever had about her evaporated.

Putting one finger to her mouth, she closed the door soundlessly and hurried toward me, whispering, "I was afraid you'd be dead! Come on! Let's get out of here before he gets back."

She untied my hands and started to work on my feet while I pulled the tape from my mouth and hair, ripping out what felt like a few solid handfuls in the process. I gulped air and rubbed my wrists to get the circulation going, then turned my attention to the rope around my torso. "I was afraid he'd killed you," I said, keeping my voice low. "Where did he go?"

"Outside somewhere, but I don't think he's gone far. We have to get out of here now." She freed one foot, then another, and I stood shakily. She scowled up at me. "Can you walk?"

"Yes. Let's go." I didn't want to spend one more second in that room.

We slipped out of the office and closed the door behind us, but then we faced a dilemma. If we went to the right, we'd have to cut through the ladies' dressing room, which would at least give us hiding places if we needed them. But on the other side of that was the long corridor with nowhere to turn until we reached the lobby. If we turned left, we'd go through the rehearsal hall. Fewer places to hide, but it was a shorter run to the front door. Or we could jog a few steps to the right and shoot straight through the auditorium to the outside door.

All three options zipped through my head in about a second and a half. Making a snap decision, I grabbed Paisley's wrist and tugged her toward the auditorium. We raced up the ramp and into the deserted room. Images of Laurence's body lying on the stage rose up in front of me, but I pushed them away resolutely. Nothing was going to stop me from getting out of there.

Nothing.

Two minutes later, we pushed out the front doors into the frigid night. The cold had never felt so good. We didn't take time to lock the door behind us. All that mattered was getting away. We paused for only a second to get our bearings and look for Jason, before plunging off the curb and racing across the street. By unspoken mutual agreement, we headed for Alpine Sports and the obscurity it provided where it blocked the light. It would also provide shelter from the wind that buffeted us as we ran. From there, we'd just have to cross one more street before we reached the safety of the Curl Up & Dye.

The raging storm swept the sound of our footsteps away as we ran, and I hoped that meant that Jason wouldn't be able to hear us if he was nearby. Just as we slipped into the shadows cast by the sporting goods store, the lights of an approaching car swept over the spot where we'd been just a second before. My heart thumped madly as I glanced over my shoulder. Was it Jason? Had he come back? Had he seen us?

To my surprise, Jawarski's big black truck turned onto the street and came to a stop in front of the Playhouse. He'd probably gone to my apartment, and when I wasn't there he came looking for me. That touched me in a way I didn't have time to analyze right then.

I stopped running but either Paisley didn't notice or she didn't care. "Hey, Paisley, it's Jawarski," I called after her. "Everything's going to be okay."

If she heard me, she ignored me.

Nothing on earth could have compelled me to go back into that building, but I wanted to catch Jawarski before he went in. I didn't want him to run into Jason unprepared, especially since I was pretty sure Jawarski wouldn't be carrying his gun.

The street was empty, so he'd parked directly in front of the doors. I called out to him, but the wind carried my warning away. I shouted again and kicked myself into high gear, hoping I could stop him, but he ducked his head into the wind and let himself into the Playhouse before I could reach him.

Terrified and gasping for breath, I stopped at the corner of the building. Jawarski was walking into a dangerous situation completely unprepared. Everything inside rebelled at the thought of going back into the Playhouse, but I couldn't let him run into Jason without warning.

There had to be some other way. I could follow Paisley to the Curl and call for help, but that might take too long. I could call Jawarski on his cell, but there were so many places in the Playhouse where he wouldn't receive a signal, I discarded that idea immediately. No, it was either go in after him, or wait where I was and pray he made it out alive.

That was no choice at all.

After glancing around to make sure Jason wasn't nearby, I darted across the street and into the theater before I could change my mind. Inside the lobby, I stood for a minute, straining to hear Jawarski moving around and trying to figure out which direction to go.

When this was over, I promised myself, I was going to avoid this theater like the plague.

Outside, the wind howled and the glass doors rattled. I jumped and whipped around, convinced I'd find Jason there. When I realized I was still alone, I sighed with relief and forced myself to choose a direction. Opting for the auditorium again, I inched aside the velvet curtain and looked inside to make sure Jason wasn't there before I stepped inside.

With every minute that passed, my muscles wound tighter.

If Jawarski was here to look for me, wouldn't he be making some noise? Calling out for me? Turning on lights? Instead, an ominous silence echoed through the theater, and my nerves felt as if they were on fire.

I hurried through the auditorium, taking advantage of the cover the curtain provided to check the hallway and shop area before I stepped out into the open. And still I couldn't hear anything that would let me know where Jawarski was. For all I knew, he'd doubled back and gone outside again while I was in the auditorium.

I'd almost convinced myself that's what had happened when something several feet ahead of me hit the ground with a loud bang. I heard voices, but only for a second before a gunshot exploded in the silence.

I held back a scream and gulped back tears that sprang into my eyes before I could stop them. I silently begged anyone who'd listen to let Jawarski be the one with the gun, but I was terrified that he wasn't.

The Playhouse wasn't a large theater, but as I tried to figure out where the shot came from, the twisting mass of rooms and work areas separated by eerie-looking props and dust-covered backdrops seemed to stretch on forever. Fear paralyzed me, but I couldn't let it gain the upper hand. Jawarski might already be hurt. I had to find him before the unthinkable happened.

Desperate, I plunged along a narrow path that led through abandoned sets and props. The pain medication was wearing off, and my head throbbed as I ran. As I neared the back of the building, I heard someone moving around in the distance, so I stopped running and slid behind a listing backdrop from some long-ago play.

Instinct urged me to hurry, but I forced myself to move cautiously. As I drew closer, I heard Jason talking but I was still too far away to pick up what he said. My breathing sounded unnaturally loud in my ears as I strained to make out what he was saying.

"A cop? You're a goddamn cop? What in the hell am I going to do *now*?"

A large box several feet ahead of me tilted, then fell heavily to the floor. I held back a gasp and pulled back into the shadows. In the dim emergency lighting, I could see Jason in the scene shop, which was little more than a clearing in the middle of the chaos. The stage crew used that area to build the backdrops and platforms needed for each production. If I could get to it, there'd be plenty of items I could use as a weapon. But that was a big *if*.

Jason paced from one end of the clearing to the other, then stopped and looked down at something on the floor. I assumed that something was Jawarski.

Please, I begged silently. *Be alive.* Because if he wasn't . . .

I couldn't even go there. Every doubt about our relationship I'd nursed for the past two years evaporated as I tried *not* to contemplate a future without Jawarski. But the more I tried not to think about the unthinkable, the more firmly my mind locked on it and refused to let go.

Be alive, I pleaded again and slipped a little deeper into the shadows. I had no doubt that Jason would kill me if he saw me, and the fear that realization brought with it nauseated me. Whatever I did now, I'd have to be more careful than ever.

Chapter 33

I stood in the shadows for what felt like hours, studying my surroundings and trying to formulate a plan. I'd have to catch Jason off guard, but that wasn't going to be easy. The box that might have helped keep my location secret had fallen to the floor a few minutes ago, so the distance between us—which I calculated at about thirty feet—was completely open. The instant I left my hiding place, it would be open season on Abby.

Jason paced the floor, talking to Jawarski every once in a while. Obviously, the idea of killing a policeman bothered him more than the murder of your ordinary civilian. It was a small point in our favor, but I'd take anything I could get.

I couldn't hear Jawarski responding, but I didn't let myself lose hope. Jason was talking to him. That had to be a good sign.

Each lap Jason made was six steps long as he paced between a large piece of castle backdrop from last year's production of *Cinderella* and a row of wooden palm trees used in *Joseph and the Amazing Technicolor Dreamcoat*. That didn't give me much time, but if I judged it right, I could take advantage of the element of surprise. And *if* I could catch him off guard, I might be able to push over that row of palm trees. If Jason was in just the right place when I made my move, the trees would hit him and buy Jawarski and me some time to get away.

If that plan wasn't shaky enough, Jason clutched a pistol in one hand. No amount of surprise would give me the upper hand against a gun. I had to make sure he didn't get a shot off.

Piece of cake.

Obviously agitated, Jason made another pass the length of the floor. As he reached the far end of the open area, he whipped around and aimed the gun at Jawarski. "Shut *up*. I told you, let me *think*."

Jawarski *was* alive! Relief so strong it almost buckled my knees swept over me and tears filled my eyes. He was alive, but I had to assume he was injured; otherwise, he'd have been on his feet. He must have said something else, because Jason mopped sweat away from his temples with the back of his gun hand. "That's easy for you to say," he snarled. "That son of a bitch killed my sister, same as if he held a gun to her head and pulled the trigger. He killed my mother, too. Don't talk to me about forgiving."

While he was distracted, I dropped to all fours and crawled through the jumble of scenery and props toward him. As I drew closer, I began to pick up on what Jawarski was saying, but I still couldn't see him. I crawled past a few loose boards and a pile of stage swords. I considered using both as a weapon, but I didn't trust myself to grab one without giving myself away.

I forced myself to focus on the plan and inched around a wooden platform that probably hadn't been moved in at least a year. Dust billowed up from the floor, and I fought back the urge to sneeze. The effort made my nose hurt, my eyes water, and my throat sting.

"You don't know what it was like, watching my sister suffer. Watching my mother wither up and die." Jason's voice rose higher. "Everyone thought he was such a great guy. Everybody loved him—until they got to know him. He used people. Like a vampire, he sucked the life right out of everyone he met."

I could make out the low rumble of Jawarski's voice now, and the relief of knowing that he was still alive made my eyes water again. Not more than five feet from my goal, I crept past another abandoned backdrop and something soft brushed against my arm.

Instinctively, I jerked. My hand swept the back of a Grecian pillar, and it tottered on its flimsy base. I caught it as quickly as I could, but I was too late.

"Who's there?" Jason demanded.

I froze in place and held my breath, cursing myself silently for making such a stupid mistake.

"Whoever it is, you'd better come out. *Now*."

I didn't move. I'm not sure I even breathed.

"*Now*!" he demanded again. "Unless you want the cop to die right here and now."

Frustrated and angry with myself, I got to my feet. I was close enough to see over the last row of storage that stood between us. Jawarski lay on the floor, alive but pale and obviously weak. A trail of blood spread out from beneath his shoulder.

I'd never seen Jawarski looking anything but buff and healthy. Seeing him like this made my stomach lurch, but it also filled me with a resolve that surprised me. No matter what it took, I was going to keep him alive.

"I want your hands where I can see 'em," Jason ordered. "Now, come on out here."

Jawarski rolled his head to the side and saw me. His eyelids flickered, and I realized that he was close to passing out from the loss of blood. "Abby," he croaked. "Get out of here."

With a roar of anger, Jason shouted, "Shut up! How many times do I have to tell you?" and before I could move, he planted a boot in Jawarski's side.

Jawarski's skin grew deathly pale and a moan escaped his lips. I decided the time was now or never. I lunged for the palm tree backdrop and shoved it as hard as I could. It didn't move.

I threw my whole body into the effort and shoved again. Just as it began to topple, I saw Jason spot me and level the gun in my direction. As the shot rang out, I crumpled to the floor. I heard the explosion, saw the flash from the end of the muzzle, and felt something scorching hot fly past me.

The palm trees fell with a loud crash and dust billowed up from the floor. I looked frantically for Jason and found him beneath the fronds of one tree. He was dazed, but not out. I couldn't see Jawarski anywhere.

I knew that Jawarski and I had just one chance to escape with our lives, so I wasted no time. Gathering my strength, I let out a bellow that surprised even me and charged Jason. I saw him stagger to his feet. I saw the moment he realized I was aiming for him. Watched his arm rise slowly until the pistol was aiming at my chest.

This is it, I thought, and a strange sense of calm settled over me. I hit him dead-on. My head and neck snapped backward from the impact. Pain shot through my ribs and down into my knees. I stumbled after the impact and fell into the castle backdrop. It fell backward, and I heard the sound of splintering wood.

Jason rolled to his side. He looked stunned, but I couldn't count on that lasting long. I looked around for something—anything—to use as a weapon. My gaze lit on a stage screw someone had left on a box about two feet from where I stood.

I could hear Jason coming close, so I lunged for it and slipped my hand into the handle. I swung with all my might as Jason came up behind me and the long screw plunged into his chest, just below his shoulder.

The impact stunned him, but he had momentum going, and he fell forward. Blood poured from the wound, spattering the scenery around me. I threw myself out of his way and narrowly missed being pinned beneath his body.

He landed heavily, and the gun skittered away from his hand. I dove after it and aimed it at him, determined to make sure he wouldn't get up again. I'd never shot a person before, but I was pretty sure I wouldn't hesitate if Jason made any attempt to come at me again.

He groaned and rolled to one side, and a cold knot of anger formed where my heart used to be. "Try it, Jason. Go ahead. I dare you."

Very slowly, he turned his head to look at me, and he must have seen the conviction on my face because he lay back down, skewed slightly to avoid applying more pressure on the screw embedded in his chest.

Somewhere in the distance, I heard shouting and then lights popped on all around us. *Paisley must have called for help*, I thought. And it was probably a good thing. If I'd been left alone with Jason for another minute, I don't know what I would have done.

"Abby?" Jawarski's voice was so weak, I could barely hear him.

I let my gaze flicker toward him, but only for a second. "Yeah?"

He lifted his head about an inch from the floor and made a valiant effort to smile. "Thanks."

Before I could respond, he collapsed on the floor. The last thing I remember about that night was the sound of my own voice, screaming for help.

Chapter 34

"It wasn't supposed to end up like this," Jawarski said from his hospital bed the next morning. "I came back to surprise you. I was kind of hoping we could spend a little time together."

I stood at the foot of his bed, stretching as much as my poor, aching body would let me to work out the kinks I'd picked up overnight. Nate had called for an ambulance to transport Jawarski to the hospital in Leadville. I had followed in the Jetta. When the nurses kicked me out a little before two that morning, I'd grabbed a few hours sleep on the world's most uncomfortable bed in the cheapest hotel in town. When I awoke, I'd been so stiff it had taken me a good twenty minutes just to stand up.

Through the windows of the hospital room, I could see thick flakes of snow falling, and I gave serious consideration to calling Karen and telling her I'd be staying overnight so I wouldn't have to drive through the canyons in the middle of a storm. I'd been hanging onto the Jetta for a long time, but I was beginning to think I should buy something built for the mountainous area I now called home again. I guess that meant I was committed to staying.

"Don't worry about it," I said, trying on this commitment thing for size. "I'm just glad to see you, and I'm very glad you're okay."

"Yeah. Me, too." He poked at a shapeless piece of meat on his lunch tray and grimaced. "You've got to get me out of here, slick. This stuff is going to kill me."

"I doubt that," I said. "Apparently, you're kinda hard to

kill." I said it jokingly, but every time I thought about how close I'd come to losing him, my stomach turned over. He abandoned the plate and started to battle with a can of Coke and a straw.

I moved to stand beside him and held the straw so he could find it with his mouth. "What made you decide to come to the Playhouse anyway? How did you know I'd be there?"

"I didn't, but it seemed logical. You'd been spending an awful lot of time there, so when Liberty said you hadn't come back, I figured that's where I'd find you."

He knew me too well, but that wasn't a bad thing. I took the can from him and returned it to the tray. "That's it? You weren't playing knight in shining armor riding in to rescue me?"

He leaned back against the pillows and shook his head. "I'm afraid not. Not this time, anyway. It might have been different if someone had told me about the attack on you and Colleen."

"I tried! I called you a couple of times, but you never answered." I'm not sure how much I would have said if I'd been able to reach him, but I saw no reason to admit that.

"I was on the road, heading home. There are some long old stretches of road between here and there with no cell phone signal." He closed his eyes briefly, and I could see exhaustion making his face tight. "So you were right. Richie had nothing to do with the murder."

"Nothing at all," I agreed. "But you look tired, and I'm starving. Why don't you catch a nap and I'll run down to the cafeteria. Do you want me to bring you anything?"

He shook his head without opening his eyes. "Just you."

Instead of walking away, I stood at his bedside and studied him for a long time. I'd turned a corner in our relationship. I couldn't deny that. Nearly losing him inside the Playhouse had opened my eyes—and my heart. I still didn't like the idea of being vulnerable, but I'd realized that I was going to be vulnerable with this guy whether or not I wanted to be.

One eye opened, and he studied me curiously. "Something wrong?"

I shook my head and kissed his cheek lightly. "Just the opposite," I whispered. "Something's very, very right."

The other eye opened, his exhaustion forgotten for a moment. "Yeah? What's that?"

"I was just wondering what I'd do if I ever lost you," I said. "I realized last night that I don't ever want to find out."

A pleased smile curved his lips. "It's about time."

I laughed and sat on the edge of the chair. "And for the record, next time you go to Montana, I'd feel a whole lot better if you sent Bree to a hotel while you're there with the kids." It was an irrational request, and we both knew it.

Jawarski chuckled and closed his eyes again. "Yeah, I'm sure she'll appreciate that. When I suggest it, I'll also be sure to let her know it's your idea."

"Fine with me." I stood again and started for the door, but there I stopped and forced myself to turn back. I was doing it again. Dodging the truth. Making a joke to protect myself. This man deserved the same honesty from me that I needed from him. I cleared my throat and said, "Jawarski?"

"Yeah?"

"I just want you to know that . . . well . . . I've thought a lot about our relationship. About us. And I—" The words wouldn't come. I felt them. I meant them. But I couldn't force them out of my throat. Tears of frustration burned my eyes and a thick lump clogged my throat. "I don't know what's wrong with me," I croaked. "If you knew how I felt . . ."

"What makes you think I don't?" He locked eyes with me, and the gentleness I saw in his expression knocked the wind right out of me. "Go. Get some lunch. I'll be here when you get back. And Abby?"

"Yeah?"

"I love you, too."

"Shamrocks?" I stared, open mouthed, at the clovers dangling from the ceiling of Divinity, fluttering in the breeze every time someone moved. "Are you kidding me?"

Liberty bounced with excitement, her pride in her accomplishment obvious. "Do you like it? It's my welcome home present for you."

"I—I'm speechless." And I had the sinking feeling I was going to have Easter eggs hanging in front of my face next month. I couldn't think of a single thing to say that wouldn't make Karen angry or offend Liberty. Stunned, I moved further into the kitchen, holding onto Jawarski's arm. Richie and Dylan came inside behind us. They'd insisted on coming to Leadville to see us, and Richie had been adamant about driving the Jetta back to Paradise for me.

I had to admit, he'd been right. I was in no condition to drive and probably wouldn't be for a few days. Richie hustled Max up the back stairs to the currently empty second floor, where he could play with his doggie toys for a while. Dylan had been fussing over me and Jawarski like a mother hen all the way through the canyon. Were we warm enough? Were we too warm? Did we need something to drink?

He didn't let up even now that we were home. "How about some coffee? You want coffee, Abby?"

Not really. The two cups he'd bought me on the trip home had been enough, but if he didn't stop hovering I was going to scream. "Sure," I said. "Coffee sounds great."

"Already made a pot." Karen bustled into the room looking maternal and concerned. "Both of you come and sit down. I'll get it for you." She hurried away and came back a minute later with two mugs, a pitcher of cream, and a container filled with green sugar.

I could only stare at it.

Jawarski bit back a grin. "It's green," he whispered.

"Yes, it is."

Karen ignored us both and sat, propping her elbows on the table and her chin in her hands. "So? What's the word? What's going to happen to the kid?"

"Jason is no kid," I told her. "Believe me."

"He's going to face charges," Jawarski said as he carefully spooned green sugar into his mug. "He's not a child, and Laurence's murder was definitely premeditated. He's going to go away for a long time, I'm afraid."

"Well, I say thank heaven for small favors." Dylan sat beside me. "If it weren't for Abby, it would be Richie going away. I don't know what we'd have done without you, and I don't know how to thank you."

"No thanks necessary," I said. "I knew Richie was innocent. I'm sure that if he'd gone to trial, a jury would have figured it out, too."

"Don't be so sure," Liberty said, dragging an empty chair to the table. "Innocent people go to prison all the time. I've seen shows about it. But this Jason guy . . . I think it's so sad. I mean, he lost his sister. He lost his mother. That would be enough to make anybody go a little crazy."

"People have bad things happen to them all the time," I pointed out. "Not everybody goes around killing the people they hold responsible."

"Thank goodness," Karen said with a thin smile. "I *do* feel sorry for him in a way. It's all so tragic. By the way, Sergio told me that Alexander has filed a lawsuit against Geoffrey Manwaring, claiming a share of Laurence's inheritance."

Karen's attorney husband hears all the good stuff first. "On what grounds?"

"I don't have all the details, of course, but apparently Laurence borrowed some money from Alexander years ago to invest in a play. Laurence was absolutely certain it was going to be a huge hit and sweep the nation. It didn't, and he lost everything. And, of course, Laurence made sure there was no paper trail, so Alexander never could get him to pay the money back."

"Does he stand a chance of winning?" Dylan asked.

Karen shook her head. "Not a very good one. Geoffrey will probably get to keep everything."

I sipped my coffee cautiously in case the green sugar tasted like lime or something. You never know. "That hardly seems fair. A jerk like Geoffrey Manwaring doesn't deserve a fortune. But since when has a person needed to be deserving?"

"Ain't that the truth?" Karen pulled the cream and sugar

toward her. "Hey, did you get a chance to check on Colleen while you were in Leadville?"

I nodded. "Just over the phone. She's recovering from her injuries, and Doyle is being very attentive. She seems relieved."

The kitchen door blew open and Rachel came inside carrying a white bag from the bakery. "I heard you two were back. I brought croissants." She stopped midstride and stared at the shamrocks. "Ooh! St. Patrick's Day," she said, closing the door behind her. "My favorite holiday. Who wants to go out for corned beef and green beer that night?"

A chorus of "*Me*" went up around the table, and suddenly the room broke out in chaos as everyone started adding ideas to the mix.

"What are you doing?" I asked. "It's a month away."

"Oh, but you have to make your plans now," Liberty said. "Otherwise, you'll never get a reservation. Put Rutger and me down for dinner and drinks. I heard that O'Shucks is a great place for St. Patrick's Day."

"It's good," Dylan said, "but it's not my favorite. The best place is this little-hole-in-the-wall Irish pub on the road to Aspen . . ."

I smiled and sat back in my chair, content to listen. Yeah, St. Patrick's Day was more than a month away, but suddenly the idea of making plans in advance didn't seem so bad. After all, I wasn't going anywhere.

Candy Recipes

—— ❀ ——

Divine Cherry Divinity

Makes 5 to 6 dozen candies

> *2½ cups sugar*
> *½ cup water*
> *½ cup light corn syrup*
> *2 egg whites*
> *1 teaspoon vanilla (can use vanilla extract if desired)*
> *1 cup chopped red candied cherries*

Combine the sugar, water, and corn syrup in a 3-quart saucepan. Cook over low heat, stirring gently, until the sugar dissolves. Wash down any crystallized sugar on the sides of pan with a wet pastry brush a few times, as necessary.

Cover and cook over medium heat 2–3 minutes. Uncover and cook over medium heat, without stirring, to 260° on a candy thermometer (hard-ball stage).

Remove from heat.

Beat the egg whites in a large mixing bowl until stiff peaks form. Pour hot sugar mixture slowly, in a very thin stream, over the egg whites while beating constantly at high speed with an electric handheld mixer. Add vanilla and continue beating just until mixture holds its shape (3–4 minutes).

Stir in chopped cherries and drop by rounded teaspoonfuls onto wax paper.

Let cool.

Strawberry Lollipops

Makes 10

> 1 cup sugar
> ½ cup water
> 1 cup light corn syrup
> ¼ teaspoon strawberry flavor oil
>   (can substitute other flavors if desired)
> Red food coloring

Before getting started, spray the inside of your candy molds and a cookie sheet with nonstick spray. Line up your molds on the cookie sheet so they're ready when you are. Place lollipop sticks into the molds, and then put the molds and the cookie sheet into the freezer.

Combine the sugar, water, and corn syrup. Cook to 300° on a candy thermometer (hard-crack stage.)

Remove from heat, and add flavoring and food coloring. Stir for approximately 2 minutes, then pour the hot candy into the cooled molds.

If your candy hardens before it's all poured, place the pan over low heat to soften again.

Allow to cool at room temperature, or put them in the refrigerator for faster cooling. When cooled, remove the lollipops from the molds and cover with decorative bags.

Marshmallow Caramel Pillows

Makes 32 pillows

> 16 large marshmallows
> 1 cup finely chopped nuts (optional)
> 1 cup toasted coconut (optional)
> 1 cup sugar

¼ cup water
½ cup cream
1 cup light corn syrup
1 tablespoon butter
1 teaspoon vanilla extract
⅛ teaspoon salt
32 paper or foil candy cups

Begin by setting out 32 paper or foil candy cups. Cut the marshmallows in half widthwise and set aside. Place the chopped nuts and coconut in separate bowls and set aside.

Combine the sugar, water, cream, and corn syrup in a small saucepan and cook over medium heat, stirring constantly, until the sugar dissolves. Insert a candy thermometer and stir in the butter until it's melted. Continue to cook, stirring occasionally to prevent scorching on the bottom. Cook until the caramel reaches 238°. Remove from heat.

Stir in the vanilla and salt. Allow the caramel to stand for 10–15 minutes to thicken and cool to approximately 175°.

Using a fork, drop a marshmallow half in the caramel and turn it over until it is completely covered. Remove the marshmallow from the caramel and roll it in the nuts or coconut if desired until it's covered. Place the finished marshmallow caramel pillow in a candy cup so it retains its shape.

Repeat the caramel and coating steps with the remaining marshmallows. If the caramel becomes too stiff for easy dipping, place it over low heat for a minute or two until it becomes easy to work with.

Allow pillows to set fully at room temperature before serving. Store in an airtight container.